I0682009

All I Want For Christmas

Stories by

Ina Louise Jackson

B.A. Belliveau

and

Lynn Marie Simpson

ISBN: 978-1-926898-84-1

West Guilford, Ontario
pinelakebooks@gmail.com
www.pinelakebooks.ca
www.pinelakebooks.org

Table of Contents

The Christmas Tree Farm
  *Ina Louise Jackson*_____ 5
Gone!
  B.A. Belliveau _____ 115
Incubus, Tales of the Anunnaki
  Lynn Marie Simpson _____ 119
Simple Gifts
  *Ina Louise Jackson*_____ 189

The Christmas Tree Farm

Ina Louise Jackson

The Christmas Tree Farm Facts

The word 'Wendigo' (pronounced wehn-dee-go) comes from the Native American
Algonquian language, meaning 'evil spirit that devours mankind."

* * *

*650 years ago, the entire Anasazi civilization and culture vanished without a trace; after over 20 years of arduous research, archaeologists now believe the answer to be a Wendigo.

*Swift Runner slaughtered his entire family in 1878 and ate them, despite being only 25 miles from the Hudson Bay Company's supply post.

*From late 1800's through the 1920's a Wendigo made a number of appearances near a town called Rosesu in Northern Minnesota. Each time it was reported, an unexpected death followed.

*Jack Fiddler and his brother in 1907 were arrested for killing over 14 people who he claimed were Wendigo's or about to become them.

*A doctor in Fort Kent in 1921 ate all but 11 people in a town of 150. He disappeared shortly thereafter leaving everything in his home behind.

*Historically, there were many reports in the early 20th century of Wendigo spirits possessing people in dozens of communities from northern Quebec to the Rockies.

*As more and more are influenced by surrounding culture, the reports of the Wendigo have declined over the years, but as with most evils, it is doubtful that this creature is gone for good.

References

- Monstropedia : Internet reference library, established 2008–
  The Wendigo Legend
- Wikipedia: Internet encyclopaedia, established 2001–
  Algonquian Mythology

Dedicated to
Colton

Prologue

O Christmas Tree! O Christmas Tree!
Much pleasure thou can'st give me;
O Christmas Tree! O Christmas Tree!
Much pleasure thou can'st give me;
How often has the Christmas tree
Afforded me the greatest glee!
O Christmas Tree! O Christmas Tree

One

Nature knows no right or wrong ...
Only balance and imbalance

Rebecca mindlessly wiped down the telephone receiver. No sooner had she replaced it in the cradle than it rang.

"Hello?"

"I am looking for Becky Weatherspoon."

"Speaking and it's Rebecca," she corrected.

"My name is Wen Fiddler," he said.

"Am I supposed to know you?" She could not place the name, but something tugged way down deep inside, his voice silken and smooth, comfortable, like a precious memory of what came before, of a forgotten place and time. She felt as if she could have gotten lost in that voice, floating off into never, never land without a care in the world. She gave herself a shake snapping free of it.

"I am an old friend of your sister's." He was lying.

"Susanna?" she asked, suddenly feeling stupid. She thoughtlessly gave the receiver a final wipe. Of course, it was Susanna. She only had, but the one sister. She threw the cleaning cloth off to the side.

"Yes," he confirmed.

"My sister passed away quite a few years back, what is it you want? I ..."

He cut her off. "Your sister was a friend of mine and helped me out in the past and I am in need once again and I was ..."

"Excuse me?" she broke in, '*Who in hell is this guy?*'

He drew the receiver closer to his lips, "Let's start over. Your sister and I were friends," he paused listening intently to her breathing. He grinned, sensing he had hit a nerve.

"Okay ... And?" She sat down on the sofa.

"She helped me out a number of years back and I was hoping that ..."

She reined him in before he could further his sentence. "Look ... Sphen Fiddles or whatever the hell your name is."

"Wen Fiddler," he said quietly. "My name is Wen Fiddler," he repeated.

"Whatever! ... If it's money you want I'm in-between jobs right now so you're out of luck and another thing, I don't know you from Adam and after this telephone call I don't want to either." She slammed the telephone down on the receiver. "God that guy's got a lot of nerve," she muttered.

Her relationship with her sister in the last few years before she'd passed were awkward and uncomfortable, eventually dissolving to the point of nothing—no telephone calls, no letters, no emails, no nothing. She had not even known where Susanna was living when she got notified of her death. The funeral with the closed casket and few in attendance had been more than she could bear. A silent tear ran down her cheek. Her sister and the closeness they had shared, like dust in the wind gone, forever, never to return. She found herself wishing she had not picked up the telephone, had just kept right on cleaning her apartment. She had a hard enough time dealing with the death on a daily basis; she surely did not need some long lost friend of Susanna's calling her up. It was like a slap in the face.

She put her head down and cried.

The telephone rang.

She reluctantly picked it up, knowing it was him again. "Yes," she muffled.

"Becky, I am sorry we got off on the wrong foot. I didn't mean to upset you," Wen said.

"It's Rebecca." Her sister had been the only one in her life that had called her Becky and got away with it. Becky to her had always sounded like a breakfast cereal.

"I don't want money. I want to give you money."

She stood and started to pace slowly back and forth, clasping the telephone tightly to her ear. He had caught her undivided attention; she'd been out of work for too long and bills were mounting quicker than she could shake a stick. No name mac and cheese had become her main stay diet. "I'm listening," she said.

"I would like to hire you. And as I said ..."

"I know you were a friend of my sister," she interjected.

"Yes."

"Did she work for you?"

"Yes," he said, lying once again.

"Hire me for?" She paused, it was there again, that voice, that feeling ... That déjà vu, whiffing round tugging and pulling at a memory of another life. 'Dracula' had that same effect on people, women in particular, a voice of the ages, one you could get lost in. "For what?" she finally asked.

"A twelve day job," Wen said.

"Only twelve days?"

"Yes," he said. "Pays well," he added as incentive.

"Doing?"

"Caring for my daughter."

"Babysitting?"

"Not really, she is six, more caretaking I would say."

"Caretaking?" She repeated the odd word he had used. She switched the receiver to her other ear. *What an unorthodox way of putting it,*' she thought. *'It's babysitting.'*

"Yes."

"Are you in the city here?" she asked. The guy really had not said too much of anything; not where he was from, nor of himself, her sister, his daughter, nothing.

"No. I am quite a distance."

"My car isn't running at the moment and ...."

"I'll pay your way," he cut in. "Train, bus, or cab, which ever mode of transportation you would prefer."

"What are the hours and where would I be staying after work?"

"Hours are twenty-four-seven and you'll be staying in the guest room in my home. Don't worry the door locks, so do the windows for that matter."

"I don't know," Rebecca started chewing her bottom lip. *'Twenty-four-seven ... Holy Christ."*

"I'll pay you four hundred per day in cash."

She did the math in her head. "You'll pay me four thousand eight hundred dollars?"

"Do you want more?" he asked quickly.

"No that's fi ... fine." She looked down at the floor, wondering why in hell she was stuttering. "When is it for?"

"The twelve days right before Christmas."

"The twelve days right before Christmas?" she repeated him verbatim, her voice raising an octave.

"Yes."

"Jesus," she muttered.

"Do you have other plans for this time period?"

"No, my family is long gone." She looked up at the photo of her parents taken just before that horrid plane crash. Two more closed caskets.

The corners of his mouth turned up ever so slightly. "Becky?"

"Yeah."

"I know you don't know anything about me, and all this may seem over whelming to you just out of the blue."

"No kidding," she mumbled.

"I have my own home and my own business. My busy time is the twelve days right before Christmas. I recently moved to the town I am in and do not know or trust anyone enough to invite them into my home for days at a time, or to care for my daughter. Your sister spoke often of you; often enough that I feel as if I know you. I can tell you about yourself if it would help with your decision."

"You can ... Can you?" she teased. She was suddenly feeling comfortable and all that money would be a blessing, more than a blessing. "Okay shoot ... Tell me," she quipped.

Wen openly laughed. "You have long, light brown wavy hair past your shoulders. Green eyes, cute freckles, you always wear gold hoop earrings and a single stone diamond pendant that belonged to your mother. You dress casual in tee shirts or sweat shirts and jeans, your favourite slippers are fuzzy lilac ones that come up to your knee with pom-poms on them. Your favourite music is old time rock and roll ..."

"Okay ... You can stop." Wen seemed so much more personable now, and his voice, that silken, melted chocolate, 'Dracula' voice.

"Will you take the position?"

"I'll do it."

"Your word?"

"Yeah, my word."

"Mode of transportation you'd fancy?"

"Cab, please."

"One more thing," he said.

"Okay, what?"

"I'd prefer you and my daughter stay within the home at all times," he paused, and then added as if a carefully contemplated after-thought. "The weather is unpredictable this time of year."

"Sure no big deal. Oh and ..." all at once the rest of the sentence flew off and she could not remember what she was going to ask him.

"Yes."

She bit her upper lip feeling silly once again. "Nothing," she said softly. She played with her necklace wondering whether he was good looking and how old he was.

"See you in a month Becky Weatherspoon. There will be a cab outside your door at six a.m. December thirteenth, and Becky."

"Yeah?"

"I'm forty-two," he paused briefly, the need of lies seemed abundant in this conversation." The other part you can determine."

The telephone went dead.

Rebecca replaced the telephone in the cradle, mouth open, eyebrows raised, kicking herself for saying that aloud.

Or, had she?

Wen strolled over to the open front door and leaned on the doorframe staring intently into the driving snow. "She's coming Ellie," he whispered.

A dark figure stood at the outer edge of the tree line.
It was thirteen days to Christmas.
Tomorrow ... It would begin.

Two

♪On the first day of Christmas, my true love sent to me:
A Partridge in a Pear Tree ... ♪

"Stop! Stop!" Beth yelled like a crazy person.

Matt slammed on the brakes forgetting about the depth of the snow. The vehicle fishtailed, straightened, and then skidded forward and to the right. He checked the rear view mirror. Had he hit something? Had something broke and fallen off?

"Did you see that back there?"

"See what?"

"That sign!"

"Sign? ...What sign?" he asked.

"The Christmas tree farm sign."

"No," he said. He had not seen any sign recently, or for miles for that matter.

"Are you kidding me? You really didn't see it? It was big as a house and glowing," she said. She loosened her scarf then poked his knee with her index finger.

"Big as a house? Glowing?" He could not contain his amusement and started to laugh.

She scrunched her face up. "Okay ... Maybe not quite as big as a house, but almost, honest to God!" She undid her seat belt. "But it was glowing and it had a black Christmas tree on it with white ornaments with little faces or something," she murmured. Her eyes twinkled, mirroring that smile he loved so much.

Matt put the truck in reverse slowly backing.

She'd said it was a glowing sign with ornaments with little faces or something ... Okay fine ... But out of nowhere, for no reason, the 'or something' words jumped up and bit him on the back of the neck, shaking his flesh, giving him trouble. Why? ... He didn't know.

He slammed on the brake; checked the side mirrors, and the rear view. He was distracted, stuck on the 'or something.' He examined the area surrounding them. Everything seemed wrong, unfamiliar, out of place. He suddenly didn't know where he was. He had not remembered there ever being a fork in the road back there, but had taken it assuming it was a new short cut to the main road.

"Why'd you stop?" Beth asked. She was watching him intently; he seemed unnerved.

Matt lifted his hands waving them slightly back and forth in an attempt to act nonchalant. "So ... where's the sign?" He cleared his throat on purpose.

"It must be back further." She didn't take her eyes from him; unnerved had given way to unglued.

He forced his foot from the brake to the gas pedal, backing a couple feet then all at once stopping again. He opened his mouth and his tongue grabbed the opportunity, darting out and lulling to the side. He gawked about awkwardly. The 'or something' was still shaking the back of his neck. "How about we come back tomorrow? ... When it's daylight?"

"What?"

"How about we come back tomorrow? ... When it's daylight," he repeated. He again checked the mirrors, one after the other. He had grown grape sized goose bumps in-between the now erect hairs on his neck and the 'or something' had pitched a tent.

"It is daylight you idiot!" She reached over and touched the back of his hand. It was stone cold and mushy, like it had

16

died on the end of his arm. "What the hell is wrong with you?" she asked. He was way passed unglued.

"Beth, I think we're lost." He did not want to admit he was creeped out by those two little words, or something, and hoped that by saying he thought they were lost, which was true, he would defuse the crazy eye glare she was giving him; not to mention take her mind off the sign.

"Lost? ... How can we be lost? ... We both grew up around here."

"Look about. Is anything recognizable?"

"Everything looks different in the snow."

That was not the answer he was looking for. It didn't look different. It looked wrong. He put the truck in low gear, and stepped on the gas inching them forward along the road.

It started to snow.

"What about the sign?"

He crept along the road pretending it was difficult to steer the truck and taking his foot on and off the gas pedal.

"What is with you and that stupid sign anyway?" He did not take his eyes from the road.

The snow grew heavier.

"I wanted you to see it?"

"I'm good."

They travelled at a snail's pace down the road taking a half hour to cover two miles. The snow blew and drifted and whirled creating white outs.

"Look! ... Matt! Look! .... There it is! There's the sign!"

He slammed on the brakes.

It was there ... Right there ... Right up close and personal.

Beth rolled down the passenger side window reaching out her hand, grabbing hold of the edge.

"Beth don't!" he screeched. "Don't touch it! Get your hand back in!"

"It feels like velvet." She giggled stroking the edge of the sign.

"That sign was back behind us not two miles ahead of us. How could you know about it and have me looking for it, if we hadn't come to it yet? ... Tell me that! Beth!" he screamed. "Get your hand off it! ... Something's very wrong, Beth!"

Beth turned her head looking back over her shoulder at him. She did not say a word, just grinned the silliest of grins. Suddenly her body jerked, and then jerked again. She tossed side to side whipping out the window like a plastic slinky on steroids.

"Beth!" Matt rammed the truck in park and flung open the driver's door, running round to the passenger side.

Beth was nowhere. Gone. Completely gone. Without a trace. It was like the snow had simply swallowed her whole, or something. 'There were those two words again.'

He revolved in circles yelling her name.

He stepped back, his heel knocking up against something hard. He spun round picking it up. Dark, warm, red blood coated his hands, flowing over his wrists and under his sleeves like glacial rivers in spring.

His lips separated of their own accord.

He screamed screams he could not hear.

His inner circuits fused, forming a balled up clump.

He stared blankly at the object with the matted, blood soaked, tuft of hair.

Time slowed.

He watched the thing fall from his hands, spinning like a top in the snow, zigzagging along the roadside until coming to a rest against his left boot.

Beth's head severed cleanly and precisely. What remained of her face turned up to him, still wearing that silly grin. One eyeball stared out blankly, the other gone.

He stood stationary, frozen like an ice sculpture. He couldn't remember how to run. He couldn't remember his name. He couldn't remember anything.

He was still screaming.

He felt a yank on his right leg.

Then another.

Something sharp gouged into the flesh of his ankle, wrapping round three fold.

He went down, face planting into Beth's head. His fingers punched through the remaining eyeball bursting it like an over ripe grape. The insides hung off his nose and forehead.

Another jerk.

All of a sudden Matt was sliding backward through the snow, giving 'like lightening' a new meaning. Snow packed into his nose, mouth, and throat like wet cement, sealing off any chance of a breath.

One second he was there, the next he was gone. *Time waits for no one.*

Three

♪On the second day of Christmas, my true love sent to me:
Two Turtle Doves ... ♪

"Look!" Cindy thumped Steve in the back with mitted fists. "Look! ... Look!" She gestured with her arms to the side then behind sculpting them rhythmically like a cheerleader; all that was missing was the chant.

Steve slowed the snowmobile to an idle.

"Turn around! Turn around!" Cindy's voice was high pitched and full of excitement.

Steve pulled a one-eighty on the heavily snow covered road.

"Look at what?" He flipped up his face shield.

"There's a sign back there for a Christmas tree farm." Cindy was doing the cheerleader gesture thing again.

He smiled and shook his head. "You want to go and look for a Christmas tree? ... Now? ... Out here?" he asked. He looked about for the sign. He did not see it. "Where ever here is," he added too low for her to hear. He did not remember there being a fork in the road and his curiosity had taken hold. He drew his gloved hand across his lips regretting his decision. Nothing was recognizable, absolutely nothing. It was as if they had dropped through a hole into another dimension. Moreover, for some reason he couldn't put a finger on he was getting the creeps.

"Well?"

"Well? ... What?" He drew out the two words slowly, deliberately, attempting to hide his sudden confusion.

"Are you in there?" She knocked on his helmet.

"Yes ... I'm in here," he said quietly, repeating himself under his breath as his thoughts ran away with him. *'I'm in here Cindy ... You better believe I'm in here ... I'm so in here that I am having a really hard time making a decision. If I were a cartoon character, I would submit to my spider senses tingling and beat it out of here for no logical reason. Should I tell you that there was never a fork in the road and that I took it out of inquisitiveness and now, we are somewhere we should not be, and on top of that, I have an odd feeling? Or, should I do the macho thing and act like all this was part of the plan?'*

"Hey you?" Cindy chirped.

"What?" He was scanning both sides of the road as if he was looking for a missing pot of gold.

"You okay?" she asked. He had grown very quiet.

Steve nodded slowly, all the while every part of his being was screaming 'no' in capital letters. He decided not to share his thoughts; she was already looking at him as if he was severely out of his mind.

"Let's go pick out a tree!" Cindy suggested, suddenly unsure. This was only their fourth date, and this guy, the one who made her laugh nonstop and talked her ear off, was suddenly too silent and looking over his shoulder into the woods more often than he should. If he kept this up, he was going to get his name added into the definition of odd in the dictionary. She thought he would have been on the right side of normal meeting him at church and all.

Steve turned and stared at her, forcing a half smile that wasn't mirrored in his eyes. He paused before answering, paused long enough for the creeps to leap onto his booted foot, crawl up his leg, over his mid-section to his shoulder, and down his arms chilling all his skin. A simple warning sign in neon would have been better.

He swiped his tongue back and forth wetting his dry, cold lips. "Hooo ... arrr ... we are we?" He arched his shoulders stretching out his neck like a goose about to strike. He started over. "How are we ... we supposed to get it home?" He cleared his throat again. "Drag it behind the sled?" He forced another smile chewing on the right side of his inner cheek. *'Good God man, get it together, you're acting weirder than weird.'* He quickly answered his inner dialog. *'I know, I know.'*

"I'm sure they'll hold it," she said.

"Hold a Christmas tree?" he questioned. His voice crackling like a teenage boy, but at least the words were recognizable.

"Yeah why not?" she quipped, weird or not she did like him. She wrapped her arms around his chest giving him an enormous hug. "Please, please, "she pouted, with accompanying batting eyelashes.

Their relationship was too new for him to come out and say flat out 'no,' even with all the inner reasons: arms chilled, goose bumps, hair standing, creeps, and the big one, this road, the one and same that he didn't recognize or remember. He drew his gloved hand across his lips stifling the words ... *'Let's get the hell out of here.'*

"Please," she pushed.

"Okay," he replied. He slowly drove the sled forward, buckling his lips, sucking them into his mouth making his cheeks hollow. He mentally kicked himself for the answer. No would have been better, coming clean would have been better still. He had grown up in the next town over and spent all his life out on these roads, and this one was as if it had sprung up out of nowhere.

His thoughts abruptly stopped as the sign came cheek-to-cheek pressing against his flesh, as if they were lovers about to perform the 'Tango'. The Christmas tree farm sign, with an all-black tree bearing white skull ornaments. *'Skulls? ... Skulls?'* Was he seeing right? He moved the snowmobile closer. "Definitely skulls," he muttered.

"Cool huh?" Cindy was running her fingers along the sign tracing the outline of one of the skulls.

"Cool?" *'I would call it something else,'* he thought.

"Bet they're Goths." She seemed mesmerized by the sign, petting it much like one would a small furry animal.

"Would you stop touching it!" The creepy thing had stolen his idea and gotten that neon sign.

"It feels like velvet, take your glove off and touch it."

"No thanks," he said. *'Now who is acting weird?'* He smiled and nodded. *'Both of us, different reasons, but both.'*

"What are you waiting for? Let's go up the drive."

"Goths selling Christmas trees? This should be interesting."

She was still stroking the sign.

He gave the sled a burp of gasoline jolting it forward and putting several feet of distance between her and it.

She stood on the running boards, slapping him hard on the shoulder. "Why did you do that? I was enjoying it?"

"Enjoying it? You were petting a sign! It is a sign Cindy! Just a damn sign!"

"But I like it," she retorted. "You don't have to be short with me." She slapped his shoulder again.

He swivelled part way round giving her a look. It went by unnoticed. Her back was to him and she was waving bye to it like it was a long lost friend.

"Okay then," he muttered. He turned into the laneway.

This whole afternoon had fallen into the realm of bizarre and the icing on the cake was that Goddamn sign. That very odd sign. The sign that, although he knew better, he believed had pulled her in, forming an invisible hold on her like something out of an old science fiction movie. She had protested

far too much being dislodged from it in his opinion. Maybe some relationships were not meant to work, were not meant to go farther; this snowmobile ride was bringing out qualities in each of them that should have remained buried deep inside.

She was still waving as he throttled the sled into a higher gear. They flew along the snowy lane through its hairpin twists and turns, hills and valleys, spraying out a rooster tail of snow. If the pathway to hell was snow covered then this was surely it.

He pulled to a halt, after what seemed like hours of running, in the only open area they had come to, a small clearing in the middle of thick hardwood forests.

They both dismounted and removed their helmets.

He browsed the area. "I don't see any Christmas tree farm, do you?"

Cindy shook her head back and forth in a slow no, showing obvious disappointment. "We could go back to the sign and start over again?" she suggested.

He ignored her. "Let's get going. It'll be dark soon." He felt a twinge of relief. He could not wait to back track out of the hellish laneway and be on the side road he had never seen before.

Cindy held out her hand, which he too quickly grasped.

They about faced in unison.

Both gasped at the same time.

The only difference was the reason; one awe, the other horror.

Just beyond the sled stood high, red, sloppily painted wooden fencing stretching as far as the eye could see. Evergreen trees poked over top the rails. The white washed makeshift gates stood ajar. A cock-eyed open sign hung from one.

Cindy squealed with glee like a schoolgirl, toting him through the gates.

"Wow! ... Oh, wow! Look at all the beautiful trees!"

Standing front and center, as if on show, stood an all-black tree adorned with white skull ornaments.

Cindy let go of his hand running over to it. "It's the tree from the sign!" she exclaimed. "Oh my God! Isn't it amazing?"

He moved in beside her analysing the tree and skulls. "Amazing? ... No! Hideous? ... Hell yes!"

Cindy was not listening; she was enthralled once again. She ran her fingertips over one of the skulls. "They feel so lifelike."

He leaned closer. There was a repulsive odour coming off the tree. It reminded him of a backed up sewer with copper piping.

He grabbed her hand pulling it back.

"Don't!" she snapped.

"What the hell is wrong with you girl? Don't you realize your mauling skulls?"

"They're not skulls, they're ornaments!" She shot back. "Very creative ornaments."

Steve stepped back. He had no come back. *They sure look like human skulls.'*

Cindy was tracing her fingers in and out of the eye, nose, and mouth cavities. Her fingers looked like she had dipped them in red paint. She giggled profusely.

Disbelief furrowed along the lines in his forehead. *'What is that red stuff, blood?'* He grabbed her sleeve jerking her hand loose, flipping it palm side up and bringing it to his nose. His nostrils flared as he caught the unmistakable smell of decomposition.

Cindy gave him a hurt look tearing free of him. She darted off in amongst the rows of Christmas trees.

A blood-curdling scream rang out like 'Hell's Bells.'

"Fuck this!" he turned to run.
Darkness engulfed him.

Four

♫On the third day of Christmas, my true love sent to me:
Three French Hens ... ♫

Ralph Conners left the squad car idling as he slid from the seat and out the driver's door with his pen and notepad. He zipped up his police issue bomber jacket making his way down the embankment and up the other side.

He walked slowly and carefully in the deep snow over to the skidoo and inspected it for damage. It was highly unusual for a brand new sled to be sitting abandoned in the middle of a field. He wrote down the make, model, and plate number, and then turned his attention to the truck, repeating the process verbatim.

He backtracked over to the squad car, grabbed the radio and called in the plate numbers. He drummed his fingers on the steering wheel as he waited for the dispatcher to retrieve the information.

Snow began to fall.

"Hey Ralph," the dispatcher said.

He smiled. There had been a shift change. "Hi Erma, what ya got for me?"

"The truck is registered to a Matt Hammond of Lakehurst County. That boy is sure a long way from home. The snowmobile belongs to Steve Boramack, couple of counties over. You know the Boramacks? Herb and Zena? Steve's the third youngest son, the one that broke up with his wife a year or so back."

He smiled yet again; good old Erma knew everything about everyone in these parts.

"What's the scoop?"

"Don't know what to tell ya, these vehicles are sitting empty with the keys in them, side by side in this field here."

"Where is here Ralph?"

He glanced around all of a sudden unsure of his location. "Hold on there, I'm going for a walk. Be right back." He sat the radio on the driver's seat.

"Ralph location please? ... Ralph? ... Ralph? ... Crap Ralph you know you should not wander off too far alone without the two-way radio. Okay then, I'll be right here." Erma drew circles on her report pad in purple ink waiting for his return. "Shouldn't be long," she said into her head set, gazing out the window. "It's getting nasty out there," she added. She watched the heavy snow whirl around on the street outside the station.

Ralph stood silent, deep in thought, scrutinizing each vehicle in turn. There were no tracks of any kind. Judging by the amount of old snow around them, there should have been at least faint ones.

Something was off.

He trudged down the road a piece and stopped. He shuffled and padded his feet turning in a three-sixty, eyeing up all and everything. Nothing was familiar. Was he at old Ed's farm and they tore down the house and buildings? Or, mistakenly in the next county over? He could not place his position. Maybe it was that new fork in the road a ways back. He shrugged, pulling his scarf tight around his neck tucking the ends into his jacket as he about faced and walked back over to the field.

He ambled around the vehicles one more time. They too offered up nothing in the way of location.

The snow grew heavy and dense.

He unfolded the earflaps on his hat, pulling it down on his head as far as it would go. The wife would have his hide if he

got chilled again. He had just gotten over flu. He headed across the field to the fence line, following it up and over the knoll.

He stopped dead in his tracks.

His body swayed back and forth on legs that felt as if they were made of matchsticks. Too thin match sticks.

Hunks of what looked like freezer burnt raw stewing beef dotted the snow where it was still white. Sheared off pieces of partial limbs, long ribbons of skin, and hunks of internal organs lay in divots of frozen blood ponds. Entrails looped like macabre streamers in and out and around the carnage, it was as if a butcher and a sausage maker had a very bad day.

Vomit rose and bubbled in his throat. He cupped his mouth forcing himself to swallow it back down; he did not want to contaminate the scene. He took deep breath after deep breath, steadying his nerves before moving in for a closer study.

Was this an attack by a wolf pack? Bears? He looked for bite impressions. He lifted what looked like a mutilated hand with a stick. He turned it round finding imprints of teeth on the backside. His mouth opened crystallizing the salvia on his tongue. He'd been hunting game since childhood and been a cop for over thirty years. These were like nothing he had ever seen in his life. Deep elongated fanglike impressions. No—incisors. This was no wild animal or human being.

He dropped the hand, twisted round, and started to run.

His heartbeats echoed in his ears. He flung open the driver's door and grabbed the radio. "Get back up out here! ... Now! ... Get the coroner! ... Get the chief! ... Get the fire department! ... Hell, get everybody!" he screamed.

He all at once felt uneasy. He lifted his head scanning the field where he'd come from.

"Coroner?" Erma shot back. "The chief? Where is here?"

He did not answer. He was scrutinizing the tree and fence line; he would have sworn on his mother's grave that he had just heard something. Something unnatural.

"Repeat! ... Repeat! Where is here?" Erma asked.

"I don't fucking know! ... Just get them out here!"

He thought he saw movement.

Erma motioned to the other dispatcher to come to her. Ralph was really on a roll this time. "Okay Ralph ... The jigs up! Quit kidding around." Erma and the other dispatcher pulled their chairs tight together waiting for the bouts of laughter from Ralph.

There wasn't any ... But what there was made their blood run cold.

Ralph's first screams were ear shattering, the second bout shrill and hollow.

Erma had thrown her headset down onto her desk with the first lot of screams. Everyone in the station heard the horror coming from her head set and had come running. She held her stomach feeling as if she was about to throw up.

The third set of screams hissed and gurgled, and the fourth did not come.

Ralph staggered backward, clumsily clawing at his neck with both hands. His eyes rolled back in his head. He collapsed, folding in sections down onto the snow like a soggy piece of cardboard.

It had come from behind.

There was no sound as his body was dragged through the snow.

The squad car, sled, and truck sat side by side by side in the field as if making friends.

The heavy snow turned to a raging blizzard.

Five

♫*On the fourth day of Christmas, my true love sent to me:*
Four Calling Birds ... ♫

"There you are." Rebecca called out, hurriedly crossing the street in her nightclothes. She kicked and shook each foot as she went attempting to keep the snow from her slippers.

Ellie was standing on top three dark coloured plastic milk crates, her ponytail hung loosely down the back of her pyjama top, her face plastered tightly against the neighbour's kitchen window as if it had become part of it.

Rebecca smiled at the cross-patterned drag marks coming from the side of the carport to the front of the house in the snow. This six-year-old kid was sure inventive.

"What has you so intrigued, my little one?" She went up on tiptoes putting her hands on the windowpane and tilting forward.

The air felt like it all at once vaporized from around her.

On the inside windowsill laid the carcass of a brown tabby cat, its corpse twisted and distorted, and alive with white fat wiggly maggots. Its abdomen split bow to sternum. Its backbone was free of flesh and currently in use as a maggot highway. Its intestines hung decomposing on the drapery valance in perfectly placed loops.

Rebecca put one foot up on the top milk crate as she lifted the other off the ground. She held it straight out behind her using it as a makeshift balance rudder. She cupped Ellie's eyes with her hands.

The milk crates teeter-tottered back and forth under their combined weight, and then gained momentum, lifting at the

front corners. They flew backward tumbling ass over teakettle and landing in a heap on top of the ornamental bushes.

She tugged Ellie to a stand, running as fast as her feet would carry her, skiing Ellie behind her in her bare feet.

Rebecca flung her inside the entranceway and slammed the house door shut.

The power flickered and went out.

She inched her way over to the front window, no street lamps, nothing. "Figures," she muffled.

It started to snow again.

Rebecca gazed at the house across the street they had run from. It looked no different than it had since her arrival three days ago. Totally engulfed in darkness, no vehicles in the carport, no sign of life; 'Not even the cat' crawled unbidden from her mind. A mental picture of the cat flashed before her eyes. She wrapped her arms around her middle. "Good Lord," she whispered.

She glanced out the window again. It seemed as if this snowfall had brought an eerie, look over your shoulder, dread with it, the kind that allowed one to hear their own heartbeat.

Rebecca crept her way through the darkness into the kitchen, opening drawers feeling for a flashlight. The fifth drawer netted results. "Okay now let's find that number," she started flipping through papers on the counter.

"You always talk to yourself?" Ellie was gazing up at her.

"Yeah, sometimes."

"What you doing?"

"Looking for your dad's cell phone number." Rebecca flipped through another heap of papers. "Ah! ... Here it is!" She shone the flashlight along the walls finding the telephone. She punched in the number.

The kitchen table started to vibrate.

Rebecca directed the flashlight beam onto the table. The cell phone shimmered as it whirled round in tight circles. "So much for that," she muttered.

Rebecca hung up the house phone. The plunk seemed to bounce through the house changing in tone and dimension as it went.

She turned to Ellie.

She had disappeared.

"Ellie? ... Ellie?" Rebecca yelled.

Something knocked against her shoulder; something cold as ice. She whirled round going ballistic, flashing the light up and down the walls, ceiling, and floors.

Another knock.

Rebecca reeled hitting Ellie directly in the eyes with the beam. "Good God kid! You almost made me jump out of my skin!" She put down the light, scooting the child out of the corner and down off the kitchen counter.

"Would you have looked like the kitty if you'd jumped out of your skin?" Ellie whispered.

"Let's not talk about the kitty in the dark."

"In the daylight's okay?"

"Yeah, I guess so ... If we really have to."

"We don't have to."

"Good then. That's solved. Let's get back to what we were doing, okay?"

Ellie nodded in the dark.

"Does your dad have a telephone, out where he is?"

"Nope."

"Jesus Christ!" Rebecca muttered. She went back to searching drawers, this time for a telephone book.

"Looking for this?" Ellie shoved skinny yellow pages into her hand.

She didn't ask how she knew what she was looking for, leaving that alone.

She punched the police number into the telephone with her right index finger. It had not even rung once when there was a voice on the other end.

"Provincial police," said the female voice.

"May I have a constable?" Rebecca suddenly felt nervous.

"You have one. How may I assist you?"

"All the power is out here," she blurted. "And there's a dead cat and no car in the driveway and ..."

The constable cut her off. "The power is out here as well. There is a main feed line down. Next time though please call the hydro company. As for the dead cat in the neighbour's window, that is not our department. That would be animal welfare. Do you wish their number Miss Weatherspoon?"

"I ... I ... I ... didn't say the cat ... was ... was in the neighbour's window. I ... I ... didn't give my ... my name either." *'Why in hell am I nervous? Why in hell am I stuttering? Why in hell are my hands shaking? What is wrong with me?'*

"Of course you did Miss Weatherspoon, after all, how else would I know?"

The telephone buzzed and went dead.

Rebecca shone the flashlight back and forth over the telephone, her forehead wrinkled with disbelief. *'Did the police department just hang up on me?'* She pressed the talk button; a dial tone hummed. She pressed the redial button; it connected immediately blaring out a busy signal. *'What a god damn asshole fucked up place this is!'* She threw the receiver into the sink.

Ellie was by her side gazing up at her with eyes that seemed a lot older and wiser than a six-year-old.

"Want to stay with me until the power comes back on?"

"I'm okay."

Rebecca went down on one knee, putting her hands into the small of Ellie's back and bringing them face to face. "You know you and I are supposed to stay indoors?"

Ellie nodded.

"I'll have to tell him you know." Her voice faded to a slight whisper as she added, "Eventually ... Maybe."

Ellie's lips drew into a sideways smirk. She did an about face and skipped off down the hall disappearing into the darkness.

Rebecca edged her way around the kitchen, fetching the telephone from the sink. She depressed the lever. No dial tone. She threw it back into the basin.

Giggles floated into the living room hanging themselves above Rebecca's head like hot-air word balloons.

She sat the flashlight into the book page using it as a marker. She had been so absorbed in the story the world around her had ceased to exist.

More giggles.

She cocked her head listening. "What in hell is that kid up to now?" she said.

She stretched out her arms getting her bearings, tiptoeing through the kitchen and down the hallway toward Ellie's bedroom.

The short corridor seemed overly dark and unnatural with navy blue overtones. The walls felt cold and damp to her touch, not unlike an underground passage. She bit at her lip immobilizing as her fingertips slid onto the doorframe.

"Cool huh?" Ellie quipped. She snickered out of control.

"Yeah ... Like that's the best. Wish I could have seen it," a different girl's voice replied.

"It was all mangled and blown," Ellie boasted.

They are talking about the cat. That damn poor dead cat. The word 'they're' rolled around in her head before taking up point front and center. They're as in they are, two meaning more than one, separate and apart entities.

Every hair on the back of Rebecca's neck prickled and stood.

She stayed silent, attempting to make sense of all she was hearing ... Two little girls? Two little girls sitting in a bedroom in the pitch-black ... Two little girls sitting in a bedroom in the pitch-black finding amusement in a dead cat? ... Two of them like the *'Doublemint Gum'* advertisements ... Two for the price of one ... Where'd the other girl come from? ... How'd she get in? ... How long has she been here?

Another huge bout of laughter.

Rebecca stepped into the open doorway.

She could see absolutely nothing.

There should have been an inkling of light from the window. Snow reflected. The drapes were drawn.

"Ellie!" she shouted abruptly. Her breath folded back and hit her square in the face. The room felt like an ice castle. "Ellie!" she called.

Nothing but silence, silence and darkness.

Shuffling wormed out of the stillness, shuffling of little feet.

"Ellie stop this shit!"

More shuffling.

"Ellie I mean it. I'm not fooling around!"

"Yes Becky." Ellie's voice was close, very close, in her ear close.

"It's Rebecca and where in the hell are you?"

"I'm right here beside you on top of the book shelf."

"Will you quit doing that! ... Get down, right now," she ordered. "And where is your little friend?"

"What friend?"

"For Christ's sake! ... You damn well know what I am talking about! Don't play games, I heard you both."

A chilled little hand slipped into hers.

"Well?" Rebecca stamped one foot impatiently.

"It's just me in here."

Rebecca stepped into the room swiping blindly back and forth with her free arm.

"I'm the only one in here. ... Honest Injun, I was playing with my dolly."

"Ellie, you don't have a dolly! Why I don't know, but you don't."

"I do so. I make my fists into balls and pretend they are dolls and they talk back and forth to each other."

Rebecca sighed. "Yeah right, and it is ninety degrees in the shade outside too. ... I'll walk you home whoever you are, when the power comes back on."

"There's nobody else here. You don't believe me, do you?" Ellie started to fake whimper.

"No I don't." Rebecca gathered Ellie up in her arms. "Oh for God's sake, don't cry."

"But, but ..." Ellie's grin well masked by the darkness.

Rebecca cut her off. "Did she go back out the window?"

"No."

"Then what the hell?"

Ellie wrapped her arms around Rebecca's neck and her legs around her middle, molding her body into Rebecca.

"Crap kid ... You are something else!" Rebecca turned putting heel to toe, moving slowly down the hall through the kitchen into the living room. She plunked down into the overstuffed chair wearing Ellie like a piece of 'Velcro.'

She gently rubbed the cool skin of Ellie's back attempting to warm her." You always feel so cold my little dove. Why is that?" Rebecca brought her closer, folding her in and under her sweater.

"Mamma calls me dove too," Ellie whispered.

The terminology flew past Rebecca without a second's thought. "She did, did she?"

Ellie nodded against her arm. "You're not mad at me?" Ellie wiggled round in her lap laying her head against her chest, nesting like an animal.

"No ...Well sort of but ..." she did not finish the sentence. Ellie's body was heavy and relaxed. Cold, but heavy and relaxed. She knew she was close to sleep.

'What an odd little girl this one was. Did she for one minute believe she was alone in her bedroom? No ... But where had the child came from and where had she gone? Or, was she still in the house, lurking somewhere in the darkness? She would look later, much later.

Rebecca decided to wait for the power to return before putting Ellie to bed.

Hours later, she scrawled out a memo in orange crayon for Wen noting the power outage, the dead cat in the neighbour's window across the street with the no car in the carport, and lastly her telephone call to the police, which had gone south. She did not include anything else. The content seemed bizarre enough. She stuck it on the refrigerator door with duct tape.

The whistling kettle undermined the first gurgled hiss and the second; but not the third. It was there ... Peculiar ... Unsettling ... Disturbing.

Rebecca stiffened, listening.

Five minutes of nothingness passed, just long enough to make Rebecca think all was right.

But it wasn't.

It had stayed silent, waiting.

When it came again it was closer, unnerving and frightening in a way that made one look over their shoulder, find nothing, and do it again as they started to run.

She closed her eyes straining, listening, attempting resolve. She scuffled over to the front door, opening it, ears prickling, tuning in like antenna to what lay beneath the wind.

Like a cat and mouse game, it again lay dormant, as if it had known at the click of the door mechanism to withdraw and dig down into the shadows where it would be unseen, where it could fester to return another time when least suspected.

The power flickered and went out ... Again.

Rebecca trailed down the hallway sticking her arms straight out to the side using them as feelers, calling it a day.

The walls juddered. Thunderous bangs echoed along the ceilings.

She sat bolt upright in bed.

It sounded like the entire house was under siege.

She jerked the bedroom lamp cord from the wall, holding the light as a makeshift weapon as she silently stole from her bedroom into the hallway.

Deafening rapid bangs wailed throughout the dwelling.

Rebecca stood stationary, weapon ready, searching the source.

It was Wen's room. His dresser drawers were opening and closing in rapid succession. Cupboard doors were smashing into the wallboards.

Someone was in the house.

She crept down the hall stopping at the doorway just out of the line of sight.

She leaned into the doorframe one eyeing the room through the darkness.

Wen was bent over, fetching something from the floor, his back to the door.

"What the fuck Wen?" She felt like shaking him to death. "You scared the living hell out of me! ... I thought whatever made those noises earlier broke in!"

"Forgot my key, had to use the window," his voice was unusually hoarse. He coughed clearing his throat. "You heard a noise outside?" he muffled. It sounded like his mouth was stuffed full of cotton balls. His clothes were shiny and glued to him as if he was soaking wet. He smelled of rot.

"Yeah." She cupped her nose, the smell of him bringing her close to vomiting. "What the hell happened to you? Take a swim in someone's septic tank?"

He ignored her question. "Like what?"

She shrugged her shoulders. "I don't know." Rebecca watched him fumbling round in the blackness. She reached for the bedroom light switch.

"Don't," he muttered without turning round. He moved closer to the window throwing off his shirt and tee shirt. His hands slipped to his belt buckle unfastening it. "Excuse me Becky," he said slightly above a whisper.

"Sorry," she could feel her cheeks flush. She had been standing in his bedroom doorway watching him undress.

She had gone through a gambit of emotions this night, startled by a dead cat in a window, alarmed at the power failing ... twice, unnerved by a two sided conversation of Ellie's, scared by odd noises, frightened at the sounds of Wen coming in through a window; And to top it all off, ashamed. She might as well have tipped over the boiling pot and scalded her bare feet too.

Rebecca lay down on top of her bed covers listening to the sounds of the continuous banging and thudding from the room next to her. All that had taken up residence in her mind, like Ellie, the dead cat, the storm, and the power outage, flew off and away as she heard running and then the slamming of the front door.

The heavy stench of whatever Wen had on his clothing wafted down the hallway into her room. She rose with all intents and purposes of closing his door but found herself

bowed over, one hand cupping her mouth and nose, while the other rifled through his stained clothing with the pasted on chunks of something. She had no idea what he had gotten in to, only that it stunk, like road kill lying out under a hot sun. The stink seemed to form a dense cloud at the ceiling. It wafted back and forth as she moved about the trashed room. Dead center lay an open rectangular metal box. The padlock cut. A piece of old weathered silk caught up in the hinge, draping down onto the floor. She ran her free hand back and forth across the pitted metal. Something important had been in there.

She slowly ambled back to her room. Her sister had ties to this family? Where'd she meet them ... A road trip to Hell?

She sat on the edge of her bed staring out the window, watching the snow twirl and dance in the wind where shadows of unspeakable things crept just out of sight.

She remained as she was for the rest of night.

Six

♪On the fifth day of Christmas, my true love sent to me:
Five Golden Rings ... ♪

"Did you see that?" Michelle's face was plastered against the passenger window.

"See what?" Phillip did not take his eyes from the road.

"That ... That thing in the trees!" Her voice was sharp and off key.

Phillip glanced at her questioningly. All he could see was whirling snow.

"Go faster! ... Go faster!" Michelle screamed.

"Are you crazy?" he shot out. "We're in a blizzard!"

"It's keeping up with the car! ... Oh my God! ... It's keeping up with the car!" Her voice clacked and broke with each word, panic was at a premium.

"What the hell are you screaming about?"

"Go! ... Go! ... Go!" Michelle shrieked.

She unfastened her seat belt lurching over and stomping her foot on top of his, pressing the gas pedal to the floor. The car tires spun causing a giant rooster tail of snow. The car zigzagged back and forth out of control, plowing sideways into a snowdrift.

Her fingernails dug half-moon pits into the rubber window seal as she stared out, eyes whipping back and forth like lightening.

Her one arm rose, extended, hand pointed. "It's right there ... Good God in hell ... It's right there!" She started to cry.

"What the fuck is wrong with you?" The driver's window was a third of the way down and Phillip was clawing fistfuls of snow away from the side mirror.

She cupped his face with both hands forcefully turning his head to the right.

"That!"

His eyes fell on something he could not comprehend, something that looked like it should be long dead but wasn't. "Fucking hell ... What is that?"

"Oh my God ... No," Michelle sobbed.

Michelle's and Phillip's screams pierced the air like arrows launched by an archer, one after another. The screams guttural, then rumbling, then foamy, and then silenced.

They were no more.

The sounds of their bodies yanked from the car and across the snow were lost to the wind.

The set of semi-circular footprints full of blood seeped over into the soft snow and soon were lost too.

Nature had a way of keeping its secrets.

Seven

♫On the sixth day of Christmas, my true love sent to me:
Six Geese a Laying ... ♫

Rebecca poked out her arms from under the coverlet; stretching them full out, fanning at the sun stream that looked like it was full of fairy dust. She rolled out of bed, grabbed her robe putting it on as she sauntered sleepily towards the kitchen.

The smell of bacon and eggs accompanied by the sounds of endless chatter etched a smile across her lips. She crossed the kitchen bee lining for the coffee pot, giving a nod in the direction of Wen, Ellie, and a man she had never seen before. Her eyes flickered to the platter of food dead centre of the table and the four place settings. Her smile broadened.

"Hi sleepyhead," Wen said.

Rebecca sipped her coffee glancing up at the wall clock. "Twelve-thirty? ... Okay who's the wise guy that changed the hands?" She sat down at the table.

"It is twelve-thirty, really." Wen confirmed.

"What the hell? Are you sure?"

Wen nodded. "So what had you so interested in the wood shed until almost dawn?"

Rebecca gagged on her coffee going into a coughing fit. "What are you ... You talking about? I wasn't in the wood shed. I was here with Ellie."

Wen drew his hand across his lips trying to conceal his amusement. "Sure you were," he said slowly.

"How would you know anyway, you're never here?" Rebecca shot back. This was the first time she had witnessed him smile.

She could feel Wen's eyes on her, watching, studying, examining. She wondered what he was thinking; she could not read him. He wore an impenetrable mask.

"Who's for more coffee?" Wen grabbed the coffee pot topping up his and Rebecca's mugs. He glanced at the other man's cup. "You're good" he mumbled and replaced the pot on the burner.

The man never moved, just sat as he was.

Wen dished out breakfast to each of them and then folded the small town paper he had been reading in half. He picked at his breakfast then put his fork down. He eyed up Rebecca. "Have you read the front page news?" He tapped the paper with his fork giving Ellie, who was playing with her food, a stern sideways glance.

She instantly stopped.

"No. I didn't even know there was one." Rebecca bit off the end of a piece of bacon chewing it slowly. "So ... What's it say?"

The man still just sat there.

"That there's a police constable missing and some of the towns people; Fifteen in total." He was studying her again.

"Are you kidding me?"

"Yes," he said slowly. It was a lie; there really was a constable and fifteen people missing. He folded up the small paper and stuffed it into his pocket.

The man sat as he was.

Wen turned to him. "So what do you think of the state of the world affairs?" He waited a few moments drumming his fingers on the tabletop. "No comment? Good choice." Wen's eyes flickered to Rebecca, then to Ellie. He started to pick through his breakfast again.

All of a sudden, the man exhaled long and loud as if someone had pushed his start button, bringing him to life. He struggled with his one arm, moving it in small odd jerks like it was made of old brittle rubber bands. He swiped it back and forth, awkwardly steadying it with the other hand as he fumbled with his coffee mug, finally latching onto the handle. He lifted it from the table tilting it to the side and spilling the contents all over himself. As if oblivious to the spill, he stood without a word, moving with the same odd jerks in the direction of the front door, banging into it head on. He staggered backward as if regrouping, came back around in front of the door, reached for the handle with both hands, and clumsily opened it. He trudged out onto the porch, down the walkway, and onto the drive. Once he reached the end of the driveway, he straightened, pivoted army like, and then continued along the roadway.

Rebecca watched intensely, in total bewilderment as the man clomped along, jerking and weaving. She shifted her gaze to Wen, to the man, and then back to Wen who indifferently sipped his coffee and read the newspaper.

Ellie pushed her uneaten plate of food into the middle of the table and asked to be excused; leaving before an answer was given.

Rebecca rolled her tongue around in her mouth—words at a loss. She leaned across the table pounding Wen in the arm with one hand, pointing to the doorway with the other.

Nothing. No response. He was totally engrossed in that paper.

She bit her tongue on purpose, freeing herself from the fuzz of stupid. "Wen!" she yelled.

He put down his mug, folded the newspaper and stuck it back into his pocket, all the while gazing straight at her.

Rebecca swept her arm to point in the direction of the open front door. "There's something wrong with that man!" There, she'd finally found the words.

He smiled strangely. "Why would you think that?"

"He ... He ... He's not right!" She was whipping her arms back and forth pointing wildly.

"He's been like that for awhile, pay no mind," Wen said.

Rebecca sped out onto the front porch. The man was still in sight, clomping zombie like down the road, going God knows where.

"Pay no mind?" she yelled from the porch. "He's out there without a coat!" She added. *'He is out there without a coat. Good God Rebecca, of all the dumb asinine things to say, you say he is out there without a coat!'*

Wen shrugged.

She moved over to the side rail of the porch, watching the man as his pace slowed to a crawl and he started to stumble and wobble. He began vibrating like a long metal rod knocked by a hammer, and then halted, stiffened, dropped his arms to his sides, suddenly tipping face first like an old wooden plank and disappearing from sight behind the snow bank.

"Oh my God ... He just fell down ... I'm going to go help him!" Rebecca turned running across the porch.

Wen caught her by the arm swinging her around. "Don't worry about it. You're here for Ellie not him."

Rebecca gunned him down, her mouth opening and closing in silent rapid successions. She should have been saying so much. She swivelled her head like an owl, glancing at the place where the man had been walking along, if one would call it that. She wondered if he was still there lying plastered into the snow or if he had crawled off somewhere.

Wen guided her by the elbow back into the house, closing and locking the door behind them.

He placed a fresh hot coffee in front of her on the table.

She sat rigid, elbows splayed, hands palm side up cupping her chin, daggering him so intensely her eyes were watering. His pleasantness was gone and he was back to his standard stiff mannerism. The long and the short of it he was right, she was there for Ellie, but hell this was all so out there. She smirked. Her entire time at this place was so out there. She begrudgingly sipped her coffee.

"I was thinking of walking to the grocery store later with Ellie and picking up a few things." She watched him stirring his coffee; he had been stirring for the last five minutes.

"What do you need?" He did not look up. He appeared deep in thought.

"I don't know exactly, maybe some fruit and a few other things. I was going to make chili for supper so I thought ..."

Wen cut her off. "Ellie doesn't eat fruit."

"Well, she should don't you think?"

"She doesn't eat chili either," he said flatly.

He put down his spoon, which was a good thing, Rebecca had been about ready to jump across the table, grab it from his hand, and ask him what the hell he was doing, trying to churn it into coffee butter.

He stared her down, commandingly, authoritatively. "Write down what you need. I'll pick it up."

"It would be nice for us both to get out."

He came around the table, bending down and lining them up face to face. He gently brushed the fallen hair from her ponytail away from her eye. "If you recall Miss Becky, you and Ellie are supposed to say inside the house at all times." He was so close, in her invisible space close.

"I remember, but hell some exercise ... Some fresh ..." she did not go further. She did not even correct her name, she felt, invaded.

"I would prefer the two of you stay in the house as we agreed and besides ..." He paused, moving back out of her private space. "You two have already been outside for exercise and fresh air. Have you not?"

She pasted on a smirk. She didn't say a word, she didn't need to, he'd read the note.

"Besides," he continued. "The weather is most unstable this time of year; a storm can come up out of nowhere."

"Of course," she retorted. "Of course," she said again sarcastically.

There was no hint of smile on his face but his eyes were sparkling, she knew she had entertained him ... Yet again. She grabbed a pen and paper glancing at the refrigerator door in the process. The crayon note was gone.

She commenced scrawling out a small grocery list. "So what about the content of the note I ..."

"All taken care of," he cut in.

"What are you, a mind reader?" This was not the first, or even second time, he had answered her before she finished the sentence. He had done this too on the telephone call that had brought her to this place. She remembered wondering his age and if he was good looking, and he had answered with his age of forty-two and the other part he was leaving to her to decide, and yes, she decided, he had rugged good looks; he reminded her of the old 'Marlborough Man' commercials. "Well ... Are you?"

He smirked.

"So what about the neighbour? He still hasn't come home."

"He's away for Christmas ... And no, I'm not a mind reader, just perceptive." He was openly smiling now.

She put the pen down, pushing the grocery list across the table to him. "How do you know? You said you both just moved here, did you not?"

"I asked around." His smile broadened showing off his dimples.

Rebecca leaned over to him. "Do I amuse you or something?"

"Yes ... Yes you do."

"And in passing, I don't believe you asked around."

"I know."

Wen left just as dark fell.

Rebecca watched Wen turn into a shadow figure, disappearing into the darkness as if he was part and parcel of it. It no longer struck her as odd that he seemed to float above the snow as he travelled, or that he vanished as if he'd never been there at all. It was commonplace now, as was the peculiar little Ellie.

She turned on the outside porch lights, which had become habit since the dead cat episode. There were also those peculiar noises each, and every, night since. Sounds that were unnerving and indescribable. Sounds that clung onto the skin at the back of your neck and never left. She had rationalized them as being pieces of eve hanging down and rubbing against the brickwork. The only other option being it was something else; And, something else was not a good option for a woman alone most of the night with a six year old child, even as strange a child as Ellie. The muffled gurgles and growls, with the underlying hisses rotating round the house and across the windows, could be something as simple as a tree branch. *'A tree branch that circles the house?'* She did not go there. She had mentioned it to Wen, but at the time he was pre-occupied as usual. She figured that the topic would come up again, eventually. *'A tree branch that circles the house and a hanging piece of awning that gurgles, growls, and hisses?'* She bit at her bottom lip, *'yeah right'* she thought, *'that sort of topic comes up every day.'*

She glanced back and forth and up and down the street; none of the other houses had a single light on, strange for this time of year. The street should have lit up the night sky with glowing Santas and reindeers and huge air ornaments and twinkling wreaths and icicle lights, and there was just nothing.

She shut the front door locking it. The nothingness put her on edge. The kind of on edge you got when you were a child alone in the dark tucked in bed in your room and the closet door inched open all on its own.

She curled up in her new favourite chair by the living room window, staring out into the reeling snow. The living room matched the rest of the house, minimal furnishings, the missing touches of an adult female resident was obvious. She wondered why there was no Christmas tree for Ellie, or a television or radio. Ellie herself did not have any pretty girl things or toys, or even anything pink in her room. The strange little girl with the stone cold hands and the intense green eyes who still had not ate a speck of food she had prepared for her.

She shifted in the chair her thoughts turning to Wen. The odd named guy turned on and off his social skills with the flick of a switch. Quiet. Reserved. Secretive. Same intense eyes as his daughter just a different colour. The old friend of her sister, the friend she had never heard tell of; the friend who on the other hand seemed to know a disturbing amount about her. Moreover, what on earth did he do for twelve days?

Then there was the police service, with the busy telephone, who knew the cat was dead in the window across the road and her name without being told. The odd visitor who came from God knows where, who hadn't said one single word while sitting at the table like a transforming zombie,

and then left and fell down in the snow face first with no one seeming to care; no one translating to Wen.

Her world right now, was very small.

The back door slammed.

"Ellie? ... Ellie!" Rebecca yelled. She jumped from the chair sprinting through the house. "Ellie?" she screamed.

No Ellie ... Anywhere.

She went to the back door reefing on it so hard she went ass over teakettle backwards. It was stuck. "God damn kid! ... Bet she's outside again."

She ran back into the living room, twisting and turning and tugging the front door knob, forgetting it was locked. She rammed her shoulder into it glancing downward at the lock. "Jesus Christ!" she muttered, turning the mechanism and unlocking the door. She bolted across the porch and down into the snow.

"Ellie ... Ellie?" Rebecca ran around the house finding her in the side yard nestled down in the snow, pyjamas, bare feet, and all. She was sitting cross-legged her back to Rebecca and appeared to be off in another world.

"Ellie what in God are you doing out here? How many times have I found you out in the snow now? Four, five, six? You're going to catch your death of cold ..." Rebecca's words broke as Ellie turned her way. The tip of her tongue clung onto the roof of her mouth hanging the remainder like a floppy wet blanket.

"Holy shit! ... Ellie! ... Oh my God in hell!" Rebecca's eyes felt like something had removed them and stuck in pie plates.

Blood covered Ellie from her neck down. A small dead dog lay in her lap. Its head lulled down past its body and was facing backward. Its legs mangled and pointing in directions the good lord never intended. Its underside ripped open from neck to tail. Its intestines were outside its body and looped in neat little coils on each of Ellie's knees. Something had definitely been at it.

Her eyes lifted and flickered across Ellie's mouth. No blood.

"He's all broken. Can we fix him?" Ellie was gazing up at her sweetly.

"Can we fix him?" she repeated. *'Can we fix him?'*

"Can we Becky?"

She had asked again. *'Oh Lord what is wrong with this child?'*

"Where ....Where did ... Did you get that?" Rebecca's mouth dried making it difficult to spit out words and her hanging blanket of a tongue didn't help the situation either.

"The man brought him."

"The man ... What man?" She swiped her head awkwardly side to side, checking the snow for footprints. The only ones were her own. There was not even so much as a minuscule ripple in the snow from anything else. It was as if the dog had just fallen from the sky and Ellie hovered over top of the snow. *'Like Wen.'*

"The man," Ellie said, slowly turning the dog over in her lap.

"Ellie, what man?"

"The one from the kitchen."

"The zombie guy?" She did not know what else to call the strange man from this morning.

"Yes, that one." Ellie moved the dog's legs in a pretend run. "Can we fix the doggy?"

This was the third time she had asked. "No." Rebecca unhooked her tongue from the roof of her mouth running it back and forth across her lips wetting them; they were trying to stick together of their own accord.

"Can we try?"

"No, it's too late." She tried to speak with compassion to balance out Ellie's seemingly wide-eyed innocence in this horrid situation. "The doggy has passed on ... He's not fixable." *'O Lord God help me here?"*

"But I always wanted a doggy. Can I bring him in and play with him anyway?"

Rebecca closed her eyes and opened them. Still there ... All of it ... Still there. A six year old in pyjamas and bare feet sitting in the snow with a slaughtered, mangled, almost decapitated dog covered in blood, with its intestines looped on her knees.

"Can I Becky?"

"No and it's Rebecca."

"Daddy calls you Becky."

"I know, but that's not my name it's ..." She paused, "oh whatever!"

Ellie was hugging the dog so tight to her chest its stomach sac had ruptured and spewed out all over the front of her pyjama top.

Rebecca wiped at her nose, the smell of dead dog and blood stuck in her nostrils. She held out her hands to Ellie. "Give me that thing."

"No ... It's mine!" She ran off with the dog clutched to her chest.

"God Damn you!" Rebecca yelled chasing after her.

Thirty seconds later, they were rolling around in the snow.

"You grabbed me!"

"I did not ... I tackled you!" She grasped the dog from underneath Ellie tearing its head off in the process. "Christ!" she said picking up the head.

"Can I have it back?"

"Not in my lifetime! ... March young lady ... Now!"

Ellie got up out of the snow and walked stiffly toward the house. "You left the front door open again."

"I wonder why smartass. Go get ready for a bath."

"You already made me have one!" She wiped her bloody hands back and forth across her pyjama top, holding them out for Rebecca to inspect. "See I'm good."

"No, not good. You need another bath. Off with you. Go get ready." Rebecca motioned with the dead dog's body in one hand and the head in the other, for her to go.

She made the sign of the cross on the dog's head and again on the body, wrapped both in a blanket and placed them inside a garbage bag which she set out on the porch. She would try to bury it later, ground permitting. She made a mental note to write a few lines for Wen on the note pad, minus some details, after Ellie was asleep.

She ran the bath squirting in dishwashing liquid for bubbles. She had done this every night for Ellie and knew she liked it by the way her eyes sparkled every time.

"Ellie come on now. Your bath's all ready."

"I can have it myself."

"Okay if you're sure." Rebecca went to her bedroom turning down her bed and changing into clean dry pyjamas.

The front door slammed shut, then the sound of running bare feet, and then a splash and another door slamming shut.

Rebecca flew from of her room tugging her top on. "Ellie? What the hell are you doing?" The bathroom door was closed and locked. "Ellie open this door right now so help me God!"

There was a very small click, and then a slight splash.

"You're lucky young lady." Rebecca entered the bathroom stopping dead in her tracks.

Ellie had the dog's body in the bath with her; its entrails wrapped about her neck like a macabre scarf. She was strok-

ing it, puffing out her chest proudly as if showing off prize jewels.

Rebecca felt vomit rise to the back of her throat. She swallowed it back down before she got a taste. "Christ All Mighty! Give me that thing!" She ripped it from Ellie's hands throwing it backwards over her head out into the hallway. It hit the wall making a loud heavy splat, hanging there longer than it should have as if on display. Moments later, as if cued, it slowly started to slither down the wall, in stops and starts, eventually balling up on the floor in a heap.

"Where's its head?" Rebecca asked.

"Still in the bag."

"Where's the bag?"

"I'm not telling."

Rebecca picked up the tub sprayer, turned on the cold water and aimed it directly at Ellie's chest holding her thumb a hairs breathe from the on button.

"Okay. Okay. It's behind the chair you sit in the living room."

Rebecca gave her the look, the one that said 'you better not be playing games with me kid or you will meet your maker.'

Ellie bent her head pretending to cry.

"Well?"

"It's in the pantry next to the stupid potatoes."

"Thank you." Rebecca pulled the bath plug. "You stay put, and next time you decide to cry at least sniffle a bit. It will seem more real." She picked up the dog's body and walked down the hallway towards the kitchen pantry.

Screaming, shrill and loud, shattered the night air like flying darts. Rebecca threw the bag with the two parts of the dog's body in it into the far corner of the front porch. She side kicked the front door shut running wildly down the hallway into the bathroom.

Ellie was on her back in the waterless tub, eyes shut, kicking and screeching for the dead dog like a crazed wild animal.

Rebecca grabbed her under the arms lifting her straight up.

Ellie's feet dangled and swayed as she came face to face with Rebecca.

"Knock it the hell off, right now!" Rebecca gave her a slight shake letting her know that she meant business. "You hear me? ... Nod if you do?"

Ellie nodded.

Rebecca put her back into the tub. "Stand up." She hosed her down with warm water. "Turn," she commanded spraying down her back and legs. "Listen to me! Number one ... You cannot have that thing! Number two ... Quit all this shit!" She picked up Ellie sitting her down on the bath mat. She swished the bloody water from the tub putting back in the plug and dish soap refilling it.

"Is there a number three?"

"No."

"Can I get pyjamas from my room?"

"Yes and come right back. And ... And don't you dare touch that dog."

When Ellie returned Rebecca was sitting on the toilet lid smoking a cigarette. Ellie slipped into the tub swishing the bubbles back and forth like a normal kid. Rebecca shook her head watching her.

"I've never seen you smoke before."

"Is that a question?"

Ellie nodded.

"I don't smoke usually, but there's nothing to drink."

"There are drinks in the refrigerator and there's water."

"That's not the type of drink I was meaning."

"Where'd you get the cigarette?"

"Your dad's dresser drawer."

"Does he know you go through his drawers?"

She took a long drag off the cigarette. "He will now, just like he'll know about the dead dog in the bath." *'I'm bargaining and playing mind games with a six year old.'*

Ellie smiled cutely, "What cigarette?"

"That's what I thought."

She waited until Ellie was sound asleep before retrieving the dog; Rewrapping and camouflaging it, she tucked it into the cubbyhole under the basement stairs, then readied herself for bed.

Rebecca checked on Ellie a few hours later. She was sound asleep, pillow and covers thrown off the bed, night light out, curled up in a tight little ball as always. She reminded her of the pictures she'd seen of denning wolves. She picked up her blanket tucking it around her.

A putrid stench wafted up making her gag. Her eyes and nose started to run. She flipped on the bedside lamp. Her hands were covered in brownish-red guck. The blanket she had just fetched and tucked Ellie into sported a huge stain and her handprints.

"What the hell?" She pulled back the blanket.

Ellie had the dog tucked up against her chest.

Rebecca reached for it.

Ellie's eyes shot open, dark, foreboding, no pupils, no whites. She barred her teeth emitting a low growl.

Rebecca stepped back. "Christ! ... Keep the God damn thing then!"

Ellie closed her eyes.

Rebecca inhaled deep on the cigarette, leaning on the back of the open front door. The porch had accumulated a lot of snow over the last few hours. She tilted her head blowing the smoke up into the air. It looked like sculptured streamers under the porch light.

Ellie slowly, quietly, tiptoed up behind her and stood.

"I know you're there," Rebecca said. She took another drag from the cigarette.

"How?"

Rebecca pointed to the dog under her right arm.

"Becky, Daddy said we aren't to go outside."

"I'm not outside, I'm in the doorway."

"You're sort of outside."

Rebecca held her hands up in the 'whatever' pose.

"I thought you were my friend?"

"What are you saying?" Rebecca moved from the doorway out onto the porch with her half-finished cigarette.

Ellie was staring at her.

"Ellie? ... Come on, what's up?"

"You are what's up!" she squealed, slamming the door shut and locking it.

"Jesus fucking hell!" Rebecca shouted stepping off the porch. She did not bother pounding on the front door, that kind of approach with this kid would not have netted results. Ellie had the upper hand, and the dead dog to boot.

She turned her face skyward. "Whatever did I do to deserve all this? Tell me will you ... Come on I'm waiting ... No answer ... Figures!" She sat on stoop staring at all the dark houses on the street wondering what kind of people lived inside, if any.

She strolled around the house in her slippers, checking out the doors and windows ... Locked ... Of course they were locked, she had been making sure they were. Her fingers started to numb, she shoved them into her housecoat pockets. The cold was getting to her and she walked up and down the drive trying to keep warm. She moved faster and farther out with each pass.

Finding herself on the roadway, she decided to occupy her mind by checking for traces of the morning's zombie guy. She stopped about where she thought he had fallen, brushing at the snow ... Nothing.

A tree branch cracked and fell onto the snow covered lawn across the street. Her eyes flickered across it. The snow seemed off colour in the absence of streetlights.

She crossed the road. Her mouth fell open, cocking sideways as if one of its hinges had let go. Her new grape sized eyes almost thrust from their sockets as she probed the ash-filled shape of a human body with one unburned foot still in the shoe.

"Oh my God!" she shrieked, reversing and running full tilt for the house. She banged wildly on the front door. "Ellie! Ellie! Open this God damn door ... Right now! Ellie!" Rebecca moved backwards to get a good run at the door. She dashed full out jumping up and readying a kick at the same time it opened. The steel snow shovel Ellie was holding pole side down caught her square in the forehead knocking her out.

Eight

♫On the seventh day of Christmas, my true love sent to me:
Seven Swans a Swimming ... ♫

"That's a bad bump you've got there," Wen said softly.

Rebecca snatched the towel wrapped ice bag from her forehead throwing it on the floor. She swung her legs from the sofa, sitting up.

"Just rest," Wen said.

"Just rest! ... Just rest? What the fuck is wrong with you people? And where the hell did you come from? You're never here at night!" She eyed the window. It was daylight. "Fucking hell!"

He smiled. "You have a mouth like a sewer, much like your sister, you know." He wiped her hair back from her face.

She slapped his hand away. "Will you stop that!"

"Ellie came and told me you were sleeping on the front porch."

"Sleeping?"

"Sleeping ... Knocked out ...Which ever," he shrugged.

"What'd you do, come in through your damn window again?"

He smirked.

Rebecca jumped to her feet commencing to pace. "I can't do this!" She blurted all of a sudden.

"Meaning?"

"This ... This!" She stuck out her arms moving her body back and forth completing a broad sweep of the room; words absent at the moment.

"You should really, at the very least, sit down."

"Sit down? Are you crazy? The last thing I want to do in this house is sit down!"

"Fair enough," he said quietly.

She glared at him. "I want out of here. I don't want to do this! None of this!"

"As in?"

"All this shit!"

"All this shit?" He repeated her verbatim. "You mean look after Ellie?"

"Yes ... And all the rest!"

"You gave your word."

"I know, but I just can't do it."

"Why?" he said too calmly for her liking.

"Oh I don't know ... Any guesses?" she sneered cynically.

"I realize some days may be a bit trying."

"A bit trying?" her voice raised to a shrill pitch. "A bit trying?" she repeated. "Your definition and mine must be a hell of a lot different!"

"How so?"

She plunked down on the coffee table a mere foot from him. "A bit trying is *not* obsessing over a dead cat in a window. A bit trying is *not* going outside in the snow in bare feet and nightclothes in the pitch dark every time I turn around. A bit trying, is *not* prying a God damn dead headless dog from a child, more than once I might add, only to find her sleeping with the thing and then baring her teeth and growling. Do you know all she will eat is raw meat? And ... All the rest of the fucking shit that goes on around here!"

He smiled. "Like?"

"Like! Like! ... Why in hell are you smiling? Am I fucking amusing you again?"

"No." Wen covered his mouth with his hand pretending to rub it back and forth across his lips; yes, she was definitely amusing him. "So what is the rest?"

"The rest? ... Isn't that enough?" Rebecca screeched.

"You said there was more."

She gawked at him. "Yeah there's more! ... The power goes off and on, off and on, nightly. No one seems to be home in any of the houses on the street. It is as if they are abandoned. The zombie friend of yours who walked, and I use that term loosely, right out the door without a coat, and down the road, fell face first in the snow and you did not care. Now he's fucking out there burnt to a crisp, the only thing left of the guy is one Goddamn foot still in his shoe! And on top of that, there are peculiar noises at night around the house and you are never here ...No wonder you do not want us to go outside! What the hell is this place, a leftover horror movie set?"

Wen perked up, his eyes drew dark and serious, "Peculiar noises at night?"

"I told you days ago."

"Like what?"

"Fucked if I know." She was not about to tell him it sounded like a tree branch scratching along the bricks as it circled the house, or a hanging piece of awning that gurgled, growled, and hissed.

"Like what?" he repeated, his tone insistent.

Okay then here we go ...' "Low, hissing, growly, snuffling, scratchy, rubbing, something."

"How many days ago did you tell me?"

"Two, three, maybe more, I don't know exactly."

"Does it happen every night?"

"Do you hear yourself? I tell you a mountain of shit and all you're concerned about is damn noises?"

"Does it?" he repeated.

"Fuck," she plopped down in the chair. "Yes."

"Shit! Shit! Shit! ... I've got to go!" Wen ran out the front door.

Rebecca sat staring at nothing for the longest time. The house was pin drop silent.

"Okay Ellie, where the hell are you?" She swiftly toured the house, stopping, straining, and listening. A trifling sound came from the basement. "I bet," she whispered going down the stairs. "Yep," she confirmed.

Ellie was sitting in the middle of the floor playing with that damn fucked up dog again.

"Give me that!" She snatched it from her hands, walked over to the wood furnace, opened the door, and threw it in.

Ellie started screaming at the top of her lungs. If anyone had been home in the houses on the street, surely to God they would have thought Rebecca was murdering her.

Rebecca stood over top of her counting to sixty. She had to; her self-control and sanity were wavering.

She bent over and picked up the screaming, now kicking child. She turned and climbed the stairs to the main floor.

Ellie kicked her hard in the ribs.

"Enough of this shit! Stop it! And I mean now!" Rebecca put her down, grasped onto her hand, and trotted her into the bathroom. "We are going to get cleaned up and then the two of us are going out."

Ellie mocked crying, sniffling. "Better with a sniffle?"

"Yeah, the sniffle's good."

"We're going out?"

"Yeah."

"But, daddy says we can't."

Rebecca raised her eyebrows giving her that 'honestly kid are you kidding me' look. "Excuse me! You go out all the time!"

"I don't go anywhere."

Rebecca finished washing Ellie's face and hands, flushed out the cloth and threw it into the hamper. "Whatever! Today we are going somewhere."

"Where we going Becky?" Ellie was tailing her back and forth from the hall closet to the front entrance.

"Where's your winter stuff? ... And it's Rebecca for the fortieth time."

"Winter stuff?"

"You know ... Boots, coat, hat? That stuff." Rebecca pointed to hers.

"Don't have any."

Rebecca stopped herself from saying a bunch of things she shouldn't. She pulled on her runners, and two sweaters. She put her boots, coat, and mitts on Ellie, wrapping her scarf around her head and middle tying it in the back. "Well, it's all a bit big, but it works. We'll walk slowly so you don't fall out of the boots." She took Ellie's hand as they went out the front door.

"Where we going?"

"My little dove, we are going to find a store that sells a teddy bear."

"For me?" Ellie tightened her mitted grip on Rebecca's hand.

"Yeah, for you."

Ellie beamed. "You called me dove again, just like mamma does."

The terminology went by unnoticed ... Again.

They walked along the road past all the homes without cars, without life.

Rebecca glanced back behind them.

There was only one set of footprints ... Hers. *'Why isn't Ellie leaving prints with those too big of boots? Has she ever left prints?'* She could not recall. And, to tell the truth, did not want to. This was dipping over into those imaginary shadows she kept seeing and the imaginary noises she kept hearing and she did not want to go there.

The wind picked up and it started snowing lightly.

The street seemed endless, as if for every house they passed it grew four more. She felt like they were on an invisible conveyer belt walking and walking, but going nowhere.

The hair on the back of her neck stood up and prickled through the wool threads of her sweaters. She firmed her grip on Ellie's hand.

All the houses suddenly looked identical. The designs, the coloured bricks, the carports, the drapes in the windows, even the snowdrifts in the drives.

She looked side to side then back behind each shoulder in turn. Something was off. Something more than identicalness.

Something was out here with them, tagging them.

Everything was moving in slow motion.

The snow grew heavy and spun.

Then there it was ... The sound ... An off the scale wisp ... Ominous ... Sinister ... Inhuman.

"Okay kiddo let's go back." She looked down at Ellie forcing a smile.

"But what about the teddy bear?"

"I'll make you one."

There it was again—that sound; stealth like, in a way you could not ignore.

Rebecca stopped walking. Her skin started crawling around under her sweater as if looking for a place to hide.

"You will?"

"Yeah," she said through a cough. Her throat felt like it had filled itself with the lumps that should have been residing at the back of her tongue. "Let's run," she said quickly. She looked back behind her. *'Was that a shadow at the corner of that house?'*

"It will be hard to run in the snow with these." Ellie held out one booted foot.

Rebecca bent down. "Hurry climb on my back. I'll piggy back you."

"What's that?"

"Just do it."

Ellie climbed up on her.

"Wrap your arms around my neck and your legs around my tummy."

Ellie clung onto her, fitting into her like a third sweater.

"Good girl," Rebecca whispered. She gripped onto Ellie's legs and took off running as fast as her feet would carry them.

It stopped at the house directly across. Yellowish-brown drool seeped from its mouth, balling and plopping into the snow, eating right through it to the bare soil like battery acid. It tilted its head and sniffed the air.

He was coming.

It galloped back to where it had come using its hands and feet, leaving two distinct sets of prints.

The heavy snow covered them instantly.

Some secrets kept best that way.

Hours later Rebecca checked on Ellie. She was cuddled up in bed hugging the pink teddy bear Rebecca had made for her out of a pair of her fuzzy socks. "Now ... That's more like it," she said quietly.

"Thank you Becky," Ellie whispered.

"You're very welcome honey," she replied.

Rebecca turned on the porch light. The storm was all but over. She made herself a cup of cocoa, retrieved her book, propped up her bed pillows, and settled in. She had become accustomed to having no television or radio and found herself looking forward to the simple pleasure of reading. She smiled; grateful she had stuffed the book into her suitcase at the last minute.

The living room window boomed sounding out one long bellow, reverberating and clacking as the aftershock took hold.

Rebecca dropped the book and raced out of her room. Her skin beaded with goose bumps. Fear, with no reference point, squished between them and set up house.

Another boom, then high pitched scraping, like long thick nails drawn across a chalkboard.

She nervously glanced at the door, had she locked it? Would it matter? Another hit on the glass like that and it would surely shatter.

She stood silent, erect, semi-frozen, listening to the scraping and scratching, the growling, gurgling, and hissing. It sounded like it had centered its attention onto the front of the house, particularly the front door and window.

Fear engulfed her. She could not get her feet to budge; they felt encased in cement blocks.

The drape was off centre leaving a gap at one side; a bare gap of window. She grabbed the edge of the easy chair pulling herself with her arms, sliding her cement encased feet a foot to the right. She peered out the window.

The storm had picked up.

Without warning, a fire flare blasted out from the darkness, searing the gray-black air into two sections. It travelled as if in competition for a new speed record, crossing over the top most layers of snow like lightening. The snow sparkled in an 'aurora borealis' light show in red, orange, yellow, green, and blue as it went through.

Rebecca crouched. "What in hell," she muttered. She rested her chin on the windowsill, gawking out with eyeballs that had ringed themselves in white.

Another flare.

A blood curdling screech.

A hunched up something bolted from the front porch, bounded across the lawn and roadway, before disappearing from sight.

The snow spun like a cyclone, becoming heavier.

Something howled off in the distance. Long, eerie, like a great lone wolf howling for its dead mate.

Fright turned to terror.

Every hair on her body stood at attention, poking with sharp needles through the cloth of her pyjamas. She used the drape to stand, her feet still encased in the cement, her legs feeling like they belonged to an under stuffed soft toy. They wobbled and bowed in ways they were not designed for. She went down on her hands and knees, crawling through the house, visually checking the locks on all the doors and windows.

She crawled into Ellie's room using the top edge of the mattress to haul herself up on her knees.

Ellie was curled up in her tight little ball, bear hug on the teddy bear, facing out, no pillow and no blanket as usual. Her lips were moving.

Rebecca stole closer.

"It's okay Becky ... It's okay," she whispered over and over like an old vinyl record stuck on a scratch.

Rebecca let go of the mattress, sinking back down onto the floor and worming her body backwards out from the room.

Ellie rolled into the wall taking her teddy bear with her. Her eyes were wide and full. Her lips curled up showing off a toothy smile.

Rebecca dragged the living room chair across the floor facing it toward the front door. She sat cross-legged, her back jammed into the cushion, butcher knife in hand, waiting for daylight.

Nine

♪*On the eighth day of Christmas, my true love sent to me:*
Eight Maids a Milking ... ♪

"Your slippers are all snow," Wen said quietly.

Rebecca took a long drag from the cigarette ... "Fuck if I care."

"You're not supposed to be outside."

"Fuck if I care about that too."

"Did you sleep well?"

"No ... Didn't sleep at all."

"I see." He was standing directly behind her.

"Do you Wen?"

"What do you mean?"

She twisted to face him; they were so close they could feel one another's breath.

"Just what I said ... Do you see? ... Do you see anything?"

He smiled.

"Don't smile! ... Answer me!"

"Yes."

"Yes ... Yes! Is that it? ... All you can say is yes?" She did not wait for an answer. "Tell me something ... Did my sister go through all this bizarre fucking shit, with this place and the child?" Anger was crawling up her spine, flushing her skin a bright pink.

"No."

"No?"

"No," he said again.

"Why not?"

"I didn't live here then."

"Asshole! You know what I damn well meant!"

"No," he said quietly.

"Why are you making this so difficult?"

"I'm not."

"I beg to differ! ... So then answer me!"

The glint went out of his eyes. "The child was a new born when she was caring for it."

"Yes that would be right, fitting in with the time frame. The child would have been too small to give her a hard time ..."

"Not true," he interjected.

She stared him down, holding up her hands. "Finish the sentence," she said without emotion. She was tired of his sidestepping, and she knew he knew it.

"The child gave her a very difficult time."

"How so?"

"The child was a difficult birth."

"Pardon me?" She tilted her head; she could feel her legs starting to turn into old used up elastic. She started to sway. *'Here it comes ... The inconceivable ... The reprehensible ... The unconscionable.'*

"The child is your sister's ... Becky."

Rebecca gave a look straight from hell. She pulled her lips into her mouth, shoving him backward into the open door. She stepped off the porch and sat down in a heap in the snow. "Don't you fucking come near me! Just leave me the fuck alone! Fucking hell!" She put her head in her hands and wept.

Wen could feel Ellie, as he always could, there behind him, lingering, soaking up every bit of the conversation like a dry sponge.

He turned.

She was but a mere three feet from him, standing innocently, hugging a fuzzy pink teddy bear, sucking her thumb.

"Where'd you get that? ... Becky?"

She nodded sliding her bare feet backward and doing a mock-up of a *'Michael Jackson'* moonwalk, stopping as she reached the hallway. "Is she coming back in soon?"

"Probably a while, maybe a long while, but she will eventually. The temperature's going to drop and it's starting to snow again."

Ellie popped her thumb out of her mouth. "She knows now?"

"Some," he paused, and then added, "Only some, my little one."

Much later Rebecca brushed the snow off herself, coming back through the open front door and passing Wen without a glance or word. She put the kettle on, pulled out a chair, and sat at the kitchen table.

She pointed at him. "Don't you dare say one single fucking word! ... Not one!"

"I can see you're upset and you have every right to ..."

She cut him off. "That's eleven!"

He gave her the 'fair enough' hand sign and sat facing her at the table.

The kettle boiled.

Rebecca did not budge. She just sat there with stone cold eyes fixated front and centre upon his face.

He excused himself, made them both a hot drink, and then returned as he was, waiting for the onslaught of wrath.

"You forgot to mention the child's mother was my fucking sister?"

"You didn't ask who the mother was."

"You're such an asshole."

"So you keep saying."

"She didn't fucking work for you."

"No."

"What was that then?"

"A lie."

"Yes it was ... What else have you lied about?"

"My age."

"Your fucking age ... You lied about your fucking age?"

"Yes."

"If you don't stop all this fucking around with one and two word answers, I'm going to fly across this table and lose my fucking shit on you!"

"I'm older than I said. Much older. Old enough to be very, very, tired Becky." He was not about to say centuries; Right now she could not begin to understand, nor would she want to he suspected.

"You're lucky asshole ... I was getting up."

"I would call myself anything but lucky my dear sweet Rebecca," the corners of his mouth lit up in an ever so slight smile.

"Fucking hell, you called me Rebecc ... a."

He held up a finger signalling the 'wait a moment.' He stood, tilted his head, sniffing the air, whirling in circles.

He tore from the kitchen.

She could hear crashing and banging as if things were being hurled.

Seconds later, he bolted past her carrying what looked like a machine gun. He leapt off the front porch at a dead run, disappearing from sight in between the lifeless homes.

"Want another cigarette?" Ellie held a cigarette and purple lighter up to her.

Rebecca smiled; against all the odds, she could not help it. "Where'd you get the lighter?"

"I stole it from my dad's drawer."

"A lot of that going 'round, huh?" She stepped out onto the porch lighting up the cigarette.

Ellie stepped with her.

"Tell me something, does your dad even smoke?"

"Sometimes." Ellie fitted her cold icicle of a hand inside hers.

"Never seen him." Rebecca took a long drag from the cigarette blowing the smoke straight up in ribbons. "Guess I'm stuck with you, kid. No surprises today okay?"

"You mean like the doggy?"

"Yeah, like the doggy."

"I better go to my room now," Ellie said far too hastily. She had one hand behind her back.

"Hold on there ... What on earth do you have now?"

Ellie started stomping.

"What are you doing?"

Rebecca grasped her forearm.

Maggots showered onto the porch.

She flicked the cigarette into the snow with one hand while turning Ellie around with the other.

Both, as if timed and practised to the ninth, looked at the dead cat in unison, then at each other, then back at the cat; The lifeless, bloated, split open, rancid with maggots, entrails hanging, putrid, dead as a stone, cat, from the windowsill across the street.

Rebecca lunged, grabbing the cat in one fluid motion. Her fingers popped dime sized holes through the stretched plastic-like skin, right into a den of cold gooey baby maggots. Without a second thought of how Ellie had gotten hold of it, she threw it far out into the snow and slammed the door shut.

"Fucking hell," she said wiping her hands on her jeans. "Kid I don't get you."

Ellie used Rebecca's sweater to go up on her tippy-toes. "You're doing better," she whispered.

She bunny hopped out of the living room and through the kitchen, thunking her way down the hall into her room singing something too low to make out. Nevertheless, whatever it was, it was cheery.

Rebecca scrawled a note for Wen, in bright red crayon this time. 'The hell you took care of the dead cat.' She added five exclamation marks underneath the sentence to drive home her point. She put tape on one corner slapping it on the front of the refrigerator door.

She spent the remainder of the day making a toy cat out of a pair of her yellow and white striped socks, and a dog out of plain purple ones.

She loaded up the wood furnace to maximum capacity, then stood back watching the decomposed cat, with accompanying maggots, bubble, explode, and catch fire. She shut her eyes clasping her hands together and praying for God to send down a special angel to take its ashes to heaven. She knelt in front of the furnace waiting for it to be no more of body.

"First the dog, now the cat," she said. "What's next? Don't think of an answer Rebecca ... Don't you dare ... Oh brother I'm talking to myself," she said softly starting up the basement stairs. "Yep I am ... Not good," she added. "Not good at all."

All of a sudden, the basement door rumbled like it had just been involved in a head on collision. It pulsated, sucking in and out, fissuring and cracking.

Fear grew marbles on the back of her tongue as she bounded up the basement stairs two at a time.

The door thumped and banged again just as she reached the top stair.

She could hear the wood groaning, starting to give.

Her legs shook and bobbed as she shrank down onto her knees reciting her version of *The Lord's Prayer.*' "Father, may your holy name be honoured; may your kingdom come. Give us day by day the food we need cooked and raw. Forgive

us our sins and my swearing as we forgive everyone who does us wrong and do not bring us to hard testing ..." She paused, listening to the sudden terrifying sound of silence. She finished the prayer at top speed under her breath, adding an additional line. *'And Father, please make that thing at the basement door go away ... Far, far away if you will.'*

She inched along the hallway toward the living room. The living room with the undrawn drapes ... The living room with the undrawn drapes and huge picture window ... The living room with the undrawn drapes and huge picture window that you could see out of as well as see in to.

She felt like she should be a participant in an old black and white film, creeping along with close ups centered on her heaving chest, and accompanying garish heart beat sound effects dubbed in. Her palms wet the paint as she slithered along to the corner. She slimed into the wall becoming part of it, peering at the window with one eye open and one closed.

Dark ... All dark ... Dark living room ... Dark window ... Nothing but dark everywhere.

She shuffled along the living room wall toward the window and the drape, the drape she was hell bent on drawing.

She clenched the curtain hem and began to pull it sideways, eyes riveted on the dark window.

A scream shivered in her throat as it stepped forward into view.

It had been waiting.

Rebecca's bulging eyes worked as separate entities, tracing over the thing on the other side of the window. The thing out in the snow. The thing so close, that if there had not been a pane of glass with those two degrees of separation, they could have swapped breath.

Her eyeballs rolled up and over the massive antlers. The deer like head with the tiny doe ears and no lips; The massive canines; The elongated tongue that hung five or six

inches out of its mouth; The matted covering of coarse brownish hair with the exception of its ribcage, which was all but bone. She could see the internal organs pulsating within. It stood erect on two hind legs. Its elongated arms had tufts of hair at the shoulders, the remainder bare skin. Its elbows bent and nestled in at the hip. It was gaunt and disfigured.

Its black orb eyes were fixated upon her, tracing over her, studying her as she had done it.

Their eyes locked and held.

It lifted one front limb pressing three massive toes against the glass.

Without warning, it turned and was gone, galloping on all fours, like a monkey, into the storm, and disappearing.

The sky lit up in orange-red flames.

All the windows of the house rattled.

A long eerie howl came out of the white blindness.

Rebecca's body turned limp, pasting itself to the window glass. She turned her head sideways opening her mouth, gulping in air, her tongue felt like a piece of dried, folded up cardboard. Her eyes ticked back and forth clock like.

A dark figure stood motionless, high on the hill, and without warning suddenly disappeared too.

She gazed into the storm. It was as if neither had ever been there at all.

Ten

♪*On the ninth day of Christmas, my true love sent to me:*
Nine Ladies Dancing ... ♪

"On the first day of Christmas my true love sent to me, a partridge in a pear tree ... On the second day of Christmas my true love sent to me, two turtle doves and a partridge in a pear tree ... On the third day of Christmas ..." Rebecca bopped her head joyfully as she sang.

Wen rushed her. "Why are singing that?"

"I can't get it out of my head. It's like no matter what I do or where I go, I hear it. But it is Christmas time." She beamed with delight. "I can't think of anything better to dance around in my head."

He caught her by the arm whipping her round so they were face to face. "How long have you been hearing it?"

"A few days."

"How many?"

"A few days, like I said."

"A few?" He wrapped both his hands around her sweater-covered forearms.

"Maybe more than a few." She glanced down at his hands, then into his eyes, and then back at his hands, letting him silently know this hand thing was not sitting well with her.

He let go.

"Jesus ... Wen." She shook her arms up and down; he had been cutting off the circulation.

"How many?" he repeated.

"How about I don't know, and I don't care ... Is that fucking good enough for you?"

"How many?" he repeated again.

"Christ! ... Three, six, nine ... I don't know! Shortly after I got here I think." She pulled at her sweater arms fixing them. "What is with you and all this third degree shit about such silly asinine things?" She walked over to the kitchen sink picking up the dishcloth, humming the song.

She knew he was staring again, she could feel the burn holes in her back. She stopped humming, throwing the dishcloth on the counter as she turned his way. "It's a fucking Christmas song! Just a God Damn Christmas song! You can stop that stare any time now ... Fuck!"

"Why didn't you tell me?"

"Tell you what?"

"About the song." *'Only three days left ... Soon ... Soon.'*

"Tell you I'm singing a song?" She did not wait for his reply. "For fucking Christ's sake ... Here we go ... Again! Do you hear yourself? You are grilling me over a stupid ass song!" She folded her arms across her chest. "You both could use some Christmas around here. You know like lights, decorations, presents, a turkey thawing in the refrigerator, a tree! Why is there no damn fucking tree Wen?"

"I don't believe in Christmas anymore."

"What kind of hellish thing is that to say? You have a little girl, in case you have forgotten."

Wen glanced over at Ellie who was sitting at the end of the table jabbering away to the three stuffed toys Rebecca had made her. She pranced them up and down then sat them down on their bottoms, arranging them at precise points around her plate. She dunked their heads each in turn, pretending they were eating the raw hamburger meat.

He cleared his throat on purpose, and then stared at Ellie.

Ellie stuffed her mouth full of meat, grabbed her toys, got down on all fours crawling as fast as she could for her bedroom.

Rebecca pounded the tabletop with her fist in anger. "Why do you do that to her?"

"What?"

"That ungodly death stare of yours! She's only a little girl!" she said. "Odd little girl," she muttered adding, "but she's still just a little girl."

Rebecca cleared the table of dishes. She turned her back to Wen, swiping up Ellie's left over raw meat with her fingers and cramming it all into her mouth. She chewed quickly, putting the dishes in the sink to soak.

She pulled a chair directly up in front of Wen flicking miniscule morsels of meat off her fingers.

His eyes flickered across her hands.

"Don't you find it a tad odd that your daughter only eats raw meat?" she asked as a diversion, positive he had noticed the hamburger bits on her fingers.

He sighed heavily. "How long's she been doing that?" His eyes scanned her hands again.

Rebecca shoved them into her sweater pockets. "Has been since I arrived." She drew her chair up close and personal. "Always I would guess ... And you damn well know this all ready. I have asked you several times to stop playing fucking games. Now I'm telling you." Her eyebrows drew together showing her annoyance.

"Your eyes grow dark, just like your sister's when you're angry."

"Leave Susanna out of this ... You asshole ... Friends my fucking ass."

"You still on that?"

"Fuck off ... Just fuck off."

He riddled his hands together hiding his outright amusement. "Can you stop swearing?"

"I know what you're doing. You and your bullshit smoke screen. So cut the fucking crap. Quit the games and tell me what the fuck is going on around here."

"You swore ... Again ... Many, many times actually." He glanced at the clock.

"Jesus Christ!" She stood and placed her hands on each of his chair arms, penning him in. "Before you run off, or in your case fly off like a lunatic again, I saw it last night."

"Saw what?"

She sighed laboriously, "I think you damn well know what I'm talking about. Now ... I'm asking you one last time, what the fuck is going on here?"

He gently removed her hands, leaned back in the chair, balancing it on two legs, and pulled his lips into his mouth. He looked down at the floor. "You wouldn't believe me if I told you."

"Try me."

"For one thing, Ellie's not quite right."

"No kidding!"

He skimmed the clock again.

"I take it you are going to run out without answering me." He smiled that same smile.

"This conversation isn't finished asshole ... There's way more than Ellie going on here."

"You are stronger than your sister."

"Strong? ... I am mentally ill! And it is all your God Damn fucking fault! I was fine before I came here."

"Were you really Rebecca?"

He ran out the door.

"Holy shit, he called me Rebecca again," she mumbled.

She watched him run off between the houses and disappear. "I saw a lot of things last night Wen," she said. And then added, "far, far, too many things."

"Come on little one," Rebecca yelled. "Let's get bundled up and go outside and make a snowman."

Ellie came running, clutching the three toys under her one arm. "Can they come too?"

"Of course."

"I've never made a snowman. Can we eat it?"

Rebecca shook her head. "If you like, sweetheart ... If you like."

They went outside leaving the front door open, just in case.

Eleven

♫On the tenth day of Christmas, my true love sent to me:
Ten Lords a Leaping ... ♫

Edmond pulled off the road fitting the school bus as close to the shoulder as his skill and the snow banks permitted. He turned the key shutting it off. The engine clunked and hissed then silenced. Steamy fog wafted out from under the hood.

"What's up?" Vivian asked.

The substitute teacher tag that read *'Hi I'm Miss Maggie!'* swung loosely back and forth on the end of the chain around her neck, clipping the top of the steering wheel with each swipe. Maggie was scheduled for the field trip but became ill, Vivian was asked to fill in at the last minute. She had only agreed to this one-month teaching position for extra Christmas money, and here she was in the middle of nowhere, on an old broken down school bus packed full of squirming eight year olds.

"What's up?" she asked again.

"The bus over heated." Edmond was studying a map, turning it this way and that. He had not noticed any of the points of reference on the road, like Bensford Bridge, Willard's Hill, the lilac groves, or even the split road. "And I think we're lost," he added. He turned the key on and off and on and off, at the same time pressing the gas pedal, mirroring the action of the key turns.

The bus sat dead, it might as well been on its roof with its tires up in the air.

"Are you kidding me?" She glimpsed at the children.

"I've never had a bus over heat or not start, and I don't remember there being a fork in the road way back there. It's not on the map."

The overpowering smell of gasoline wafted down the aisle between the seats. He flicked the gauges with his thumb and index finger.

"Try the key again," Vivian urged.

"The engine's unresponsive, the battery light doesn't come on when I turn the key."

"Crap. I'll get my phone out of my bag and call the school board for someone to come out."

Less than a minute later Vivian was back at his side. "My phone's out of range."

"Great ... Just great." Edmond got out of the bus and opened the hood checking the battery.

It started to snow.

Ten minutes later he climbed back in, shaking his head, the bus was a no go. "I saw a sign for a Christmas tree farm back there a ways, maybe they can help us out." He started doing up his jacket.

"Okay children. Listen up." Vivian instructed. "Unbuckle your seat belts, make sure your coats and hats are on, we are going for a walk to see a Christmas tree farm."

She flashed a fake smile at Edmond.

"Well done," he muttered. "No sense scaring the little tots. A walk will do them good, so it will. They've been jittery the last half hour." He nodded at Vivian. "Shall we?" He motioned to the door.

"Are we still going to the Christmas museum?" One of the girls asked.

"I hope," Vivian replied too low for her to hear.

They marched single file along the left side of the road, turning up the laneway with the Christmas tree farm sign with the black tree and white ornaments.

Edmond sidetracked over to the sign studying it. He signalled for Vivian to come. They both stared at the sign scrutinizing the atrocious black Christmas tree adorned with white skull drawings, and then looked into one another's eyes, both thinking the exact same thought. '*Oh my God.*'

Vivian raised her hands, gazing at Edmond mouthing, "should we even go?"

He shrugged nonchalantly, stepping closer to the sign and running his finger tips across it. The skulls felt amazingly like velvet. His head started to swim gently, drowsily; he felt as if he was floating, suddenly all he wanted was to stay right there stroking that sign for eternity.

Vivian touched his shoulder.

He snapped out of the trance, shaking himself like a soaking wet animal. He pivoted up onto his heels forcefully snatching his hand from the sign with the other. He shoved his hands deep into his coat pockets.

He stared at the sign, yearning for it.

Vivian grabbed his arm pulling him away from it; everyone was waiting for him and getting colder by the second.

"Sorry," he murmured. "Don't know what got into me."

"Think we should go up the laneway?" Vivian whispered.

"Sure ... Probably just kids fooling around and painting stuff for a laugh." Edmond fought back the urge to stroke that sign.

"Way out here?" "Wherever here is," she added under her breath.

"Sure, kids are kids wherever they might be." Edmond kicked the snow at the bottom of the signpost. Maybe on the way back out he would touch it, just to say good-bye and all.

Vivian gave an onward wave to the bunched up ball of children, packed in a circle so tight they made her think of a ball of elastics.

They started up the narrow laneway, automatically forming two lines, tramping hand in hand, with Vivian and Edmond bringing up the rear. They tracked along through dips and hills, twists and turns, stopping and fanning out in the only clearing, where a yellow and black skidoo, pickup truck, an older model car, and a black and white police vehicle sat side by each. Just beyond the vehicles was a red painted wooden fence with evergreen trees poking over the top. The white washed gates were ajar. A cock-eyed open sign hung from one.

The children rushed through the gates.

Vivian and Edmond followed.

"Wow! ... Look at all the pretty trees!" said a little girl. She stretched her arms full out whirling in circles like a ballerina.

"Wowee!" Chirped a boy, running up to one of the trees and handshaking 'howdy do' with one of the lower boughs.

"Here's the cool tree from the sign," yelled a third child.

"Good God! Those skulls look so lifelike," said Vivian, resisting the sudden urge to move closer.

The children ran off in all directions, disappearing from sight in the massive maze of trees.

"There's one thing in our favour," Edmond pointed to the police car.

Vivian smiled, feeling more at ease; the help they needed would be forth coming and soon they would all be on their way.

"I'd be willing to bet, we find the officer, we find the person in charge," Edmond said feeling more comfortable than he had.

"And the other customers," Vivian quipped, sizing up the snowmobile, car, and pickup truck.

"Let's split up, it will be faster to find them that way," Edmond suggested.

Vivian nodded her agreement already striding toward a row of trees.

The trees aligned in tight knit rows with T intersections, making the Christmas tree farm resemble a labyrinth more than anything else.

Without warning, a blood-curdling scream snapped through the air like an electrical current gone awry; then another, and another. Then many—all different in pitch, tone, and volume as if auditions were being held for screamers for a horror flick.

Vivian panicked, running mindlessly through the rows, dead-ending time and again. She attempted to plow through the branches into the next row over to no avail. It was as if the trees had anticipated a cross over attempt and intertwined their limbs making them impassable.

Edmond had been luckier, finding clear passageways. He charged as fast as his feet would carry him down the rows in the direction of the screams. As he turned left at the last T, he abruptly halted.

The snow was saturated with so much blood it had melted and formed a deep red pool with copper scented, foggy streamers. Shredded carcasses of better than half the children were covering the snow and lower boughs of trees, as if someone had used the body parts in place of ornaments and had decorated over zealously.

The carcasses were interlaced with massive amounts of minced and chunky something that resembled raw hamburger and stewing beef. Tattered clothing hung about like garland. A small arm, stripped of flesh and severed at the shoulder, was up-ended and off to one side like a macabre cane. Part of a scalp with a single tuft of long blonde hair was tangled up on one of the skull ornaments on the black tree, as was a dripping red meaty hip joint. Hoof and three toed claw prints filled to the brim with blood mixed throughout

the carnage as if someone had detailed an intricate plan for a grisly puzzle project.

Edmond stood transfixed, face drained of colour, remnants of vomit trickling down the front of his jacket.

Something way down deep inside told him to turn and run for his life. He listened.

He flew uncontrollably through the aisles, running like a man chased by the devil himself. He glanced back over his shoulder, turning back too late and smashing full force into a tree. His forehead spouted blood. He sank down to his hands and knees crawling with his head cocked at an awkward angle.

More screams trumpeted, shrill, panicked, and full of terror. They grew in volume and intensity and then abruptly silenced like a snuffed out candle.

He rounded a corner, stopping mid crawl. His breaths rapid and harsh. His heart felt like it was about to explode.

The pulverised corpses of the remaining children littered the snow as if a hay rake had mowed them all down.

Then he saw it. Really, saw it.

The thing, hunched over the dead, dining on them, gobbling, stuffing, cramming its lipless mouth so full it was overflowing and falling out down onto the corpses. A single eyeball dangled by its optic nerve from one of its fangs, bouncing up and down like a small rubber ball on the end of a bungee cord.

Without warning it stopped eating, turning his way, eyes surveying him.

Edmond's body knew terror before he did, freezer burning him in place. Fresh urine dripped from the crotch of his coveralls onto the snow.

It shifted, jumped into the air, coming straight at him. It bounded with tremendous speed, in ape like movements, pushing out its elongated front limbs, bringing up the hind.

Its deer like head with massive anthers held low in a rutting manner. Its lipless mouth was open.

It was on him ripping and tearing at his flesh before he had the chance to scream.

He felt as if he was having an out of body experience, watching as it carved into his flesh pulling out his liver, gulping it down whilst he still breathed. He felt no pain as it severed him into two separate pieces; only a warm fuzzy darkness. He exhaled his final breath as blood bubbled from his lips.

It feasted, gorging itself on the warm meaty flesh of the man once called Edmond. It remained on him, devouring him entirely, stripping his bones so clean they looked like they'd been boiled in a science lab. Once done it moved back over to the strewn about little carcasses, scraping them up into a pile and stuffing its self.

A coo, like that of a dove, whistled through the wind.

It halted, cocking its head, tuning its ears. It sniffed the air.

Vivian had not been quick enough with her hand to muffle the little girl's cough.

It hurdled itself through the maze, bounding over top of the rows of trees effortlessly, coming to a halt directly in front of Vivian and the two remaining children.

It stepped forward towering above them, swaying the top half of its body side to side almost mockingly.

Vivian whipped the children behind her back. They pressed against her, clinging to her coat and jeans as if they had been crazy-glued.

It scrutinized them, starting with their feet and ever so slowly working its way up to the tops of their heads.

Without warning, it lunged forward seizing Vivian in one hand, embedding its claws deep into her neck. It lifted her off the ground turning her round slow and purposeful before set-

ting her back down. It grasped the two children in the same manner, holding them up, rotating them, and returning them to the ground.

It gripped Vivian with one claw, the two children with the other. It turned round, moving through the snow dragging all three behind.

The thing stopped at the base of an enormous hollowed tree trunk. It mercilessly tossed them at the tree, stared momentarily, and then turned its attention to a headless corpse.

The girl to the right of Vivian started to scream.

It crooked its head eyeing them with contempt.

It scratched up three small clumps of the kill, grasped each in turn, and forcing their mouths open stuffed in one clump, clinched their lips shut, massaging their throats until they swallowed.

It plucked them one by one out from the snow heaving them up and into the tree trunk.

It scampered away, bounding over treetops to the first pile of dead, gulping down the leftovers before they started to freeze.

Vivian and the two girls huddled together using one another's body heat to keep from shivering.

"What ... What do you ... You think is it doing?" The one little girl to the left asked. Her knees were knocking uncontrollably. Her snow pants reeked of feces and urine.

"I don't know," Vivian said. But ... She did know. She even knew what the thing was.

Vivian wedged herself down sitting cross-legged. She motioned for the two girls to draw in as tight to her as they could. She started to hum a tune she learned as a child. She could hear the thing moving around out there. She hummed louder.

She gazed up at the sky. There was not even a single star to wish upon. She had no idea how long it had been dark, or how much time had passed.

The silence shattered.

It sounded like a freight train had just roared through.

A blood-curdling squeal bounced in and out of the tree trunk.

Again the roar ... Closer ... Thunderous.

Another squeal ... Tormented, farther off.

"Anybody out here?" He yelled. He walked slowly through the butchery. "Anyone here?" he called out again.

"Here! Here ... We are here!" Vivian hugged the two girls. All three started to cry with unbridled raw emotion. They were saved.

"How many of you?" he asked. He was standing directly adjacent to the tree trunk surveying the snow at the base.

"Three," Vivian yelled. "There are three of us," she confirmed. She wiped at her tears smiling.

"Did it do anything to you?" He untied the rope from his utility belt, snapping it along the ground releasing the coil.

"It put us in here," Vivian said. She helped the girls to their feet.

"Did it do anything else?"

"Yes ... Yes ... It made us swallow a piece of something."

He dropped the rope. "All of you?"

Vivian checked with the girls, they nodded in unison. "Yes, all of us."

He dropped his head remaining still and silent. The world at large did not need more of these creatures. If they had not been possessed yet, they had eaten the flesh. Either way their fates were sealed.

He backed a good distance from the tree trunk. He went down on one knee, sighting in the flamethrower.

"I'm sorry," he whispered. "I'm so sorry."

He flipped off the safety, pulling the trigger repeatedly until the tree lit and caught fire.

Vivian and the two girls started to scream and scream and scream.

He stood resting one arm on the butt of the gun as the tree turned into a vertical inferno and the smell of burning flesh choked the air.

He remained so until all reduced to bone fragments and cinders.

Twelve

♪On the eleventh day of Christmas, my true love sent to me:
Eleven Pipers Piping ... ♪

"You didn't come home last night." Rebecca folded her arms across her chest showing her displeasure.

"No I didn't," Wen replied staring out the front window.

"And why not?"

"Busy."

"Busy?" Her eyebrows raised of their own accord in tune to her thought ... *'Asshole.'*

"Yes, that's what I said."

"It's almost Christmas and you do have a daughter if you remember? You know, long brown hair, little turned up nose, six years of age, eats raw meat, kind of odd."

Wen seemed twenty miles away.

It started to snow.

"Are you in there?" She stamped her foot resisting the sudden urge to backhand him one.

"Yes." He stared directly into her eyes. "We need to talk!" he blurted. He grasped her hand tugging her down the basement stairs, back booting the door shut behind them.

He stood motionless, arms at his sides like a soldier.

"I'm listening," Rebecca said.

The sudden silence had turned uncomfortable, eerily so.

"Well?" she demanded.

He clutched both her hands, holding them. "I don't know if you are going to believe me or not ..." He paused briefly and then continued, "and I guess it doesn't matter. You are hearing the song."

"You are making as much fucking sense as always, just like everything else around this place ... Which is none!"

"You saw the creature?"

"No, I just said that for something to say."

"Becky, please ..."

She shook her hands free. "Yes you asshole! ... I saw it and it saw me."

"I know ..."

She cut him off. "What is your fucking point, then?"

"I've been trying to keep it away but I can't."

"No kidding Einstein!"

"Becky," his tone was soft, gentle. "I ..."

She broke into his sentence. "Get on with it ... Spit it out for Christ's sake!"

"It caught your scent the day you went outside to fetch Ellie from the neighbours ... And that was the day you first started to hear the twelve days of Christmas lyrics, right?"

"Okay, and?"

"God you're so much like Susanna ..."

Rebecca flushed with rage. She balled her hands into fists, hitting him hard in the chest, knocking him backwards into the wall. "I've about fucking had it with you and your bullshit! Course I'm like her, we were sisters!" she yelled. "Can we fucking go back to the 'I don't know if you are going to believe me or not' ... Now? ... Like *right* now."

"I don't know how to tell you."

"So we're just down in the fucking basement for something to do?"

"I need to talk to you. I have to talk to yo ... u." His last word trailed and broke off.

He snatched Rebecca up in his arms, whirling, moving them both away from the exterior door as the wood simultaneously thumped, rumbled, and reverberated, shaking its frame so radically it looked like it was about to implode.

94

"Go upstairs!" he yelled. "Now!" he screamed. He shoved Rebecca toward the staircase.

"Don't look back!"

The door splintered.

Three hooked claws clutched at a plank pulling it free.

He fired a flare through the opening.

A horrendous scream recoiled, and then cannon balled back through the hole, up the stairs, and along the ceiling.

He flung the basement door open, stepping out into the snow firing the remaining two flare guns in rapid succession.

The snow heaved.

A long spine-chilling howl broke the air, disturbing and haunting beyond words.

Rebecca and Ellie stood side by side watching out the living room window. Ellie slipped her hand into Rebecca's. "It's okay Becky ... it's okay," she whispered.

Rebecca gazed down at Ellie. She gave her hand a soft squeeze.

Thirteen

♪*On the twelfth day of Christmas, my true love sent to me:*
Twelve Drummers Drumming ... ♪

Eleven p.m.

The front door boomed open back lashing into the wall. It squealed in protest uttering bouts of thunderous claps.

"Quick! Come! Come!" Wen shouted. He pulled Rebecca out from under her blanket toppling the easy chair. "I'll get Ellie!"

He ran wildly down the hallway.

"Hurray," he urged. He ushered them both through the open front door, across the porch, down the walkway, and out onto the road.

"Run! Run!" he shouted.

Ellie and Rebecca sprinted after him through the maze of dark houses and yards.

He slowed as he approached an open field, gazing in all directions as if scouting it out, and then halted. "Rest," he said.

"Good God Wen!" said Rebecca breathlessly. "What the hell?"

In one fluid motion, he took the machine gun out of its sling, slipped in a black canister, and snapped the safety off. He repeated the process with three smaller guns.

She had seen the machine gun before. "What on earth are you doing?"

He held up the machine gun. "This is a Black ops two, twelve shot, flame thrower" He held up the other three. "These are British T Calibre world war one, one flame shot, very hot, very powerful." He tucked the three smaller guns in his belt, barrel down. He gripped the largest in his right hand.

"And!" Rebecca held up her hands. Confusion was at a premium.

"Fire is the only way ... Come now ... You've rested enough." He started running again.

"Fire?" Rebecca shouted out after him. "Fire ... For what?" He did not answer.

They ran for what felt like an eternity, across fields, fences, unplowed roads, down and up dips and knolls.

Rebecca veered slightly to the right as they started up a narrow laneway skimming a Christmas tree farm sign with a black tree and white skull like ornaments.

Ellie grabbed onto her hand. "It's okay Becky ... It's okay." She stared up into Rebecca's eyes holding them longer than a child should.

Rebecca felt unnerved, almost frightened. Ellie's eyes were black, the green gone, more orb than almond in shape, and if words could be put to it, her demeanour was brooding, dark, unnatural. And ... On top of everything ... she was floating along like Wen, effortlessly. Wen, who was steaming full ahead, as natural as if he was born of snow, all the while toting four guns.

She must have lost her mind over the past twelve days. Here she was, with no questions asked, following this guy, running like hell through the snow beside his six-year-old daughter, in the dark, in slippers and no coat, after eleven o'clock at night on Christmas Eve.

The laneway opened up into a clearing where a skidoo, pickup truck, an older model car, police vehicle, and a school bus sat side by each. Wen's pace slowed to a measured jog as he went through the gates of the wooden fence with the cock-

eyed open sign. He motioned with his gun for them to come through.

Ellie still held Rebecca's hand.

"I have to let go for a second," Rebecca said breathlessly. "I need a tissue." She fetched it from her jeans pocket wiping at the saliva on her chin, not giving it a second thought.

Wen's eyes flickered to Ellie and back.

Neither said a word.

Eleven-thirty p.m.

Wen sauntered over to a forlorn looking picnic table and sat. "Becky we need to talk." He pushed the snow from the seat patting it.

"You want to talk? ... Here? ... Now?" she muffled. She doubled over, hands wrapped around the back of her knees, attempting to catch her breath.

"Yes."

"All right, but give me a minute." Her side had a stitch in it and her breath still had not regulated. She scratched at the back of one hand ambling over to the bench. It felt like a flock of mosquitoes had descended on it, feasting to their hearts content, the itch was way the other side of intense.

"Before you start ... Couldn't we have talked at home? ... You know it is Christmas Eve, chestnuts roasting over the open fire and all that."

"No. We had to come here."

"Had to come here?" She gawked around at the rows and rows of Christmas trees. "Why might I ask?"

"This used to be a magical place. This is where it all be-gan." He set the machine gun down in the snow leaning it up against a table leg.

She pulled her lips into her mouth. "I'll say one thing for you. You are true to form. You're making absolutely no sense, as usual." She stared into his eyes. "I'm waiting," she said. "Or is it still?"

Rebecca forced a smile at Ellie who was rolling snowballs and piling them in a heap.

"Ellie, go play somewhere else." Wen motioned for her to leave them.

"You're sending her off ... Yet again ... Here ... At night ... On Christmas Eve?"

"She'll be fine."

She gave him a disparaging scowl. "Whatever." She watched Ellie skip off down one of the rows of trees. No coat ... No hat ... No boots ... No footprints.

Eleven-forty-five p.m.

Wen stared at her intensely, allowing his eyes to take her all in.

She hunched her shoulders suddenly feeling like a science project.

"You can stop staring any time now," she said gruffly.

"My first name isn't Wen, it is Jack," he began. "I have been on this earth six-hundred and fifty years as has this Christmas tree farm." He paused; the corners of Rebecca's mouth were curling upwards. "When I was a young man I accepted a mission in return for the gift of long life. It was a mission of protection and preservation of the line of mystical wood spirits known as the 'Noel Wendigo.' To protect them from humankind, and vice versa, to protect humankind from them, and to ensure and preserve their lives. As long as they live, I live."

She dipped her head. "Say that again?" She had a cynical grin smeared across her face.

"My first name is Jack. I have been around six-hundred and fifty years, as has this Christmas tree farm. When I was

a young man I accepted a mission in return for endless life. It was a mission to protect and preserve a line of wood spirits."

"Okay," she sucked her lips into her mouth. "That's what I thought you said." Rebecca's grin was mature and full-blown. She was eyeballing him as if he had just downed a whole jar of crazy pills; A very, very, large jar.

It was snowing heavier.

He continued, unfazed by her obvious amusement. "Wendigo translated means, 'The evil spirit that devours mankind,' a cannibal."

"I am quite aware what a 'Wendigo' is, but thank you very much for clearing that up anyway." She got up, shaking the snow off herself.

He gripped her arm. "I'm not finished."

"I am," she shot back.

"No, no you're not."

She sat back down, sighing heavily. "Whatever, asshole ... Get on with it, then."

"Around eighteen hundred sixty is when I first started to run into trouble ..."

Rebecca flicked his hand loose, springing back up onto her feet. She shook her head back and forth. "What in fuck are you on?"

"No ... No, please hear me out. If you do nothing else in your life ... Do this."

"Jesus Christ," she muttered looking him smack dab in the eyes. She sat at the far end of the table, out of grasping range. "You know, a nice normal Christmas tale would have been enjoyable," she said sarcastically. "Go on, finish this fucking shit." She wiped at the drool at the corner of her mouth then scratched at the back of her hand again.

"As I said, it was eighteen hundred sixty when I first ran into trouble. Some of the creatures escaped from this tree farm, and ..."

She cut him off. "Hold on shithead! ... You brought Ellie and I to the place in your cockamamie story where these bullshit, asshole, fucked up creatures were kept? ... Wen! ... Jack! ...Whoever the fuck you are, I have had about enough! ... I'm leaving." She whipped around the other side of the table tramping off through the snow in the direction of the gate.

"How long have you been eating raw meat, Rebecca?"

She stopped, digging her slippers into the snow, whirling round scowling, shooting invisible daggers at his forehead.

"Well? ... Tell me." He held up his hands waiting for an answer.

Her eyes started to tear. She opened her mouth to give him a smart-ass retort, but snapped it shut instead. She could have picked from any one of a dozen or so responses, or even said she had just wanted to try it, but that was a lie. She had been eating it for quite a while in secret. She just could not get enough of it.

"None of your fucking business," she finally said.

She wiped at her eyes, scratching her cheek in the process making it bleed. Her fingers were cumbersome and not functioning probably. It was as if she had just been released from *Frankenstein*'s' laboratory. She held her hands up in front of her face. Her four fingers were webbing together, as if forming a set of two from four. Her thumb seemed elongated. Each had a thick nail like nub protruding from the end as if she was about to grow eagle talons.

She kicked at the snow mindlessly with her right slipper. "Go on," she said quietly.

"A 'Noel Wendigo' is rare and very different from generalized Wendigo's."

"So what!" She shoved a finger into her mouth chewing at the side of the nub, attempting to rip it off.

"Please, hear me out."

"Cut to the chase!" She flipped her hands over studying the back of them. They had sprouted a fine downy hair. The itching was worse now.

"The Noel Wendigos at the farm had always been allowed to hunt here freely." He glanced down at the machine gun, then at her hands.

He moved the gun closer.

"That is until eighteen sixty, when the escaped ones started to breed, and flourished at man's detriment. Do not get me wrong, I did damage control. But sixty years ago when I was rounding up the last survivor of the free wills," he cleared his throat. "The ones that escaped, it was then that I made the first of the two greatest mistakes of my life."

"What is it you're saying?" She started chewing at another nail. *'What the fuck is he on? ... Better still ... What the fuck am I on?'*

"The Noel Wendigo's as I said ..."

She chopped him off again. "I'm growing tired of this fucking ass shit!"

"One more minute, please."

She gave him the 'whatever' shoulder hunch.

"The last one loose had an infant. A daughter; A daughter with the most beautiful sea green eyes I have ever seen. When its mother was killed, I took the infant to a famous shaman. He performed a magical rite of passage and transformed the infant into a human. That human being your grandmother."

"My grandmother? ... Yeah right!" she scoffed. "Say, can I have some of the drugs you are taking? ... I could really use some about now." She cupped her hand holding it out to him. "Guess not," she whispered.

"Can you be serious, please?"

"Me? ... Me! Have you heard yourself?" She shoved her hands into her pockets. "Fucking hell! Go on then, but get this shit over with sooner than later. I'm getting cold."

"Did you ever meet your grandmother, Rebecca?"

"No, she passed just after my mother was born."

"Yes ... Yes she did. She died over the Christmas season, did she not?"

Rebecca gave him the ungodly stare of all stares. 'If looks could kill he'd be dead.'

They held one another's eyes for what seemed like forever.

"I'll make it short for you ... The rite of passage changed the blood line, allowing them to live in a human form up until the age they'd hear the Christmas Song. 'The Twelve Days of Christmas.' At that time, they revert to their creature form. The transformation occurs at midnight Christmas Eve. There are two distinct varieties. One lives as a human for the twelve days of Christmas, the remainder of the year as the creature; the other as a human except for the twelve days of Christmas. After years, the rite's spell diversifies and weakens to the point where both types will only be able to take human form for twelve minutes after midnight Christmas Eve."

Rebecca sat in the snow cross-legged, staring up at him as if she was in the story circle at kindergarten class.

Wen squatted down to her. "Susanna used to be human except for the twelve days of Christmas but has succumbed. "He clasped Rebecca's three fingered hands in his, rubbing the fine hair on the backs of them. "She lives as human for twelve minutes each Christmas." Tears flowed from the inner corners of his eyes. "Ellie lives as human for the twelve days of Christmas ... This is the reason I said I didn't believe in Christmas any longer."

Rebecca hung her head not uttering a word. Her answer to what she was on was there, loud and clear. She wondered

if she would remember who she was. Drool dripped from her mouth into the snow staining it a yellowish brown.

She looked up at him. She didn't need to ask of his second mistake, she knew in her heart it was falling in love with her sister.

Wen wrapped his arms around her. "Shhh ... It's okay Becky. It's okay," he said. "You are the last of the line ... I brought you here so I can take care of you just like I do Susanna and Ellie."

Rebecca shut her eyes, fitting herself into his warmth. She felt so cold, like there was ice in her veins.

Eleven-fifty-five p.m.
A branch snapped.

Rebecca's eyes shot open.

There ... In amongst the first row of trees, bathed in Christmas Eve moonlight, stood the creature, stood Ellie, side by side.

Rebecca pushed back from Wen, coming to a stand, hastily pacing, tramping the snow into a trench. Ellie's crudely made snowman sat nearby, the three sock toys tucked neatly in behind its stick arms.

She ran a clawed finger over her head. She had sprouted two boney cores. Her ears had relocated and morphed into a different shape. Her tongue was elongated and hanging out her mouth. Her lipless mouth—Her lipless mouth full of massive pointed teeth. Her ribcage was hollow and bonelike. Her feet moved like clubs. Her stomach rumbled from hunger. She towered above Wen in height.

Eleven-fifty-eight p.m.
Rebecca and the creature with Susanna's sparkling sea green eyes locked gazes, in a connection long extinct to humankind.

The air began to mist and whirl.

The two had held one another's eyes mere days before with one degree of separation, a window glass.

Now there was no glass.

As Wen had said so many days ago, a lifetime ago, the creature had caught her scent on the first day ... Caught the scent of kin.

The creature raised its arms holding them out for Rebecca to come.

Rebecca took two steps forward, her hooves leaving half-moon imprints in the snow.

"Come to me Becky," the creature slurred. "Come be with me for eternity."

Without warning Rebecca halted, reeled, hurdling herself toward Wen. She grasped onto him lifting him from the ground with one hand.

"Kill me!" she screamed. "Kill me! ... Kill me now!" she slurred.

He looked down at the ground shaking his head back and forth in a silent no.

She dropped him into the snow, fetched the massive flare gun and handed it to him.

She stepped back holding her massive arms out. "Kill me you bastard! ... I know you know how! ... Do not let this happen to me! ... Please Wen! ... Do it! ... Do it now!"

Wen stared into her eyes, searching them for remnants of humanness.

"Please!' she garbled. Drool balled and dripped off her fangs. "Please," she whispered.

A single tear escaped the outer corner of her eye wetting the hair that lay beneath.

"Please Wen," she begged.

He backed ... Went down on one knee ... Sighted in the gun aiming directly at her heart. He paused, wiped at the stream of tears raging down his face, and pulled the trigger.

Rebecca stood silent, arms stretched out like a scarecrow, the green in her eyes darkening by the second.

The first of many flares hit her square in the heart.

Again and again he fired, dispensing ten of the flares.

Rebecca closed her eyes and smiled as the fire torched and seared away her flesh. She felt warm all over and relished in it for the second or two before her heart bubbled and exploded and she reduced to nothing but black ash.

It started to snow.

Twelve a.m.

The air turned magical, swirling and shimmering as it filled with gold dust.

Wen stood back from them, transfixed as the creature and Ellie stood facing one another holding hands; transforming like macabre butterflies.

"Merry Christmas dove," Susanna said softly. She cuddled the creature within her arms.

"Merry Christmas mamma," croaked Ellie as the final remnants of her humanness resided into oblivion.

A multitude of tears rolled off Susanna's cheeks as she watched her scamper away.

Wen wrapped Susanna tightly within his arms kissing the top of her head.

"What would you like to do?" he said softly.

"Let's sit and hold one another," she murmured.

They strolled hand in hand to the picnic table, sitting on the top facing one another.

Susanna snuggled up against him, resting her head on his shoulder. "Sing my song to me my love," she said.

"On the first day of Christmas my true love sent to me: a partridge in a pear tree. On the second day of Christmas, my true love sent to me: two turtle doves, and a partridge in a pear tree. On the third day of Christmas, my true love sent to me: three French hens, two turtle doves, and a partridge in a pear tree. On the fourth day of Christmas my true love sent to me: four calling birds, three French hens, two turtle doves, and a partridge in a pear tree."

Wen momentarily stopped singing, running his left hand through the lengths of her long silky brown hair. He turned his forearm inward. His watch was gone.

"Why did Becky choose to leave us?" Susanna whispered.

He drew her closer. "Free will," he murmured.

"She was family."

"She will always be family," he said quietly.

"Sing the rest of the song for me," she said.

He continued where he left off. "On the fifth day of Christmas my true love sent to me: five golden rings, four calling birds, three French hens, two turtle doves, and a partridge in a pear tree. On the sixth day of Christmas my true love sent to me: six geese a laying, five golden rings, four calling birds, three French hens, two turtle doves, and a partridge in a pear tree. On the seventh day of Christmas my true love sent to me: seven swans a swimming, six geese a laying, five golden rings, four calling birds, three French hens, two turtle doves, and a partridge in a pear tree ..."

Susanna had never requested him to sing this song before, he smiled as he continued with the verses; it was snowing heavier now. He closed his eyes relishing the warmth of her; there was no place on this earth he would rather be than with her. Their time was so short, twelve minutes a year. Last year they had gone for a walk in the trees picking one and decorating it. The year before they'd had a picnic, and before that, she was gone for the twelve days of Christmas

and back for the year. How he wished he could go back to that time.

The sound of a Christmas tree crashing down to the ground jolted him back into reality.

Ellie ...

Ellie was out there ... Out there waiting ... Ellie, now the thing of darkness and hunger.

"What verse was I on?" he asked.

She lifted her head, her green eyes dancing in amusement. "You lost your place while you were singing?"

"Yes."

"The eleventh," she said.

"You want the whole song?"

"Yes."

"On the eleventh day of Christmas my true love sent to me: eleven pipers piping, ten lords a leaping, nine ladies dancing, eight maids a milking, seven swans a swimming, six geese a laying, five golden rings, four calling birds, three French hens, two turtle doves, and a partridge in a pear tree. On the twelfth day of Christmas my true love sent to me: twelve drummers drumming ..."

Another tree crashed down.

Ellie again ...

"Eleven pipers piping ..."

His thoughts turned to Rebecca; the spirited, strong willed, wonderfully out spoken, beautiful, and kind sister of Susanna. She had touched and melted his heart in so many ways. Moreover, he had never once had the fore thought to say so to her.

"Ten lords a leaping ..."

He smiled at Susanna pressing kisses into the nap of his neck.

"Nine ladies dancing ..."

Another tree toppled.

"Eight maids a milking ..."

Susanna nipped his neck.

"Seven swans a swimming ..."

He turned his arm checking the time, forgetting his watch was gone.

"Six geese a laying ..."

He ran his fingers across his dry lips. His eyes tracked over the snow. The flamethrower was out of reach ... All the guns were out of reach.

"Five golden rings ..."

Cold drool dripped onto the side of his neck.

"Four calling birds ..."

The song had taken longer than expected. Twelve minutes, put in perspective is but a mere flash in the pan, gone before you knew it.

He glanced over at the four guns again, all laid out in the snow like little soldiers. He smirked. He was tired. So, very tired. Six hundred fifty years worth of tired.

Claws pierced into his sweatshirt right on through to his back muscles. He could feel the blood starting to spout and stream.

He closed his eyes.

"It's okay Susanna," he said. "It's okay," he whispered.

"Two turtle doves ..."

She sawed her teeth into the top of his shoulder blade, whipping her head back and forth violently shaking him.

Ellie bounded from the trees, leaping through the air to land at his feet, immediately sinking her razor sharp teeth into his calf muscle and severing it from the bone.

"And a partridge in a pear ..." His voice blew out little red air bubbles as he attempted to sing the last remaining word of the song.

Blood spewed from between his teeth sliming his neck as it raged down under his sweatshirt. His chest heaved errat-

ically as the two creatures tore, ripped, and shred his flesh, eating him alive. He felt no pain as the smallest creature slit open his chest cavity, pulverized the bones of his ribcage, reached deep inside, and pulled away his beating heart ending his long stay in this world.

The heart shuddered once before stopping midway down its throat.

The creatures feasted and gorged, then sucked the marrow from the bones.

They darted off between the rows of Christmas trees, bounding up and over the containment fence.

Fourteen

Ten years later

"See it yet?" Milly asked. She peered over Andrew's shoulder.

"Nope." He pulled the old map from the hotel bed placing it on top of the twenty or so on the floor.

He picked up another, unfolding it ever so carefully as if it was made of glass. "There's only four left," he said.

Milly stretched out on the bed beside him studying the map, using the tip of her index finger as a guide.

"Wait a sec ... Does that say Bensford Bridge?"

"Where?"

"Right there ... Right damn there!" She moved her finger back and forth invisibly underling the two words.

Andrew shoved his face so close to the map he could have eaten it for dinner. He pulled back beaming. "Well ... Well ... Missy, if it isn't your lucky day!" He spoke with a mocked up southern drawl.

Milly jumped up and down. "We found it!"

"Yep we did."

"See I told you it was real."

"The town's not on the map."

"How can a town with no name be on the map? Tell me that one smart ass!"

He shrugged his shoulders.

"They say the town is a mere twenty or so miles north west of the bridge."

He smirked. "They also say, whoever the hell they is, that the town is a ghost town with a magical Christmas Tree farm

on the outskirts that's said to only appear for the twelve days of Christmas. They also say that said town is riddled with dark secrets and a ghastly history."

"They, my fine feathered friend, happen to be a closed group of cryptozoologists on the internet," she said smugly folding up the map. "You said you wanted an adventure for Christmas ... Did you not?" she started to laugh.

He mirrored her laughter. "Yeah I did. I hate to admit it, but I did."

"Well then," Milly paused, putting her hands on her hips swaying her shoulders arrogantly back and forth. "Remember I said I couldn't wrap your present this year?"

"Yes as a matter of fact I do."

"Merry Christmas! ... I'm giving you this adventure as my gift. What is more festive than investigating said ghost town with a magical Christmas Tree Farm that only appears for the twelve days of Christmas?"

"Tomorrow is the start of the twelve days of Christmas, want to leave at first light?" he asked.

She nodded.

It started to snow.

Two dark figures stood at the outer edge of the tree line.
It was thirteen days to Christmas.
Tomorrow ... It could begin.

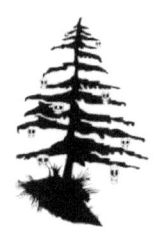

Epilogue

They're everywhere
They're nowhere
But ...
They are there.

Author's Note

Dance with me before I am but a ghost of a memory ...

Sincerely
I.L. Jackson

Gone!

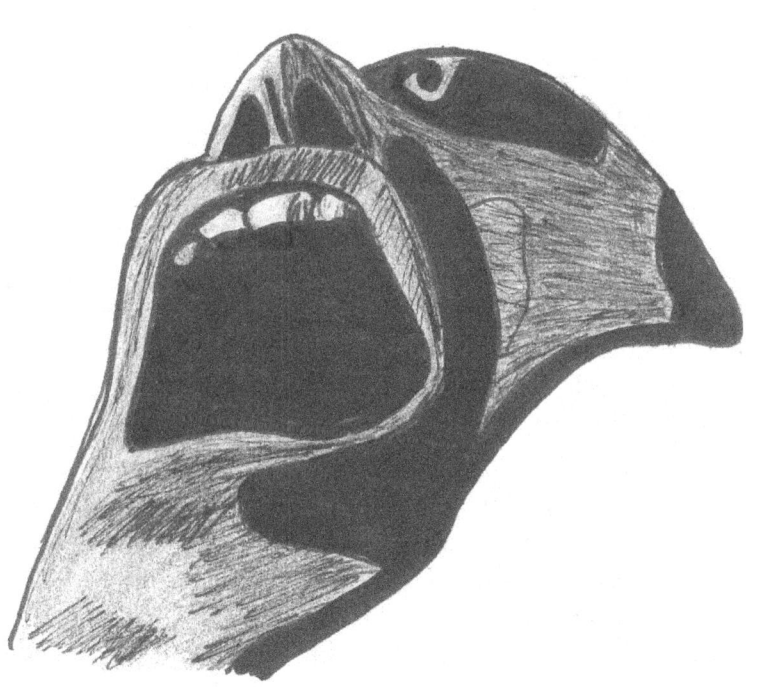

B.A. Bellliveau

I opened the door and expected to be bombarded, as usual, with "Hi Mom," a grunt or two acknowledging my existence, tales of woe, squabbling kids, questions like "What's for supper?" "Can you drive me..." or "Mom, where is..."

At the very least, I expected Tinker-dog to greet me with yelps of joy and welcome.

But on this Wednesday, all I heard was nothing. Absolute silence rang in my ears.

I dropped my purse on the small table beside the blinking Christmas tree. "Hi! I'm Home!" I yelled.

Nothing

"Where is everyone?"

No answer.

I started for the kitchen, sure that someone had an *Ipod* plugged into teenage ears and did not hear me, but halfway down the hall I noticed another sound. Running water. Aha! I thought. Susan is taking a shower. I climbed the stairs, calling her name as I went. The bathroom door was closed so I knocked and opened it a bit. "Susan?" I asked. She didn't answer so I entered. Sure enough the shower curtain was closed and the water gushed from the showerhead. I peeked around the curtain, calling her name so as not to startle her, but she was not there. Her shampoo was there, body wash was there, but she was not there. I turned off the water and cussing her roundly for being so careless, I went to her room. Today's clothes were strewn over her floor, but the room was empty. Where in heck could she be?

I checked Tommy's room. I could tell from the bed he had flopped down on it lately, but he was not there either. His earphones and his *Ipod* lay on his pillow just where his head had left an indentation.

What is going on?

Entering the kitchen, I encountered the meat burning in the fry pan and the potatoes dry of water and beginning to stick to the bottom of the pan on a stove still turned on. I rescued what I could of supper, turned the burners off and began to worry. What could have happened to cause such a panic that my family had been so careless? The back yard must hold the answer.

The yard was empty. Tommy's soccer ball was in the middle of the lawn, looking sad and alone. Tinker-dog's chain still attached to his house but the clip end lay abandoned mid-yard.

There was a very strange odor assailing my nostrils. Was it sulpher? No, not quite. More like formaldehyde. A queer smell I couldn't quite place.

Our good neighbours could probably shed some light on the situation so I hurried to their back door, which was open. I entered. I was stunned. I found the same situation at their house, meat turning black on the stove, a pot of rice smouldering, and no answer to my calls.

I was beginning to panic.

I raced back home and picked up the phone to call 911 for help. The phone line was dead. I tried my cell, but all I got was the message "No Service".

What was I to do?

And that queer smell was getting stronger and stronger.

I sat down on the couch and tried to think. Closing my eyes to concentrate and fight the nausea the stink was causing.

"I'll go to the fire department." I said to myself, opening my eyes and reaching for my purse and car keys.

I looked in horror. My hands had disappeared. I screamed and tried to stand. My feet were gone. I screeched for help and sat terrified as I watched myself disappear until only my head remained—then only my face—then only my mouth. I shrieked in horror until there was no sound.

Incubus
Tales of the Anunnaki

Lynn Marie Simpson

For all the angels in my life

Prelude

His strong warm hands gently massaged, moving lower to caress the small of her back, her hips, and her buttocks. The heat coaxed a purr of contentment from her throat. Encouraged by the sound He slipped his hand in front of her hip and urged her to roll onto her back.

His hands and fingers continued their magic as he caressed her firm small breasts, the small brown areola darkened and her nipples peaked. His hands slowly travelled lower, tracing the curves of each rib, smoothing the already flat abdomen, squeezing her inner thighs.

Almost of their own volition, her knees bent and her legs fell open offering him easy access. She moaned in frustration when he ignored her offering and continued to massage her inner thighs, the edges of his hot fingers teasing the edges of her desire. She was a puppet and he the puppet master. He, Matthew Trusler and she his Stradivarius. He played her body until it sang to his tune.

When his mouth closed over her lips and his tongue dove deep inside she screamed in ecstasy. Her body arched as he proceeded to drink her essence until there was nothing left but an empty, dried up husk—with a hideous smile on its face.

He stood over the empty husk and stared as if wondering from where it came as her strength ran through his veins, entering his organs, gorging them with life. He stared at the empty husk and heard the human female in his head. She didn't like the dark. She was scared and wanted to go home. She should never have gone out tonight, and she most definitely should not have gone to The Dungeon.

She was only twenty-five, with long blond hair that swayed from side to side as she approached the sexy stranger. Her intention was clear in the seductive tilt of her lips and the provocative sway of her hips. Her smile was full of promise as she sat on the stool closest to him and leaned in.

"Can I buy you a drink?" Her naturally husky voice cracked slightly, but she didn't back down.

Her skin glowed with life and He could smell her soul, sweet and fresh. She didn't usually act this way, provocative and daring, but she had just caught her boyfriend with another woman and wanted revenge. He was perfect. Tall and dark, with the chiselled face of a god, tantalizing golden brown eyes full of mystery, and he was alone. She'd been watching him for an hour now and nobody had gone near him. Sure the women had looked, and why not? As eye candy went, he was mighty fine. Hell, she'd been staring at him for an hour, and after three drinks finally got the courage to move ahead with her plan, to hurt her boyfriend as much as he hurt her.

She was so young and full of life as she made her way purposefully toward him. He should have politely declined her offer and left, but he was getting hungry—and you wouldn't like him when he got hungry.

So—he took her to his lair, and now he had to hide the body.

One

HER PALE BEAUTY titillated his appetite like so many others before her. He didn't know her name. He didn't want to know her name. Names were power but He already had all the power He needed.

Hunger tore him apart like a jackhammer on a sidewalk. His control crumbled and slipped like sand through his fingers. The dark interior of the dance club did nothing to hide the red of his eyes, a red much like all the other addicts that frequented The Dungeon. Only he wasn't addicted to crack cocaine or heroin. He was addicted to life—others!

He stalked across the darkened dance floor as graceful as a panther on the prowl, and just as lethal, only unlike the panther He drew his prey to him like moths to a flame. He ignored the fawning eyes and grasping hands of those nearest him and made his way to his chosen prey.

"Come with me." His voice was low and compelling. Several patrons, both male and female, turned toward him but he kept his focus on the pale female.

His intended victim raised one quirky eyebrow, looked him up and down as if he were a used car she was considering purchasing, rolled her eyes and said, "Not likely."

As if to prove her disinterest, she began to grind against the tall, skinny, pale faced boy wearing a black cape and fake fangs, and pretending to be a big bad vampire.

He couldn't grasp what just happened. Nobody refused him—ever! He nearly lost control when she turned to him with a sneer on her garishly painted red lips and asked, "Are you still here?"

Rage welled up and his vision turned red as hunger roared in his ears. He took a step toward her, gained a modicum of control and grabbed the nearest female, and dragged her to the exit leading to the back alley.

His new victim tripped and began to struggle against him. "Hey baby," she simpered coyly. "Slow down. We've got all night."

He stopped abruptly, yanking her roughly to her feet when she would have hit the ground. "Don't talk," he commanded.

"Fine," she attempted to purr but it came out a cross between a growl and a grunt when he tugged her through the door. When he caught her up against him, she began a slow grind against the bulge in his pants, sudden desire making her mind numb.

A quick scan of the alley told him they were alone. He quickly lowered his mouth over hers and began to inhale. When she started to struggle, he held her still with one arm wrapped around her waist and his other hand on her chin. She only struggled for a moment more before falling limp.

He should have stopped then, it was never a good idea to leave bodies lying around willy-nilly, but rage and hunger won out and he drank the last of her essence before tossing her into the open garbage bin like yesterday's garbage.

She took the edge off but it wasn't enough. He wanted more. He hadn't hunted for over a month, had left it too long and now one wasn't enough. At least he gained enough control to realize he couldn't hunt that club again tonight.

He moved quickly amongst the shadows, a part of them, until he came to The Fox and The Hound. He usually avoided this particular bar. It was a well-known hangout for Hunters, the kind that hunted His kind.

Feeling reckless he pushed open the door and entered the, compared to The Dungeon, well lit bar. It was almost empty.

He shouldn't have been surprised. The Hunters would be out making their rounds, patrolling the city's bars and alleys for creatures such as him. He was lucky they hadn't been at The Dungeon. Hunger had made him careless but he was under control now—for a while anyway.

It made him laugh the way humans played at being vampires while deep down believing such creatures didn't really exist. If they had even an inkling of what actually shared the streets with them they would lock their doors and hide quivering beneath their beds. Lucky for his kind they didn't believe.

He let the door slam behind him and moved gracefully to the bar. "Beer," he told the bartender, a male in his early twenties who was worried about a major test he had in the morning. His name was Todd, and Todd was supposed to have the night off, but when Mary called sick he agreed to cover her shift. He needed the money almost as much as he needed the time off.

Todd placed a coaster and a beer on the counter in front of Him and then went back to studying the book at the far end of the bar. He knew it wouldn't get busy until much later and was taking advantage of the moment.

He spun his stool around so he could lean against the bar with his arms resting on it, and studied the occupants of The Fox and The Hound. There wasn't a lot of choice. A couple in the farthest booth were enjoying a dinner of rare steak and baked potato with sour cream and chives. They were taking their time, enjoying a couple of hours away from their three kids. It was their anniversary.

He left their table and continued around the room. *Now, this looks promising.*

At a booth opposite the couple, sat four women. On second look, they were just kids, still in their teens, but they could prove to be amusing for a while. They were talking about

their boyfriends and drinking straight soda, but not one of them had any interest in looking for a little bit of fun.

He sipped his beer and watched them idly. They were so full of life it hurt to watch them, but it didn't matter how hungry he was, he refused to eat any more children.

It was the sadness drew him to her. It permeated the atmosphere like a dark cloak. She sat in a corner booth, her back to the wall. She was also watching the four girls having fun, and it was bitter sweet because they were having so much fun and there was no more time for her to spend with her girlfriends laughing and talking about boys, if she had any girlfriends.

She spent her time studying and being a "good girl" so her parents would be proud of her. Now it was too late. She would never find a man of her own; never experience the joy of that "first time." She had waited too long and now it was too late. She was going to die without having ever lived.

He kept his eyes on the four girls while he visited her memories.

The doctor had called to say he needed her to come to the office as soon as possible. Becky didn't think much of it. She'd been feeling tired a lot lately, and was having trouble sleeping—Not a great combination. The doctor was checking her blood for iron deficiency, and a few other things. She figured a few iron pills and she would be good as new.

It didn't happen quite that way.

"I'm sorry, Rebecca. There is nothing we *can* do. I suggest you put your affairs in order."

Affairs. Now that was a laugh. She'd been too busy working and studying to have time for any *affairs*.

"How long?" She'd managed to ask through a throat so tight she could barely breathe.

"A week. Two at most. At the rate you are shutting down it is hard to tell."

Her eyes burned with tears she refused to let fall. She didn't want pity. She'd come out tonight to live a little, and here she was, nursing a warm beer, feeling sorry for herself, and watching life pass her by—again. So much for living.

It's not too late.

The low masculine voice was compelling, but what did it know?

Of course it is. She answered the voice in her head. It wasn't real, but at least it was someone to talk with. *I was only kidding myself when I came out tonight.*

You are a desirable female.

Now that's a funny word to use, 'female.' Not 'woman,' because she wasn't yet. She might be age wise. but she would never experience life as a woman, not now. She was too old to be a girl; that ship had sailed a long time ago. She was a college graduate, old enough to be married with children. But she refused to refer to herself as 'spinster'—that just sounded dreadful, never mind old fashioned. Female was a good word.

Don't forget desirable.

Yeah right! She had no illusions that long, mousy brown hair, somewhere between straight and curly so it always looked messy, plain brown eyes, she'd always wished there were specks of green or something in them but there wasn't, and a nose too large for her added up to desirable. All right, she would admit that her face was cute in a small elfish way, but definitely not desirable.

She snorted in her beer, *Great! Now that was definitely desirable.*

Becky was glad that there was nobody in the bar to notice her. The happy couple had started to gather their stuff to leave, thought better of it and ordered another drink instead, but they were too engrossed in each other to notice her. The four girls at the table across from her were so busy gossiping

and giggling together that they hadn't even notice the hot guy sitting at the bar watching them.

Holy shit! When did he come in?

A few moments ago. You were preoccupied.

Oh yeah, I remember. I was mulling over my doctor's appointment earlier today and feeling sorry for myself when he came in and got me thinking about sex instead.

Is that a bad thing?

Becky felt her face flame and was glad that the hottie— Could you call a man with the face of an angel and the build of a Norse god a hottie?—wasn't looking at her.

I don't see why not.

Right! Just between you and me, if I look at him much longer my eyeballs will burn right out of my head. He's already fried my brains.

Fried your brains?

Duh! I wouldn't be thinking like this if my brains weren't fried. Or talking to you for that matter.

Lucky for me then that you have fried brains. The masculine chuckle that followed that thought surrounded her like her father's embrace when she was a small child and had been hurt or scared.

She wanted her father now. She wanted him to put his arms around her and tell her that he would make everything all right, but she knew that, even if her father were still alive, even he would not be able to fix this.

You are sad again.

Sorry, she snapped. *It is rather difficult to keep one's spirits high after being served a death sentence.*

Would it be better if you didn't know?

Would it be better if she didn't know? Becky took a moment to mull this over.

Life would go on as usual. She would get up every morning, shower, dress into her normal work attire of a skirt and

blouse, eat a meagre breakfast of fruit and cereal, if she could stomach it, brush her hair back into a ponytail, and drive to work where she would spend the next eight hours shuffling and filing paperwork. After work, she would drive to the local market where she would buy the makings of a salad and whatever else she felt like eating that night, which lately hadn't been much of anything. She would drive home to the small comfortable apartment she had rented when she was still going to school and that had somehow become home to her, where she would change into a pair of comfy jeans and a tee, make her dinner if she felt like eating, and curl up on the sofa with a good book. If there was something on television that looked interesting, she might watch a little. At eleven o'clock she would go to bed so that she could get up the next morning and start over—except on weekends. On the weekend, she would drive over to the home and spend the day with her mother.

Maybe today would be the day that she finally met someone who she wanted to spend time with, they would date, get married, have children—or maybe today was the day she would get hit by a bus and it would all be over.

Her landlady would have to clean out her apartment because there was simply nobody else to do it. Then Mrs Brown would call the home where Becky's mother spent her days staring into oblivion since her stroke five years ago. The nurse would pass on the message that Becky would no longer be coming to visit and her mother would just sit there staring. Perhaps somewhere deep inside her mother would realize that she was gone and a single tear might escape, but Becky doubted it.

But Becky knew how much time she had, or didn't have. She'd left the doctor's office and gone straight to her work office where she had given immediate notice and cleared out her desk. Then she had gone to the bank where she had

withdrawn enough money to pay three months rent and more than enough to live on for a couple of months, she was being optimistic at this point.

Her next stop was her lawyer's office where she made arrangements for the remainder of her estate. Becky wasn't poor by any standards. She had nearly two million dollars in trust from her father's estate that she had never touched, plus a couple hundred thousand of her own that she had invested and now amounted to nearly a million. She arranged that her father's trust transfer into a trust to look after her mother. It would have gone to her mother anyway, if she hadn't had a stroke. After her mother's inevitable death, the remainder of the trust would transfer to the home. She had no other real family, and the nurses at the home were like family. Then there was her landlady, Mrs Brown, who reminded her of her mother, and to whom she was leaving the remainder of her estate.

Next, she stopped at her apartment where she packed up her meagre belongings. There was surprising little that she wanted to take with her. Her entire life fit into two suitcases, and the only things she had of any value were the pictures of her parents and herself. After a last look around, Becky loaded her little brown Pinto and then went upstairs to her landlady's apartment.

Mrs Brown was shocked and saddened to hear that Becky was leaving. "Is there something wrong with the apartment," she worried. "If there is I will have it fixed."

"No! No. The apartment is great. I love it. That's why I stayed all these years. This is my home, and you are like family." Before Mrs Brown could get started, Becky continued, "The thing is, I've been transferred and I need to leave immediately, so I was wondering."

"Would you like me to hold the apartment in case you don't like it where you are going and you want to come back?" asked Mrs Brown quickly.

Becky had to smile at that. If only you could decide that you didn't like being dead and could come back. "No. That won't be necessary."

"Then what dear? I'll do anything you ask."

"I can't take anything with me. The place I'm going to ... is ... already fully furnished," she added hurriedly. "I am only taking my clothes and my personal items. Everything is relatively new. As you know, I bought everything new this past year." She had finally felt secure enough to spend some of her money. "I was wondering if I could leave the furniture behind. You could rent the apartment furnished that way."

"What a lovely idea. How much do you want for the furniture?"

"Nothing! Don't worry about it Mrs Brown. Consider it an early Christmas present."

"Oh dear, I couldn't possibly do that."

"If you don't take it I need to arrange for someone to pick it up and take it to the shelter."

"I will gladly take the furniture," assured Mrs Brown. She shoved the rent money back at Becky. "At least take this to help toward the cost of the furniture. Three months rent in lieu of notice is way too much anyway."

Becky hugged Mrs Brown goodbye before she could start crying again, and on her way out she placed the three months rent and the key to her apartment on the little hall table by the door. Mrs Brown would find it in the morning, after Becky was long gone.

Becky climbed into her ancient Ford Pinto and drove to the nearest bar, but The Dungeon was too crowded, too full of the underbelly of the city for her liking and so she ended up here, at The Fox and The Hound.

Was it better knowing the end was near? Becky wasn't sure, but at least there would be no loose ends. She would rent a motel on a weekly basis and when the pain got too much to handle on her own she would check into a hospital.

Maybe she would travel. Head north. It would be nice to see snow for Christmas. She had always wanted to see the snow.

So, is it better knowing or not knowing?

Are you still here?

A low chuckle and, *I don't have anywhere I need to be.*

That makes two of us. Becky lifted her beer bottle as if to toast. *To us*, she thought and nearly choked when the hottie on the bar stool raised his own beer at the same time the voice in her head repeated, *To us.*

He was looking straight at her with smouldering, tawny eyes that held a challenge. Slowly, without taking his eyes from hers, he lifted his beer bottle to his lips.

Don't be a fool, Beck, she scolded herself. *It's a coincidence. He just happened to look over here and take a drink of his beer at the same time as you.*

Becky took a determined sip of her warm beer and peered surreptitiously at the stranger over the tilted bottle. He was slouched comfortably on his barstool with his back and one arm resting against the bar, and she could still tell he was much taller than most of the men she knew. His eyes were perfectly set into a face that should be chiselled in granite. His nose was a little too long, not that she was complaining, and his chin was a tad too square, but the total effect was mesmerizing.

The stranger put his beer bottle down on the bar and turned once again toward the four girls. Becky placed her own bottle back on the table and let her eyes feast on the rest of the man. His shirt did nothing to hide the muscles in his arms and chest. The top two buttons were open and Becky glimpsed a few golden brown hairs. His slacks were not tight, but they bunched enough when he sat that they couldn't disguise the well-toned muscles on his thighs and legs.

Becky sighed. *He's like a love god,* she thought wistfully. *Too bad he's into young girls.*

What makes you think he has a thing for young girls?

Well, just look at him. He has been staring at them since he came in.

Would you rather he stared at you?

Becky sat back abruptly at the thought and glanced furtively around the almost empty room before staring at her own beer bottle in an effort not to look at Him again. *Of course not! That would just be creepy.*

The girls don't seem to mind.

Those featherbrains haven't even noticed him yet. They are too involved in their own little dramas.

The girls chose that exact moment to giggle loudly drawing Becky's attention to them. *I guess I was wrong.* All four girls were now primping while they continued to whisper and giggle only now their attention was completely on the hottie at the bar.

Becky finished off her beer in a determined swig. *Oh well, it's time to move on.*

Where do you go from here?

Where did she go from here? She should have thought of that before leaving her key with Mrs Brown. The Fox and The Hound didn't offer rooms for rent. The Dungeon did, but Becky could not imagine staying there without shivering in disgust. *Good thing it is still early.* Well, early for this town anyway.

Becky grabbed her purse and empty beer bottle and headed to the bar, aware that the stranger had turned to watch her approach. Not wanting to be rude, Becky acknowledged his presence with a nervous smile and a quiet, "Hi," as

she leaned on the bar, putting as much distance between them as possible without appearing to do so.

"Todd." She remembered the bartender's name from the tag he wore when he served her beer and burger. When he jumped up she said, "I was just wondering if you had a phone book I could borrow."

"Sure." Todd reached under the counter and pulled out a thick phone book. "Here."

"Thanks." This time her smile was more natural.

"No problem. Are you sure I can't get you anything else?"

"I'm sure."

Todd turned his attention to the man on the stool beside her, who had turned to face the bar and was now openly watching Becky. "How about you, can I get you another beer?"

The stranger glanced at his nearly empty beer bottle. *When did I drink that?* "I'm good," he answered in a deep, masculine voice. He couldn't help but notice the slight shiver in the female beside him at the sound of his voice. At least she wasn't immune to him.

God! His voice is like warm honey. Becky braced herself against the heat that surged through her veins. Her knuckles were white where she gripped the phone book in an attempt to hide her reaction from the others. It seemed to go on forever, but in reality, her strange reaction lasted only a heartbeat and, luckily, nobody else seemed to notice.

Becky opened the phone book with stiff fingers and managed to find the page that listed motels. If she was going to stay in town for a few more days then she didn't want to worry about night crawlers. She felt the man beside her stiffen.

What do you know about night crawlers? The voice in her head demanded.

Not now, Becky insisted. *Can't you see I'm busy here?*

Incubus

Night crawlers? The voice persisted.

Becky quickly scanned the room from beneath her long lashes. She was getting pretty good at it. Nobody was paying any attention to her. Todd was back studying his book and, He, was back studying the four teenagers, now completely focussed on him. Must be a side effect of the meds the doctor prescribed for her. Oh well, at least she had someone to talk with, even if he was rather pushy sometimes.

Night crawlers are 'guys' who tour the bars at night looking to get laid. They don't care who they pick up. They don't want to know anything about them. If truth be told, they don't even want to know their names. All they are looking for is a Wham! Bam! Thank you Ma'am! Hell, you'd be lucky to get the thank you.

You seem to know a lot about night crawlers. Is that from personal experience? The voice seemed more relaxed.

I've run into a few. Mostly during my stint as a cocktail waitress during college. My dad would have paid my way, but I wanted to prove I could do it on my own.

Maybe they weren't night crawlers as you call them. Perhaps they were simply compelled by your beauty to approach you.

Becky choked. This time everyone looked at her. Even the Adonis glanced her way. Embarrassment flamed her cheeks a delightful pink.

"Are you okay?" asked Todd as he handed her a glass of water.

Becky took a quick gulp and then thanked him, setting the glass on the bar. She tapped the open phone book in an attempt to draw the attention away from her. "Do you know where I can get a room around here? Some place safe."

Todd reached over and flipped the pages. "You don't want any of those. The one's close by will be booked, or else they

135

rent rooms by the hour. You want some place like these." He pointed to a list of rooming houses.

"Myself, I like the Cottages over on Dauphine. There are seven cottages, one and two bedrooms. Some have their own courtyard. There are a couple that share yards, but then it is only with one other cottage. They offer a continental breakfast over at the Dauphine Hotel, and they have parking there if you are driving. There's no parking at the cottages but they are only a block away from the hotel, where they also serve a continental breakfast." He grinned charmingly, "Ah, I mentioned the breakfast already, didn't I?"

Becky smiled at Todd. "Sounds like you know a lot about it."

Todd grinned. "Sure do. My sister, Sandi, and I lived at one of the cottages for almost two months when we first came to New Orleans. Oh yeah, I almost forgot the best part. They have swimming pools."

Sounds perfect for you. Private and safe.

Maybe I don't want to be safe. But she did. It was bad enough to die without it being tragic. "Sounds perfect," she told Todd. "Can you write down the number for me?"

"I can do you one better." Todd pulled his cell phone from his pocket and flipped it open. His fingers did a rapid dance and after a few moments, he spoke into the phone. "Hey, Sis, you got any cottages available? Yeah? Hold on." He covered the mouthpiece with his hand and said, "Did I forget to mention that my sister still works there? Anyway, they have two cottages available. Cottage 5, that's the one Sandi and I stayed in. It has two bedrooms, each with its own bathroom with shower, and a separate living area. It has French doors that open into the courtyard that it shares with Cottage 9, which is also available. Cottage 9 is one bedroom and a bath. It adjoins Cottage 8, and sometimes they rent it out as an extra bedroom for Cottage 8. Cottage 9 is nice, but it doesn't offer a separate sitting area."

Becky definitely didn't need all the room, but she couldn't stand the idea of spending the rest of her life cramped into a small room, and liked the idea of a separate living area. "I'll take the two bedroom cottage. My name is Becky," she added. "Becky Bonneville."

"Her name is Becky Bonneville and she wants Cottage 5. I don't know. Let me ask." Once again, he covered the phone, "How long do you want it?"

Becky hadn't thought that far ahead. She hadn't planned on hanging around, which was why she gave up her apartment, but something had drawn her to this bar, and once she was here she ordered a burger and a beer, something she had never done before, which probably explained the voice in her head. Beer and meds! She shouldn't have mixed, but it was too late now. And now, she didn't want to leave. She had the strangest feeling that if she left now she would miss something very important.

She should have said she would take the cottage for a week. She could afford to pay the rent, and if she decided to leave in the morning it wouldn't matter because they would have their money. If the doctor was right, and Becky had no reason to believe he was wrong, she wouldn't need the cottage for more than two weeks at the most. "I'll take it for the month if that is okay," she said recklessly.

Aha! An optimist.

Not really. Just stubborn.

Not necessarily a bad thing. Where is this place we are going?

The Audubon Cottages. Sounds pretty.

"Yeah. Yeah! I'll let her know." Todd hung up and turned to Becky. "Sandi says just drop by the Dauphine Orleans Hotel over on Dauphine." Todd wrote the address on the back of

a napkin. "She will get you checked in and someone will take you over to the cottage. Did I mention that they offer a continental breakfast at the hotel?"

"This is only the third time. Thanks, Todd. I'll make sure I take advantage of that breakfast."

"No problem. Can I get you anything else?"

"I think I'm good, thanks."

The sound of the door closing drew her attention, but nobody came in. Becky's brow furled in puzzlement as she looked around the room. The young couple in the far booth were still there, although they were finally getting ready to leave. Becky remembered when they came in. They were laughing about something their youngest child had done. They said it was their anniversary and they were planning to enjoy their first time out without the kids in over a year. The four teenage girls sitting across from her table were there when she came in. They looked confused for a second before they shrugged in unison and continued chatting and giggling about boys. Other than her and Todd, there was nobody else in the room. Nothing had changed in the bar in the couple of hours she'd been nursing her drink. Nobody came and nobody left. Quiet. Like the rest of her life.

Then how did that empty bottle get on the bar beside her?

Todd noticed the empty bottle, scooping it up along with Becky's empty bottle and not giving it a second thought. He put the empty bottles into the case beside the bar and dropped the wet coaster into the trashcan before wiping down the bar with the ever present bar cloth hanging out of his front pocket.

Becky continued to stare at the empty barstool beside her. *What am I missing?* She wondered, worried that she was already too far along and was losing her mind, just another fun symptom to look forward to. She gave her head a shake to

clear the fog and grabbed her purse. "Thanks, Todd. I'll see you around."

"Yeah! See you around, Becky."

Becky pushed open the doors, still trying to figure out what she was missing when her head began to ache. She went around to the back parking lot and was almost to her car when she heard them.

Two

HE HAD ALL the information he needed. With a quick smile and a wave of his hand, he ensured that the patrons of The Fox and Hound wouldn't remember him, and if they tried to think about the evening in too much detail, it would result in a vicious headache. This was going to be one of those nights of hazy memories.

He stepped onto the sidewalk and froze. He wasn't alone. A quick scan told him there were Hunters coming from both directions, and they were looking for Him.

Damn! How? Shit! He had been so furious when his intended dinner at The Dungeon refused him that he hadn't taken the time to wipe any memories. This was His fault. That's what happened when He got hungry. He got careless.

He should know by now that he had to feed regularly to stay in control. He didn't like the consequences of his hunger any more than its victims did. As the hooker he ate earlier this evening could attest too. She was still bitching. All she'd wanted was a little action, and look at her now; trapped in a dark fog, scared, alone.

He wished he was alone. His only consolation was that she would eventually give up looking for a way out, sit down—in a manner of speaking—and shut up. Then her soul would die like all the others, and there had been plenty in his long life. Most souls never lasted for more than forty-eight hours, unlike the children. The children sometimes cried for weeks, and it made his head hurt.

He refused to eat any more children. He shouldn't have finished off the hooker. He was going to need a clear head.

Where are you? The hooker whimpered for a minute and then she started to yell again. *What did you do to me? Where in hell am I? Let me out of here you bastard.* If she could find something solid she would pound on it until he came and let her out. But there was nothing solid for her to touch.

Shut up! He needed to think, and it wasn't easy with all that yelling.

Hmmph! Well at least you're talking to me now.

He rolled his eyes. *The back.* He'd slip around the back and escape through the shadows. There had to be a doorway around here somewhere. What other reason would the Hunters have to frequent this place?

"There he is." The shout immediately followed by the sound of running feet.

He spun on his heel and headed for the, unfortunately for him, well lit parking lot; More evidence of the difference between The Fox and The Hound and his normal hunting grounds. For a sheer second he thought it was the end.

And then he saw it.

At the farthest corner of the lot, a light was out and the shadow behind it was moving.

A door!

He was almost there when something struck him in the chest. He staggered but forged on. The wind whined as it rushed past him. It was too late. The cord wrapped around his knees too quick for him to sidestep. He crashed to the ground and they were on him before you could say "Jack Rabbit."

Their fists rained blows on his face and chest. He tasted blood. He hated the taste of blood—especially his own. He saw the toe of a large black boot and turned his head at the last second. The crack echoed in his brain as pain and darkness filled his mind.

"What are you doing?" The sultry voice rose in anger but he would have recognized it anywhere.

Run! He sent the command with all the strength he could muster.

Don't be stupid! Someone needs our help! Becky ran to the men surrounding the body on the ground beneath the broken streetlamp. She swung her purse at the man nearest her, catching him by surprise and knocking him back. She didn't pause to see his reaction. Screaming like a banshee she kept on swinging at the remaining men until someone caught her arms from behind.

"Stop!" The command was low and precise, and spoken with the authority of one used to being obeyed.

Becky quickly looked from one man to another and realized they were all dressed exactly alike in tight black sleeveless shirts that moulded around their bulging muscles, black trousers made out of some sort of stretchy material that although not taut did nothing to hide their physiques, and tall, black, square toed motorcycle boots. Blood still dripped from the toe of one of the boots and her stomach churned, threatening to spew her burger and beer all over the pavement. Another glance revealed they were heavily armed, although it appeared they liked to use their hands on their victims.

"You shouldn't have interfered."

The grating voice was more frightening than the male, and on reflection, perhaps he was right. After all, she was one small woman against four, very large, and obviously very dangerous, men. She risked a glance at the body sprawled on the dirty pavement with blood seeping from the wound at the back of his golden brown head.

Holy shit! She knew that man. But where had she seen him? Her head suddenly started to ache again reminding Becky that she didn't have all that long to live anyway. Still, she didn't intend to go out a victim of some street gang in a dark parking lot behind a bar.

The bar! He was at the bar. As the memory of him at the bar flooded back, her headache disappeared.

"Get rid of her." The man with the bloody toe was obviously the leader.

Panic gave Becky added strength. She lifted her foot and brought her heel down on her captor's foot, and then dropped down and twisted out of his grasp when he tried to adjust his grip *and* move his foot out of harm's way. Spinning around she pulled, what looked like a gun, from the surprised man's holster, and, stepping back out of his reach she waved it at them.

"Move away from him," she ordered the three closest to the man on the ground. "You," she waved the barrel at her captor. "Get over there with your friends."

"What do you think you are doing lady?" The man didn't seem the least bit intimidated by the huge gun she now waved at him from a shaky hand.

"Saving my life." She indicated the unconscious man with the end of the gun, "and his. Now drop your weapons and get out of here."

Becky nearly pulled the trigger when the smallest man, he was probably only six foot two, snorted in derision. "Don't be stupid," he sneered. "You won't get all of us."

"I know that." Becky smiled at him. "But, do you know who I will shoot first?"

"Enough!" the leader commanded, and the other men came to attention, much like Becky imagined a soldier would. "Drop your weapons."

"But?" The mouthy one shut up when the one sporting the bloody toe glared at him.

"She is human. Drop your weapons."

Human? To Becky's surprise, and relief, they undid their weapon belts and placed them on the pavement in front of them. Then they proceeded to remove knives from their boots and place them with the guns. Next they removed various other weapons from various pockets, and wherever else Becky wasn't entirely sure, and stacked them neatly with the guns.

"We're done here, for now," said the leader, and all four turned on their heels and disappeared into the shadows.

Becky blinked. *What the?* If it weren't for the pile of weapons in front of her, some she didn't even recognize, and the gun in her hand; Becky dropped the gun to the pavement and it landed with a loud clatter. She couldn't believe what she had just done.

A moan drew her attention to the man lying on the ground. *At least he's alive.*

Of course I am alive. It would take more than a couple of Hunters to kill me.

Hunters? Must be the name of the gang. Becky stared at the pile of weapons on the ground perplexed.

Get rid of them. The Hunters will track them. Now that was a strange thought, but, just in case it was true Becky gathered all the weapons, carried them back to the dumpster, and tossed them in.

"Oh my god! Did you see what I did? I was amazing. I've never even held a gun before. Heck, I've never so much as raised my voice. It was awesome ... I ... I ..."

Still babbling, Becky turned back to the stranger she had risked her life to aid and, he was gone. Vanished! Disappeared! Gone! The only thing that remained was a coil of some sort of wire with two large metal balls at the ends.

Becky sat on the ground and burst into tears. *It's happening. I'm already losing my mind.* She sat there in the parking lot with tears streaming down her cheeks for at least five

minutes before she swiped them away and climbed to her feet. She picked up the wire and balls contraption and tossed it in the dumpster with the other weapons; Even if it couldn't be tracked, she didn't want anyone else to find and use it. It never occurred to her that the weapons were real, and therefore everything else was as well.

She found her purse where she dropped it and dug through it until she found her keys. *The next time I go straight to my car and leave,* she promised herself.

Once inside the vehicle she locked the doors and started the engine. Pulling down the visor, she checked herself in the small mirror and gasped. Her face was white and streaked with dried tears. Her hair looked like she'd been rolling around in bed. There was no way she was showing up at the Hotel looking like this.

A quick rummage through her bag uncovered a comb and some wet wipes. What she really needed was a hot shower, but she fixed herself up the best she could.

At least I don't look *like I was in a brawl.*

Becky replaced her comb, tossed the used wet wipe in the garbage bag, and put the car in gear. Fifteen minutes later she was unpacking her belongings at what would be her home for the rest of her life—if she wanted it. She offered up a silent prayer to her guardian angel and explored.

The cottage had two bedrooms, a kitchen sitting room combination with a countertop burner, microwave, sink, and bar-sized fridge. A small wooden table with four chairs completed the kitchenette area. A sofa that turned into a bed, two comfy chairs, a low table, a television, and a radio made up the living area.

Becky felt a momentary pang of guilt taking the larger suite. She didn't need all this space. It was far larger than her tiny apartment. She should have taken the single and left this one available for a family unit. She would tell Sandi

tomorrow that she'd changed her mind and would move to the single.

The glint of moonlight through the window caught her attention. She moved over to the patio door and looked out into the courtyard. The full moon provided more than enough light.

A small round ornate table surrounded by four chairs sat on the portion of the patio immediately outside her door. There was a small in-ground pool in the center of the courtyard with plastic white deck chairs placed strategically around its sides and a couple of small tables. There were a few umbrellas placed on one side to provide shade during the day, while several tall palm trees growing in a garden of other small shrubs provided shade for the other side. Reddish brown cement surrounded the pool giving the appearance of dirt, without the mess. Across the pool in front of the building sat a small ornate table with four chairs identical to hers. The courtyard enclosed on three sides by walls, one of which had no windows and a tall stone fence on the fourth side. Vines grew up the walls and fence giving the entire courtyard a wild, abandoned appearance, while guaranteeing privacy to the two units that shared this particular courtyard.

The peacefulness of the courtyard beckoned her and Becky decided that she was going to keep the cottage. She would tell Sandi that she would be willing to switch to a smaller cottage if a family needed the larger unit otherwise she was staying right where she was.

Becky chose the largest bedroom that looked out over the courtyard. It didn't take her long to unpack her belongings, and within a few moments she was enjoying the stinging spray of the shower. Towelling off quickly she chose a pair of cut-off jeans and a yellow tank top. A quick run through her hair with a brush and she was ready to answer the summons of the courtyard.

She made a pit stop at the fridge to grab a bottle of water, which Sandi had assured her would be there, and then she stepped through the sliding glass door into wonderland. Becky ignored the loungers in front of her door opting instead to sit on the edge of the pool where she dangled her feet in the warm water and looked up at the starlit night.

Beautiful isn't it?

Oh! You're back. I thought you had moved on.

Becky leaned back and relaxed, moving her feet idly. She noticed a light in the top window across the courtyard just before it flicked out. *Guess my neighbours have gone to bed.*

It's just you and me now.

Yeah! Speaking of you and me something has been bothering me.

What is it that has been bothering you?

If you are a part of me, why do you sound like a man?

A warm deep chuckle sent shivers along her heated skin. Her head spun from side to side as she tried to peer into the suddenly dark courtyard. That sounded too real.

Who said I was a part of you?

Becky pulled her feet from the water and stood up too quickly. She lost her balance and fell into the pool with a loud splash. Breaking the surface, she reached for the side of the pool to pull herself up and, found herself staring at the squared toes of midnight black boots.

The first thought that entered her mind was the gang from the parking lot had found her. *Hell no!*

Her first instinct was to duck beneath the surface and swim to the other end of the pool to try to make her escape, but before her head could go under two strong hands grabbed her shoulders and lifted her completely out of the pool. It happened too fast for her to react, and to her surprise, she was set gently on her feet on the edge.

"Are you all right?" The warm masculine, way too sexy, voice was like warm honey, and very familiar.

Becky looked up, way up, into the warm tawny eyes of her stranger. She fought the instinct to throw herself into his arms and smother him with kisses, as a way of thanking him for helping her out of the pool of course—No other reason. She noticed his long hair was clean and damp and there were no signs that he had ever been in a fight, much less covered in cuts and bloody bruises.

"You," she muttered, allowing anger to fortify her. "Where did you come from?" Before he could reply, her small hand fisted and she punched him as hard as she could. "That's for leaving me alone in the parking lot." She hit him again. "That is for making me worry about you." She belted him again and tears ran down her face. "And that is for letting me think I was losing my mind."

When she finished punching him, He reached out and gently wiped the tears from her cheeks. The moment his fingers touched her face he felt her tremble. For the first time in a very long time, he wondered what it would be to have someone feel something real for him, and not a result of his curse.

I must be getting soft.

Three

"Soft! You?" Becky looked up at his chiselled chin. There wasn't an inch of softness anywhere. "I need to sit down."

He led her to the loungers closest to her entrance. From there she could see the stars, and he could see if anyone, or anything, entered the courtyard.

"So, where *did* you come from?" Becky finally asked when she was once again in control of her emotions.

"Over there." He told her pointing to the door on the other side of the courtyard.

"You're staying here!" Becky couldn't believe her ears. Of all the places in the city, he was staying at the very one she chose. What were the odds?

"IIey!" Becky jumped up and put the lounger between the two of them. "Are you following me?" she demanded.

"Me! Following you?" He attempted an air of shocked indignation but Becky wasn't buying it.

"Yes. You following me. I saw you at the bar when I was there." Becky absently rubbed her temple when pain stabbed there. "Stop that!" she almost shouted at him. "I don't know what you are trying to do but it won't work. I know you were there. I saw you. You were there when Todd told me about this place."

"Are you sure about that?" The words were spoken so low Becky wasn't sure if she actually heard them—or they were just in her head."

Yes I am sure about that. I'm not crazy—am I? "I am not crazy." She repeated the words aloud hoping the sound of her own voice would drive away her doubts.

"Then tell me this," he never took his eyes off her face. It was as if he thought he could hear her thoughts if he stared hard enough. "If I was following you, then how is it that I was in the parking area when you came out?"

Becky sighed and sat back down on the lounger before she fell down. Her legs were shaking and she felt like she was going to vomit. During the entire conversation, he sat in his lounger without moving an inch. She was beginning to wonder if he even saw her, or if he was looking through her to something only he could see.

Asshole! His left eye twitched, the only indication that the voice inside had surprised him. She'd been quiet so he thought she had expired. Apparently not. *Quit playing with our food. I'm hungry.*

He wondered why he was bothering to get to know her. It was only delaying the inevitable. He needed to feed and she was dinner. He didn't usually play with his food.

Then why are you now? You didn't play with me. Oh no, with me it was just 'Wham Bam Thank you Ma'am.' But then again, I didn't get the bam or the thank you, did I? Hell, I didn't even get paid.

He shook his head trying to quiet the annoying voice.

Hey! What do you think you are doing? Her arms swung out in an attempt to grab onto to something, anything, to stabilize herself. She felt like she was on one of those spinning rides at the carnival—the kind she abhorred. There was nothing within reach. There was nothing, period. Just the disorienting blankness she'd been dwelling in for the past hours. Why oh why had he chosen the Dungeon? She'd heard the rumours, but had simply laughed them off as, pardon the pun, ghost stories. After all, New Orleans was full of them. If it wasn't the ghost of a serial killer, it was vampires or zombies. When she'd dressed for work tonight, she hadn't really expected anything but her usual fare. Drunken tourists look-

ing for a night on the town and a cheap thrill; Her being the cheap thrill. She started to giggle. *Sam's gonna be pissed.*

Who's Sam? He didn't mean to interact with her but she'd piqued his curiosity.

Just my stepdad a.k.a. pimp. The stupid bastard. Thought he'd make a fortune off me tonight at the Dungeon. Wish I could be there to see his face when he finds out I won't be making him any more money—or anything else for that matter.

"Are you okay?" Becky eyed the scrumptious stranger warily. He looked like he ate something that didn't quite agree with him.

"What? Oh, yeah, I'm good." He didn't feel good. He wanted to throw up. How could he not have known how young she was—again! This was getting to be a bad habit. The young never agreed with him. They didn't know enough to roll over and say good night. Christ, he wished they would quit playing dress up. Everybody wanted to grow up too fast these days. It made feeding unpredictable.

Young! Now that's a hoot. I'm almost twenty-two with forty year's experience, thanks to dear old dad.

Shut up! He roared.

"Excuse me?" Becky's brows furrowed, a sure sign she was growing annoyed. "You are the one doing all the talking here."

I like her. The female voice mocked. *Maybe we shouldn't eat her. Maybe we should go look for some old crone.*

He knocked the lounger over in his haste to get up. "I have to go," he said abruptly, giant strides carried him across the courtyard and into the opposite building in a matter of seconds, but he was unable to outrun the echo of female laughter.

Becky stared after the retreating figure feeling as if she had just received a reprieve from an unknown sentence. Ei-

ther he was the strangest person she'd ever met, or he didn't actually exist, in which case it didn't matter whether he had vanished, or she simply thought he'd vanished. She didn't know what was real and what wasn't anymore, and at this point, she didn't much care. The drugs were doing a strange song and dance routine in her head, and her body suddenly wracked with shivers despite the warmth of the night air, her soaked clothing clinging like a second skin.

She managed to drag her tired body kicking and screaming to a stand, then to the door of her room, and finally inside where the added chill of the fan had no problem enticing her teeth to a chattering duet with her limbs. Switching the air conditioner off on the way by, she went to the master bath and filled the tub to the brim with water than was almost too hot to suffer. It did nothing to stop the chills.

The water had cooled to the point where it was almost too cool before Becky managed to drag herself out of the tub. Donning her warmest pair of pyjamas, she went into the kitchen to make herself a hot cup of chocolate before crawling into bed. She was sitting with her back against a pile of pillows watching the moonlight play across the pool's surface and sipping her drink when a different sort of chill crawled along her spine. Becky spilled her cocoa in her haste to draw the blinds. If she could see out so clearly, then anyone or anything could see in just as easily, and she knew she wasn't alone. Switching off the bedside lamp and ignoring her suddenly tasteless cocoa, she pulled the covers over her head and resolutely closed her eyes. To her surprise, sleep claimed her within moments.

Four

"Just shut up, would you," he growled. She'd been at him since they returned to the room, and he'd pretty much worn a path in the carpet with his pacing. Why hadn't he simply eaten her? He couldn't answer that—no matter how many times she asked.

The female tittered. *'You know you're talking to yourself, right.'*

He grabbed two handfuls of hair and yanked, but all he succeeded in doing was hurting his head. She laughed louder. *'You are too funny. I have to admit this is much better than the way I usually spend my nights, or days for that matter.'*

She suddenly went silent. He listened for a sound, any sound that would indicate she was still there. Just when he thought she had finally expired, she spoke. *'It's really dark in here. I don't normally like the dark, but this is peaceful. Well, if you don't count the crazy thoughts running 'round in here with me. How old are you anyway? There are enough memories in here for an army.'*

"I was sent here when I was thirty sars ..."

'You mean years, right?'

"Where I come from they don't count the passage of time as they do here. One sar is equal to 3600 of your years. That is the time it takes our planet to complete its orbit of your sun. I was a mere boy when I met Ishtar."

'Hmmph! Mere boy. You were like what, ten thousand years old? Holy crap! You're shittin' me right? There is no way you are over ten thousand years old. Hey, what do you mean, "Your planet"?'

He laughed despite himself. "No, not shittin' you, as you so crudely put it. I am well over ten thousand of your years. Where did you learn math anyway?" She snorted, and he continued, "I come from Nibiru. Your ancients called it the Planet of the Crossing. We were once thought of and treated as gods."

'Yeah right! Although I must admit, you do look like a God, or at least you did right up until you ate me. Becky thinks so too. That you look like a god, she doesn't know you ate me. At least I don't think she knows. But that is neither here, nor there. Go on with your story, please.'

"I don't understand why I am so hungry. A soul as lively as yours should have been more than enough."

'Sorry,' she quipped. 'Well, not really. It's not like you asked my permission or anything. Perhaps if you had I would have said, "sure you can eat me. I didn't really want to go home tonight anyway." But you didn't ask and I have no intention of satisfying you. Now, get on with your story before I get bored.'

Despite himself, he couldn't stop the memories from coming.

He leaned over her, her guardian angel, so beautiful, his eyes so brilliant the light blinded her as they offered to take her away from the pain. He was going to kiss her. Her own lips curved into a loving smile. A pale blue mist hovered between them, hesitant at first and then slowly it moved from the dying woman to her angel and she sighed with pleasure, the first pleasure she'd felt in a very long time, all pain forgotten.

He stood slowly careful not to dislodge the delicate soul. 'What about my baby?' The question came from within, from the soul he carried.

He glanced at the midwife and the still child cradled gently in her large, capable hands. Tears fell upon its face. Tears for them both; the young mother who hadn't asked for this, and for her child who never had the chance to take its first breath. '*He will be with you. It will be okay.*' With those words, he bent toward the still child held tenderly by the midwife despite it having no visible vitals, and gently inhaled gathering its tiny soul into his keeping. Straightening once more, he turned the dial on his wrist and stepped through the open portal; leaving the midwife to mourn, the only person who would mourn either passing.

Nibiru! Home!

It was the same every time he stepped onto the soil of his homeland. It mattered not whether he was gone for days, months, or simply hours. The rush of emotion as he inhaled, bringing the sweet air to fill his lungs.

'*What is this place?*' The female he carried spoke to him. It was no more than a mere whisper in his mind, but he heard it all.

"Home." It was but a single word and yet it said it all. The gentle soul relaxed.

'*Home,*' she repeated, his emotions brushing over her as if they were her own. '*I've never had a home of my own before.*'

She saw the land through his eyes. A sun so brilliant she was surprised it didn't burn her eyes. A sky of cadmium swirling with all the colours of the rainbow she remembered seeing as a child. Grass, so sweet smelling it brought tears to her eyes, and the plush softness beneath her feet made her want to lay down and go to sleep. Everywhere she looked there were people, smiling, shouting hellos, happy faces, nothing like the scowling, vicious faces of her homeland. She gazed down with loving eyes at her son swaddled in soft blankets and cradled gently in her arms.

"Are you ready?"

The question came as a surprise to her and she instinctively stepped closer to her angel, wondering how she had come to be here, and why there was no pain. She'd been in pain for months now and couldn't believe it was truly gone. "For what?"

"To begin your journey of course." To her surprise, the answer didn't come from her angel but from a small child who looked no more than five or six at the most. She had long flowing blonde hair and eyes as colourful as the sky above. The child giggled. "I know I don't look it, but I am much wiser than I look. Come with me and I'll introduce you to everyone."

The young mother looked down at her baby, such a tiny form cradled protectively in arms no more substantial than his ethereal body. With a last smile at her angel, she turned to follow her guide, knowing without knowing how she knew, that everything would be all right.

He watched the newest members of the community for a few minutes before closing his eyes and folding his wings into himself. He was anxious to go home and see his family; His mother and baby sister, his father, and even the thought of his older brother, Sorush, brought a smile to his lips.

When he opened his eyes, there she was. Ishtar. No wonder she was the goddess of love and sex. He wanted her immediately and he was willing to die for her; which would explain why she was also the goddess of war; she could, and had, inspired nations. He knew she was wife to Marduk, but he didn't care. Not then. He was young and wild and she was hot; strutting around like a peacock, thriving on the lust she inspired, and growing stronger every day. He was caught in her spell and when He followed her home, she was more than willing to open the door.

Unfortunately, Marduk came home early that day and went ballistic. Marduk stripped him of his key home and flung him back to Earth. Even if there'd been a trial, it wouldn't have mattered. Marduk was the chief God and his word was law. He'd spent an eternity trying to find a way home but Nibiru was gone, and although he tried to calculate when it would be close again the earth calendars kept changing and he just didn't know. It was time to face the fact that He was never going home again—but never was a long time, for someone like him.

'*Poor baby.*' The voice was soft and gentle and for a flicker of a second it sounded like she meant it. '*You're right. Forget them. I know!*' The voice rose in an excited pitch helping to push out his morose thoughts. '*Let's go eat Daddy!*'

"What!" He was so startled he actually spoke aloud.

'*I said, "Let's go eat Daddy".*' Her tone was that of a patient mother speaking to a slow child.

"I heard you," he grumbled. "I just couldn't believe what I heard."

'*Why not?*' She pouted. '*If anyone deserves to die that bastard does. If it wasn't for him I wouldn't be here right now. The bastard wormed his way into my mother's life, got her hooked on drugs, and convinced her to let him turn me into a Whore! Do you know he trained me himself? Disgusting old man with his even more disgusting, wrinkled dick. God! I wanted to puke every time he came near me. And did Mom stop him?—No! She needed the next fix and didn't give a rat's ass where it came from. When he thought I was ready he rented me to his friends, let them act out their fantasies; the bunch of sick, putrid pigs. And when I cried they laughed. LAUGHED! Well I wasn't giving them that. They could do what they wanted to my body but my soul was mine, at least until you stole it. I learned how to act like I loved it. Learned every little trick to get their rocks off and open their wallets. I've been squirreling away tip money for a couple years now. I was planning on blowing this town. Thanks a lot by the way.*'

He didn't know what to say. For the first time in a very long time, he felt remorse for taking a life.

'Oh suck it up buttercup.' She was laughing at him—Him! *'I'm not taking it personally so don't you. But you can see my point right? And if you won't do it for me, do it for my sister. She is almost twelve and I've seen the way he's been watching her. The same way he used to watch me. I would have taken off years ago, taken my chances on the street, but I couldn't leave Wendy. There was no way I was letting him do to her what he did to me. I'd kill him first. I will kill him first.'*

That's it! She reminded him of the last soul he carried home. He'd seen the way those men had used and abused her and it made his blood boil, and through it all, through the pain and fear, she still had a kind word and gentle touch for the other girls in the same position. He couldn't do anything then, it wasn't his right. His job was to carry the souls to Nibiru to be judged and delivered. There were others who dealt justice, like his older brother, Sorush. He had always followed the laws, that is until Ishtar.

There were others who refused to follow the rules, who refused to follow Marduk—the fallen ones. Those who lived by their own rules. Those were the ones he searched for, following every tale of daemon possession in the hopes of snagging a way home, but they were always one step ahead of him— even now in this age of great technology where all you needed was a computer and an internet connection and you had instant access to every sighting.

But with the increasing knowledge of the so-called daemons came the daemon hunters like the ones who'd almost had him earlier today. They would have had him if not for Becky. Her courageous interference had saved him from whatever fate the hunters had in store for him. He owed her. He wished there was something he could do for her—but she

didn't have much time. Her soul was weak. The best he could do was end her misery.

'*Way to get off topic, buddy.*' The voice was sharp, snapping him back to the present. '*God! You're like an old man with Alzheimer's. Could you at least try to focus?*'

"Sorry. Where does this bastard live?" He couldn't do anything for Becky but he could help this one, and in so doing, help her sister.

'*That's my boy.*'

Five

He stood in the shadows silently watching the scene acting out before him. The child glanced up when he shifted position, her pale blue eyes shimmering with unshed tears. She sniffed, wiping the back of her hand under her nose and then on the leg of her jeans. He could see the resemblance between the two girls, although one had dark hair and the other was a bleached blonde, gaudy even in death.

'*I would have let it grow out. I hated that colour but most men are willing to pay more for blonds.*"

"Are you here to say goodbye to Tracy?" The words broke on a sob, but the tears didn't fall.

"Who are you talking to?" The man might have been good looking at one time, but now with his features so contorted with greed and hatred that time had long since passed. Even his voice was ugly.

The child turned to her stepfather, Sam, and back to the shadows, making a decision. "Nobody. I thought I heard someone come in to say goodbye to Tracy, but I was mistaken."

The man's features twisted, making him even uglier. "Her name was Angel. I've told you a million times. Angel *not* Tracy."

The child's spine straightened and she wiped her nose. The quiet strength in her voice stopped her stepfather's movement toward her. "Her name is Tracy. That is the name our Father gave her and that is her name. Angel was just the girl that worked for you to keep us alive. And for the record, my name is Wendy."

"Why you ungrateful, little bitch!" Sam flung his arm out intending to backhand her with enough force to knock her from her seat. It was about time the ungrateful wretch showed him some respect and started earning her keep. Instead of connecting with soft flesh his hand connected with something substantially more solid. Shocked, the stepfather looked up at the face of a stranger.

The stranger stood between him and Wendy; at least six inches taller than him and built like a brick shithouse. The stranger held the fist meant for Wendy, and squeezed.

"Who the hell are ..." The words shut off when the stranger's free hand snaked around his throat and lifted him off the floor. Sam kicked and squirmed but the man lifted him as if he were no heavier than a ragdoll and of even less consequence, until they were eye to eye. Sam found himself looking into familiar orbs and the sour milk scent of raw terror filled the room.

"Hello, Daddy." He recognized that voice. He should. He'd spent many pleasurable hours moulding Martha's oldest daughter into the perfect sex machine. He'd recognize the voice—and those eyes—anywhere. His bladder let go and the scent of urine mingled with that of sour milk.

The man holding him sniffed the air and a grin of pure malice twisted his lips. His form grew in size and ebony wings sprouted from his shoulder blades. "Miss me, Daddy?" The voice purred, more terrifying than anything from of his worst nightmare.

'*You might want to look away, little one.*'

Wendy didn't even blink at the warm, soothing voice inside her head. "No thanks," she answered aloud. "He killed Tracy. I want to see this."

Wendy stared, transfixed, as a soft blue mist exited her stepfather's mouth, open wide in horror, and entered into the slightly parted lips of the dark angel. Sam's legs stopped twitching and he hung limp as the blue mist completely left his body. She didn't even blink when the angel released his hold on the body and it landed with a loud plop on the floor.

Their mother looked up then, blinking once when she saw the much taller man standing over the limp body of her husband. The sight of her husband crumpled on the floor shocked her into movement in a way that the lifeless body of her eldest daughter hadn't. She jumped up from her chair and ran over to the body. Falling to her knees, she cradled his head on her lap and wailed. "What have you done?"

Martha glared at the stranger before turning unseeing eyes upon her youngest child. "What am I supposed to do now? First Angel. Now Sam. What am I supposed to do?"

Wendy stood beside her sister's open coffin and tucked the hand she'd been holding all this time in beside the cold body. "Her name is Tracy," she said to nobody in particular. She leaned over and placed a kiss on her sister's cold, pale cheek. Even in death, Tracy was the most beautiful person she knew. Wendy brushed her sister's hair off her face and shoulder, pulling her hand back when the voice inside her head said, '*What is that?*'

Wendy slowly traced the three white spots on her sister's collarbone. Sam used to complain they marred her sister's perfect body, but Wendy thought they were perfect. "These? We used to say they were her victory marks. She was born with this one." Wendy touched the one closest to her neck. Daddy would tell us the story of the night Tracy was born. The cord wrapped around her neck and she stopped breathing. Even her heart stopped. The doctor said she was dead, and then she started crying. 'My miracle baby,' Daddy would

say. The only mark on her perfect body caused by the tongs they used to try and turn her."

Wendy glanced at her mother still holding Sam and weeping. The sight disgusted her. Her mother hadn't even one tear to spare when they'd called to say they found Tracy dead, but this monster she wept over as if her heart were breaking. And maybe it was. Wendy didn't know her mother anymore.

Ignoring her mother, she turned back to Tracy, tracing the middle mark. Her mother couldn't see the angel; maybe he didn't really exist, maybe Wendy was crazy. At this point, Wendy didn't really care. If she had gone crazy and killed her stepfather, then he got what he deserved. "This one happened when Tracy was ten." Her voice cracked but she continued. "Daddy, Tracy, and I were coming home from the movies. Mommy stayed home to bake a cake. It was Daddy's birthday and we wanted it to be a surprise. We were driving along, laughing about the movie, when suddenly there were bright lights right in front of us. Daddy and Tracy were in the front seat. When I woke up, Daddy was dead. They said Tracy should have died too. It was a miracle. There wasn't a mark on her except where a piece of glass from the window stuck in here."

Wendy's fingers slowly traced the last mark. "Sam caused this one." She glared at the body cradled in her mother's arms. If he wasn't already dead, she'd kill him again. "Tracy didn't want to do what he said she had to do. She told Mommy, but instead of protecting Tracy, she told him. He was furious. He beat Tracy for hours, finally leaving her crumpled and bleeding on his bed while he went out drinking. I snuck in to the room as soon as he left the house. I was so scared. She wasn't breathing. I wasn't even sure if her heart was beating. I cleaned her up the best I could. I wanted to kill him then, but what could an eight-year-old girl do

against someone like him. I was so afraid that I would hurt her, but she didn't even whimper when I washed off the blood. When she finally woke up hours later, she had this mark. Three victory marks. One for each time she beat death."

Wendy took a deep breath, letting it out very slowly. "I was sitting here waiting for the fourth mark to appear so I could take her home." The tears she held in for so long trailed down her cheeks. "It's not coming, is it?"

"No, little one. Not this time."

When the angel held out his hand Wendy placed her much smaller one in his. She didn't even look at her mother as they walked out the door. "Where are we going?"

"Somewhere safe."

Six

He was falling, faster and faster. The wind rushed past spinning him first one way and then another. His first instinct was to reach out and stop his fall but there was nothing to grab. His arms flailed like a drunken dancer. Something caught in his throat making it impossible to catch a breath. He wanted to cover his eyes but he could not find them. He couldn't see anything in the pitch.

Something brushed his cheek and his blood ran cold. He felt the scream growing in the back of his throat and tried to swallow it. He wasn't falling anymore, but he hadn't landed yet either. He seemed to be hovering in a black void, unable to move, his arms and legs immobilized by invisible restraints. A flicker of light came into view and disappeared just as quickly. His heartbeat quickened and he swallowed hard to keep his heart escaping by way of his mouth. He fought to keep it inside him and to calm its erratic thumping.

Samuel Frost was not afraid of anything since the day he stood up to his abusive father when he was ten. He'd always been the biggest, strongest kid in school and used his size to bully and intimidate everyone into doing anything he wanted. And Samuel wasn't afraid now.

No—Sam wasn't afraid—He was terrified.

He hated the dark. He always had. Being in the dark reminded him of the times his father locked him in the steamer trunk in the basement of their old farmhouse. That had stopped the day Sam turned ten and had broken his father's nose and arm when he'd tried to put him in that damned trunk. This reminded him of then, although instead of curled

in a box he stretched out like a sacrificial lamb; in the same position that he restrained Angel during many of their more intimate lessons.

"Who's there?" he demanded, unwilling to be afraid any longer. "Show yourself you damned coward."

He tensed. Something was moving closer. He couldn't hear it, or see it, but he knew it was there. He felt it. Felt its warm breath. Felt the tip of a long fingernail touch the side of his neck and ever so slowly trace the pulsing vein. He shivered when the nail traced the curve of his collarbone and continued to move lower, drawing slow circles above his pounding heart. Despite his terror the blood flowed to his groin making him rock hard. Sam groaned. Only one person could make him this hard just by touching him. He'd known she would be a money maker the first moment he saw her at the grocery store with her mother. When the police told them they'd found her body outside that club he didn't want to believe them. Even after they brought them to the morgue to identify the body, he didn't want to believe it. It hadn't taken much to get them to release the body for burial. Nobody worried too much about a dead whore, especially one who died of a heart attack, and so the coroner released the body to her mother to prepare for burial and they brought her home. He refused to believe she was dead. Like her sister, he had been waiting for her to wake up.

"I knew you weren't dead."

"No, Daddy." She knew he liked it when she called him Daddy while fucking him. The sick bastard. She spoke with a soft rasp in her voice. Sam said it was sexy and turned men on. He used to beat her until she got it just right, the way he taught her everything else.

She laid her hand against his chest feeling the rapidly beating heart in her palm. "No, Daddy. I'm not dead." She closed her nails around his beating heart and ripped it from his fleshless form. "But you are."

The scream broke free, reverberating throughout the dark cavern. It lasted several minutes until Samuel Frost realized he was truly dead, and everything went silent.

 # Seven

"What's your name?"

It was hard to concentrate on the tiny female sitting on his sofa with all the noise going on inside him. He was beginning to think eating the girl's stepfather wasn't such a good idea, but then when he looked at the little girl sitting with her hands folded meekly on her lap, and looking at him with such trust, he knew there was no other choice. They could never have left her to the same fate as her sister. Then, just that quick it was over and everything went quiet. What was he supposed to do now? He'd learned some very interesting things this night.

"I'm sorry, little one. What did you say?"

"My name is Wendy. I asked you what your name is."

"Oh!" Nobody had asked his name in a very long time. He lived amongst the shadows and when he did interact with humans, there was no need for names. "Remiel." It sounded strange on his lips, like it didn't belong in this time and place. He said it again, louder. "My name is Remiel." He was surprised she wasn't asking how they got here. One minute they are outside the house, the next they are in the courtyard of the cottages. But no, she wants to know his name.

Wendy's lips twisted into a half grin, her eyes glittering still, whether from unshed tears or sheer exhaustion, he wasn't sure, although sadness marred her pale face. "Can I call you Rem?"

Rem. He liked that. He hadn't really been Remiel since his banishment to this place, no longer the one to carry the souls across, but rather the one who destroyed them. "Of

course you can." He glanced around the small cottage, spying a small fridge. "Are you thirsty? There might be something in the fridge. There is always water."

"No thank you, Rem." Wendy examined his face the way an architect would examine a great project. "Are you going to take me to Tracy now?"

"What? No! What made you think I was taking you to Tracy?"

"You did kill my stepfather and then take me from my mother." Not that she had any intention of staying with her mother.

This human child was much older than she looked. "Do you want me to take you back to your mother?"

"Hell no! I mean, no thank you. That woman hasn't been my mother since Sam came into our lives. Tracy is the only one who took care of me and now she is gone." She chewed her bottom lip for a few minutes, emotions flitting across her face. "Do you think I could get a job? Will I have to go to one of those foster homes? I think I'd rather to go to Tracy if you don't mind."

'Don't you dare!' He grinned at the fury in her voice. Maybe he was getting used to having her around.

'Don't worry. I have no intention of having the two of you yammering away inside me.' When he grinned his entire face softened.

"Who are you talking to?" Wendy eyed Rem with such intensity he felt she was trying to see into his soul, and it gave him the willies. Inside his head, Tracy laughed.

"What makes you think I'm talking to someone? There is only you and I here."

"You are buzzing like a telephone pole with a party line. You know the noise they make when the world outside is quiet and you can hear the power running through them. You

were buzzing earlier too. That's why I knew you were there, just before I saw you."

Interesting. "Do you often hear or see things that others do not see or hear?"

"No! Sometimes. I don't talk about it. When I tried to tell Mommy she took me to a bunch of doctors. After lots of tests they said it was all in my head and that if it continued Mommy should put me in a special hospital where they could help me. I don't talk about it anymore." *'I'm only telling you 'cause you're in my head.'*

"Okay. Let's say I'm just in your head. Tell me, Wendy, and be honest, where do you think you are right now?"

"Oh that's easy. I'm sitting on the chair in the parlour holding Tracy's hand and waiting for her to wake up, or for the police to come and arrest me."

"Why would the police want to arrest you?"

"For killing Sam of course!" She sounded convinced of her guilt. "Do you think they will send me to prison for a long time. I hope so. I don't want to go to a hospital for loony cakes. I'm glad Sam is dead. He is dead, isn't he?" Suddenly she didn't seem so sure.

'Crap on toast! Do something. Don't let her think she killed that bastard.'

'What do you want me to do?' "Why do you think you killed Sam? More important, how do you think you killed Sam?"

Wendy thought about her answer for a long time before answering. "I was the only one there besides Mommy and Tracy. Mommy would never hurt Sam. She loves the drugs he gives her too much to do anything to jeopardise them. And Tracy," her voice caught on a sob. "Tracy can't hurt anyone. She is dead. That leaves me."

"What about me?"

"You!" She scoffed at the idea. "You are a figment of my over active imagination; the product of a brain malfunction. You couldn't possibly have done it."

"If I'm not real then why are you talking to me?" He was starting to like this strangely intelligent little girl, almost as much as he was beginning to like her sometimes funny, sometimes annoying, and always present like a conscience, sister.

'Gee thanks, Rem. I was beginning to think you didn't like me.'

"You're easy to talk to," Wendy said. "Mommy never talks anymore, except when she needs more drugs and then she is just plain mean. Sam, well when Sam did talk it was only to tell me how much I owed him and how I would soon be earning my keep like Tracy. I'd run away if I could get a job, but Tracy doesn't want me to do what she does, did, and I'm afraid."

"You will never have to do what Tracy did," promised Rem, and he meant it. Somehow, he would make sure this child was okay.

"'Cause I'll be in jail or a loony hospital." Her voice was small and sad, and then suddenly she perked up. "I like it here. I could stay here forever. This room is nice. It even has TV. I wonder if I have enough imagination to make it work. And I'm hungry."

Wendy jumped up from the sofa, a sudden bundle of activity. She grabbed the remote from the small table and flicked it on, placing the remote back on the table and clapping her hands in delight when the TV came on. She moved quickly to the small fridge, closed her eyes, counted out loud to three, pulled open the door and opened her eyes at the same time. "Yes!" She grabbed a cola and snapped the top turning. She seemed startled when she saw Rem still sitting on the chair. "You're still here?"

"Where else would I be?"

"Oh, I don't know. Same place the rest of my imaginary friends go."

Rem shrugged. "This is my room, for now," he added. "I'm not planning on going anywhere for a while."

'Is that a cola in her hand?' Tracy yelled in his head. *'Don't let her drink that!'*

'Why not? It's just a cola. Lots of people drink them.'

'I'm warning you. If she drinks that she will get sick. Stomach cramps. Chills. Vomit!'

Rem sprang from the chair across the floor, snatching the can just as it reached Wendy's lips. "Oh, no you don't," he said, dumping the contents down the sink drain.

"Hey!" Wendy faced him, her hands planted on her hips and her eyes narrowed. "What do you think you are doing?"

"Have water. She can have water can't she?"

'Of course.'

"I don't want water. And who are you talking to? This isn't fair!" Wendy stomped her foot and stuck her tongue out. "You can't have an imaginary friend. You have to be my imaginary friend."

Remiel rolled his eyes. *'Great! Just great! Now what do I do?'*

'I don't know. I usually just play along when she is having one of her episodes. I've never pretended to have my own imaginary friend.'

'Oh just shut up and let me think.'

'You are so rude. No wonder you have no friends.' But she stopped talking.

Remiel grabbed a bottle of water from the small fridge and taking Wendy's small hand in his he led her back to the sofa. Once she was settled he handed her the opened water. "We need to talk."

"Isn't that what we have been doing?"

"Fair enough. This time, I talk and you listen."

Wendy frowned. "Are you mad at me?"

Remiel took a deep breath and let it out very slowly, sitting back in the chair as far away from the child as he could possibly get without actually leaving the room. He was getting hungry and her young soul was tempting him. "No, I'm not mad at you. I just need you to listen to what I need to say."

"Okay," she answered meekly. He marvelled at how complex such a small human female could be.

"First. You are not crazy. I am real and I am here. I'm almost certain that all, or at least most, of your other imaginary friends were real as well; At least the ones that weren't six foot, talking bunnies."

"Now you're teasing me. I've never seen a talking animal except for those parrots at the pet store Tracy took me to see."

"Okay, then. All real. No crazy hospital for you. Second, you did not kill your stepfather. When the doctors find him, they will discover that he died of a heart attack. He didn't take care of himself and he paid the price. No jail for you. Third, you are really here. And this is where the problem arises."

"Don't send me back! Please. I'll be good. I can cook and clean. I won't be any trouble. I promise I won't drink cola," she paused her begging. "Hey! How come you took my cola away?"

"Chills. Cramps. Vomit. Gross!"

Wendy's eyes grew larger than saucers. "How?"

"Let's just say someone who loves you very much told me."

"Tracy! Where is she? Is she in Heaven? Can you talk to her? Can ..."

Remiel threw his hand up to fend off any more questions. "Enough! Do either one of you ever stop talking?"

Wendy folded her hands neatly on her lap. "Sorry," she said meekly, although the twinkle in her eyes said differently. "What are you going to do with me? Send me back?"

'You can't!'

"Apparently I cannot. On the other hand, I know nothing of looking after a child, human or otherwise. For instance, right now I need to go out. What am I supposed to do with you?"

"I can stay here. I'm alone a lot anyway."

Remiel thought about it briefly. If the hunters actually found a way to track him here she would be in danger, and if anything happened to her, he would never hear the end of it. "I've got an idea. Come with me and don't say anything."

Sleep didn't last long. It never did. Becky glanced at the clock and groaned. Two hours. Two measly hours. Exhausted as her body felt she knew her brain was not letting her back to sleep anytime soon. She flicked on the small lamp beside the bed, grabbed her housecoat, and padded barefoot into the kitchen; a bottle of water and hopefully something good on TV to help pass the next few hours. She glanced out the window at the pool she shared with the cottage on the other side of the courtyard. The pool looked inviting with the stars reflecting on its calm surface, but a sudden memory of her earlier visit poolside warmed her skin. She headed for the sofa and TV.

What was that? Becky muted the volume and listened to the stillness of the night. There it was again. Footsteps. She jumped at the sharp rap on the door, hurrying over. With one hand on the knob and one on the lock, she paused. What the hell was she thinking? What if it were the men from the parking lot?

"Hello?" She whispered. Then clearing her throat she asked louder, "Hello. Is there someone there?"

"I don't know if you remember me," Remiel began. '*Of course she remembers us, you. Who could ever forget you?*' Remiel ignored her and continued, "We met earlier at the pool. I'm sorry to bother you but I have a bit of a problem, '*Let me in*', and I was hoping you could help me out."

Caution flew with the wind and Becky flung open the door, her jaw dropping. There he was. The hottie from the pool. And beside him, holding his much larger hand and looking at her expectantly, was a child of ten or so. Of course, he was married. Only a fool would have thought anything else was possible. She stepped aside. "Come in. What can I do for you?"

"I wouldn't have bothered you so late at night but your light was on and I had nobody else to turn to."

"That's okay." Becky smiled at the girl. "Hi, my name is Becky. What's your name?"

"My name is Wendy, and this is Rem." She glanced up at the tall man holding her hand.

So, he does have a name. "Would you like a soda, Wendy?"

"No!"

Becky took a step back, shocked at the aggression in the man's voice.

"He means, no thank you, Becky. I'm allergic to caffeine. I could have a root beer or ginger ale if you have one. I just can't have cola, or anything with caffeine.

'*Caffeine?*'

Tracy laughed. '*You have absolutely no social skills. Where do you usually live, a cave?*'

'*Shut up or I'll eat your sister.*'

'*Huh! You wouldn't dare. The two of us would drive you crazier than you already are.*'

Unaware of the conversation going on, Becky turned to Wendy. "I happen to have a root beer in the fridge. I don't

drink a lot of caffeine myself. The fridge is in the kitchenette, go help yourself."

"Thanks." Wendy let go of Rem's hand and headed to the kitchenette, leaving them alone.

When she was gone, Becky turned to the hottie. "She's adorable. What brings you to my door at," she glanced at the clock. "Four in the morning! Oh God! She shouldn't be drinking soda at this time of day. What was I thinking? I wasn't thinking. That's the problem. I'm so sorry. I don't sleep well and lose all track of time."

"Do all human women yammer on so?" When Becky rolled her eyes, Rem cleared his throat, suddenly unsure of himself for the first time in his very long life. "I'm sorry to bother you at four in the morning, but I need to go out and I couldn't leave Wendy alone, although she assures me it is quite acceptable."

"No, no, you are right not to leave her alone. Where is your wife?"

"My what? Oh, I don't have a wife. Wendy is not mine. I'm, uh, just watching her for a friend. Both her stepfather and her sister died earlier today and she had nowhere else to go. But as it so happens, I have some business which I need to tend to. It can't wait." What the hell was wrong with him? He was beginning to yammer on like the women in his life, and he didn't like it. He had no need to explain himself He could simply compel her to watch Wendy for him, no questions asked. So why didn't he? "Would it be possible for you to watch Wendy for a couple of hours?"

Becky smiled, lighting up her entire face. He wasn't married. Not that it mattered one iota, she assured herself. Huh! "Sure, no problem. She can sleep in the spare room."

"Thanks."

He was there one minute and the next he was gone. Becky blinked and shut the open door.

Eight

"Where are we going?"

"Hunting. I'm hungry."

"Sorry. I guess I should have left Sam for you."

"No. Samuel Frost was yours."

"He tasted bad."

"You get used to it."

"Did I taste bad?"

"You are a delicious tease. I cannot consume you."

"Why? Does that mean I'm stuck here in this limbo forever? Don't get me wrong. I like it here. It is a lot better than where I was living. But let's face it, this isn't exactly living. I didn't think it would, but it hurts seeing Wendy and not being able to talk to her, to hold her, to make everything all right for her."

"Try talking to her and not eating her."

"You monster!" Tracy laughed. "Thank you for that. For rescuing her."

"I can't look after her alone."

"Sure you can. I can help. I'll tell you what to do."

"Great! More yammering," his voice gently teased. He shoved open the door at the bottom of the steps and entered the dimly lit Dungeon. The tangy scent of lust mingled with human sweat from bodies swaying too close in such a hot, cramped space. He spied a female sitting alone at the bar, and with only a single glance he saw everything. Her streaked hair, mussed to look like she just got out of bed, her top unbuttoned to allow ample viewing of her well endowed cleavage, a skirt that barely covered her butt cheeks, and

nine inch, blood red, heels. Definitely a working girl, she was looking out over the dance floor with as much enthusiasm as a student heading in for an exam they didn't take the time to study for.

"She looks promising."

"She looks worn out." Eager blue eyes scanned the dance floor, stopping at a male, probably in his late twenties or early thirties. His black hair was slicked back, his well honed body covered entirely in black, right down to the black military boots that should have looked out of place but somehow didn't. "How about him? He looks yummy!"

"Explain yummy."

"You are so archaic. You know. Yummy. Mmmm. Could swallow that man whole. I guess you would prefer a woman. Hmm, unless you swing both ways."

"I prefer women. For the most part their souls taste better. The young taste best, but they tend to fight longer and give me a headache."

"Am I giving you a headache?" Tracy's voice purred like a contented kitten.

"You are definitely giving me something."

"So, are we going to eat him?"

"You have a lot to learn if you are going to survive. Look at the way he is dressed. More importantly, look at his boots. He is a hunter. Like the ones who jumped us outside the bar."

"Jumped you, you mean. I had nothing to do with it. I guess that means we can't eat him."

His body tensed. A shift in the air current alerted him to the opening door and he stepped further into the shadows to watch as three young males, also dressed in military garb, entered the room. After a cursory scan of the club, they moved as one toward the young male in black.

The apparent leader of the group grabbed the young male's shoulder and spun him so they were face to face. By the scowl on the younger male's face, he wasn't happy to see the new arrivals. "Come on, let's go."

The younger male shoved the new comer's hand away and sneered. "I'm not going anywhere with you." He glanced disparagingly at the others, now flanking their leader. "Why don't you leave? Don't you and your 'crew' have some demon to hunt?"

There were some snickers from the dancers closest to them, but at the leader's dark scowl they quickly moved away from the vicinity. "What the hell do you think you are doing? You know we aren't supposed to talk about those things."

The reprimand came barely above a whisper, but Remiel had no problem hearing every word, and through him, Tracy. He scanned the dark room, noting the hunters were between them and the only exit. They'd have to wait this one out, or risk drawing attention to themselves.

"Shove off, Duke. I quit. Remember? I don't want to have anything to do with your insane group."

"You can't just leave. You swore an oath to Zaapiel."

Remiel tensed at the name. Zaapiel, Punisher of wicked souls. Was it possible he was here? Or, was some human assuming the identity of a god in an attempt to command obedience.

"What the hell is with that guy anyway? Makes himself out to be some all powerful being, and yet he needs us mere mortals to carry out his dirty work. Well I won't do it anymore."

Duke grabbed the younger man's wrist and tried to drag him out of the club. "You are coming with me, even if I have to beat you senseless first."

"Yeah," the boy sneered. "What happened to Zaapiel's mandate that no human be hurt? I'm still human in case you haven't noticed."

"Oh, we noticed." There was a slight buzzing in his left ear. Duke tapped his ear once, listened, and tapped it again. "You're one lucky bastard." Duke spun on his heel to face his crew. "Leave him. We have more important fish to fry across town."

Remiel waited at least ten minutes after they left before moving out of the shadows. The boy left about three minutes after the rest of the hunters. "Looks like she's dinner," Tracy whispered, trying to shrug off the tension.

Remiel could feel her anxiety, it was his. If they weren't so hungry, he'd call it a night. "Watch, listen, and learn," he said. "You need to learn to hunt if you are going to survive."

He stood across the dance floor, confidence and sexuality rolling off him in waves. Every eye turned his way, both male and female, but he only had eyes for her and she began to shiver. The usually stale, rank air was sweet and spicy. She couldn't take her eyes off him. Heat pooled at her center and she felt herself begin to drip. Of their own volition, her fingers touched her throat, trailing lower, disappearing below the last button of her blouse. Her tongue snaked out, wetting her too red lips when he sat on the stool beside her.

"Buy me a drink, honey," she cooed. She didn't want a drink. She wanted to take him upstairs to her room and fuck his brains out.

"It's getting late. Why don't we skip the drinks?" His voice dripped sex.

Ignoring the drink already sitting in front of her, she smiled at him. "I'm calling it a night, Earl," she told the bartender. "Do me a favour and don't let anyone up."

"You got it, Gracie." Earl didn't even look in their direction.

Her room was at the top of a set of stairs behind the bar. He kicked the door closed behind them. The room was small. A double bed took up most of the room barely allowing space for the small wardrobe, the only other piece of furniture. Grace backed toward the bed, unbuttoning her blouse as she went, unclipping the front clasp of her black, lace bra, releasing her perfectly shaped, pale breasts as her legs bumped the side of the bed. She'd always thought of her breasts as her crowning glory. For some it was the hair, other's the ass, but for her it was the tits. Even now, when everything else was falling and flabby, they were perfect—and all hers.

She crawled backward up the bed. She couldn't take her eyes off his face as he crawled along with her. The heat from his perfect body sent chills dancing over her bare skin. Her panties were already wet; the scent of her mixing with the sweet spice of him. When her lips parted invitingly, he captured them with his own.

He slid one hand behind her head to hold it steady, the other slipped under her skirt. She shivered when his hand cupped her wet panties, tensing in anticipation when his fingers explored the edge and then slipped inside. It was too much to expect her to wait. The moment his fingers sank into her heated entrance she came with a gasp of pure pleasure.

He inhaled. Sweet ambrosia. The soul at its best moment.

'*Wow! This is delicious.*' Tracy shared the nourishment with her host, savouring every delicious drop. When Remiel pulled back, she continued to dine.

'*Stop!*' Remiel fought for control of his own body and mind, finally succeeding in breaking free of the limp, albeit still breathing, woman.

'*What the hell!*' Tracy complained. '*Why did you stop? I'm still hungry.*'

'*You have to learn to leave some. If you leave some the soul can heal. If you take it all you kill everything.*'

181

'You didn't leave any of me!'

'A mistake. I let myself grow too hungry. Now the hunters are on my trail and I have to move again. A mistake I may yet pay for if Zaapiel is really here. If you want to survive you need to learn when to feed and when to stop.'

'What do you mean, "If I want to survive?" You already said you couldn't consume me.'

'I also said I couldn't look after your sister alone.'

For the first time in hours his thoughts were his own, and he wondered what she was thinking.

Nine

Becky sat in the overstuffed chair she dragged into Wendy's room and watched the child sleep. She seemed to be much quieter now but Becky was in no hurry to leave her alone with whatever thoughts were tormenting her sleep. The child had tossed and turned for more than an hour, crying out the name Tracy on several occasions. So much so in fact that Becky had finally dragged the chair in instead of running in every time Wendy cried out to find the child still asleep, caught in some nightmare. When she smoothed the child's hair from her brow and whispered soothing nonsense it seemed to calm her for a while, and so Becky had moved in.

Poor child, she was so young to have lost so much, and having lost everyone that mattered to her Becky understood what she was going through. Technically, Becky's mother was still alive, if you called breathing and eating whatever someone placed in your mouth without understanding what was going on around you, living; but she was still lost to Becky.

Becky struggled to take a breath, having to think about it. She wanted to go to sleep, but she was afraid she wouldn't wake up and she promised to look after this poor child until Rem returned, and Becky didn't make promises lightly.

She drew in another deep breath and her head nodded forward. Becky jerked herself upright. Funny there was no pain. She thought there would be pain; must be all the drugs she was taking. For a moment, Becky worried that she'd taken too much of the medication, and then she wondered if

she'd even remembered to take it at all. Then she didn't worry about much of anything as the darkness embraced her.

It was cold and dark. Becky didn't like the cold or the dark—not anymore. She used to love to sit in the dark and just think, let her imagination take her to faraway places. This wasn't like those times. There were no stars winking at her through the window. There was no ribbon of light and shadow sneaking under the door as her parents moved around in the other room. Becky didn't like this dark, not one little bit. She didn't want to stay here. She still had things to do and things to see. She'd never seen snow! She wanted to see snow before she left for good.

She started to whimper. Wait! That wasn't her making that noise. Then who was it? Wendy! She had to wake up. She had to get back to Wendy. Wendy needed her. She promised. And Becky had never broken a promise.

It hurt now. The pain was real and Becky embraced it, leaned on it, forcing her eyes open, she leaned forward and smoothed the hair from Wendy's furrowed brow. "Hush baby it's okay. Everything will be okay. Rem will be back soon and everything will be okay." She knew it was the truth. Becky could feel it in her very soul. Rem would come back and everything would be okay.

Ten

"It's amazing how you do that."

"What?" Remiel was distracted and Tracy's sudden thought startled him, allowing her a glimpse of his hidden thoughts.

"Hey! What was that you were thinking about? How long have you been hiding things from me?"

"Not long enough apparently," Remiel snapped. "What's amazing?" He tried to distract her while he fought to change his thought patterns.

"Oh." Tracy quit trying to divine his thoughts and shrugged it off. "You know. The way you made those women think you were having mind-blowing sex, and it really was just fantasy sex. You didn't touch any of them. Good thing. Some of them I wouldn't have wanted to touch with a ten-foot pole. But why go to all the bother?"

"That is when the soul is at its best; the peak of fulfillment. It heightens the senses and makes the difference between a gourmet meal and a quick snack."

"Good to know. Do you ever actually, you know, do it?"

Remiel sighed, his thoughts turning to Becky before he could contain them. Her sable locks that framed the face of a lost angel. She was never far from his thoughts. It was like that sometimes, when drawn to a soul he meant to carry across. But, thanks to one stupid mistake, he was no longer capable of safely transporting souls. He usually moved on when he discovered such souls, unwilling to devour them and unable to deliver them. As part of his punishment, he was forced to live off the souls he once saved.

Her pain called to him now and he stepped through the nearest portal, one moment hunting Bourbon Street, the next standing in the courtyard across from her door. '*I am here.*'

Becky smiled. "It's going to be okay little one. He's here. My angel is here to take me home. Rem will look after you now." In Becky's mind, she saw two figures. She could see her angel, bigger than life with wings as soft as cotton and as strong as iron to carry her safely home, and Rem, bigger than life and sexier than hell. She would have liked to explore that fantasy a little more but some things were not meant to be, and she was so tired.

Becky would die a virgin.

Becky would never see snow.

'*What's wrong with her?*' Tracy asked Remiel. '*I can't find anything wrong with her. She is simply fading away.*'

'*Her soul is brave but unable to keep her body from breaking down. It happens like that sometimes. The ones who don't deserve to live do, and those, like Becky, pure of heart and soul, do not.*'

'*I like her. Look how she is fighting death so she can take care of my sister. She has a good soul.*'

'*I'm glad you like her.*'

'*Why?*'

'*Wait. I don't want to say anything until I am sure.*'

Becky glanced at Rem standing beside the bed watching her and Wendy at the same time. "Could you two talk a little quieter please? I don't want you to wake Wendy. She has finally quieted." The moment Rem appeared beside the bed Wendy relaxed into a deep, normal sleep, as if his presence alone made her safe. Or, perhaps it was the angel standing beside him in all her ethereal beauty.

"You haven't come for her, have you?" Becky placed her hand protectively across Wendy's sleeping form. "She is too young. You can't take her. I won't let you. She has a life to

live yet. Take me. I'm dying anyway." Becky wasn't looking at Remiel. She was looking past him to his right.

Remiel turned his head in the direction Becky was staring and almost choked. Tracy was standing beside him. Or at least a shimmering image of her was. How was this possible?

Tracy grinned. "You didn't think you could keep me out of your thoughts, did you? I am a part of you. I will always be, no matter where I choose to reside. Thank you for showing me the way. Now all I have to do is convince Rebecca."

Remiel blinked back the tears shimmering in his eyes. How was this possible? Tracy's soul was intact and free. He hadn't seen anything so beautiful since banishment from Nibiru.

"You *are* here for her." Becky's face glowed with happiness. "You are going to keep her safe."

"We are going to keep her safe," Tracy amended. "If you will accept my offer."

"What do you mean?"

"Your body is in a weakened state, and unfortunately, although strong your soul is not strong enough to heal it. My soul is strong, but as you can see, I am lacking a corporeal form of my own." She glanced sideways at Remiel who couldn't take his eyes from the glowing shape. "Frankly, I have no intention of sharing his form for eternity, at least not from the inside. I find your form much more acceptable, if you will agree. I will keep you strong as long as possible, allowing you to enjoy the rest of your time here, and in return you will help care for my sister. This has to be your choice."

Two years later ...

"Why do I have to?"

"Because I said so?" Tracy threw up her arms in surrender. "I give up. You try."

Becky's brown eyes flashed, replacing the sky blue eyes that indicated Tracy's presence. "What Tracy means is that if you do not clean your room right now you will not be going on that night ski with Tasha."

Wendy, hands on hips and legs spread in defiance, muttered, "This isn't fair. Two against one. And you two always stick together."

"That's why we love them. Hi beautiful," purred the masculine voice behind Becky.

Wendy threw her hands up in surrender imitating her sister's earlier gesture, and flounced into her room. Becky spun around, grabbing the back of the nearest chair when her knees grew weak. She wondered if she would ever get used to the velvety warmth of his voice, and the effect it had on her. "Hi yourself." She tried for nonchalance but she wasn't fooling any of them. "Have you eaten?"

In a heartbeat, Rem moved from the doorway to stand close enough to wrap his arms around Becky. She released the back of the chair and melted into his embrace. "Afraid I might eat you," he teased.

Blue eyes flashed and settled to brown. Becky sighed. Remiel heard Tracy's sigh in his mind, and smiled. He nuzzled her neck, lowering his lips to kiss the four white spots on her collarbone.

Becky looked out at the snow-covered mountain and remembered the first time she'd seen the beautiful white stuff. Tracy had given her that moment, as she had given her so many more. Watching the sunlight sparkle off the ski trail, Becky realized she was really looking forward to Christmas this year. She wondered, not for the first time, how she got so lucky. One moment she was dying and the next she had it all; a daughter who loved her, a best friend who was always there when she needed her, and gave her space when she didn't, and an angel who loved them all.

Simple Gifts

Ina Louise Jackson

What will be will ... And it will always find a way to be.

Dedicated to

Catlin

Prologue

Merry Christmas to You
Merry Christmas to You
Merry Christmas
Merry Christmas
Merry Christmas to You
Or Not ...

Prelude

Clara Stewart hung up the telephone with an enormous smile. The same smile that adorned her picture encased in the gold oval on the real estate sign in the front window.

She paddled her office chair backwards with her feet, out into the hallway. "Someone wants to see the Briarwood Mansion," she yelled.

"Are you kidding?" Adam retorted.

"Nope, they'll be here in two weeks." She flipped through her appointment book noting the date, time and place.

"Are you going to take the bet?"

"Do I look crazy to you?"

Friday Six Weeks Later

The fifty-three foot moving van was parked ramps down, dead centre of the circular drive at nine-hundred-ninety-nine Briarwood Gate.

The massive three-story manor complete with turret's loomed over the van dwarfing it, making it resemble a child's toy.

The mansion sat far back off the road like a daunting silent spectator privy to all and everything through its peepholes in the trees.

The new owners rushed the front door, unlocking it, their voices bubbling and pitching with excitement. The family of five, complete with dog and hamster, group hugged then disappeared through the opening to scout out the mansion's massive layout floor by floor, room by room.

The moving company owner had been analysing and scrutinizing their every movement until they vanished from sight.

He'd stood motionless, arm extended, hand up, fingers splayed as the soft yellow glow of lights rippled out from one window to the next to the next. When the illumination reached the second floor, he sneered. It was time.

He whipped his arm down like a flagman at the 'Indy 500.'

Time was of utter importance.

Harry, the company's supervisor was standing just a hair to the right of driver's door as if mothballed; the colour gone from his face, his hands were twitching involuntarily. His eyes were protruding from the sockets.

His head cocked far back on his neck at an odd angle, as if partially severed. His gaze clamped on the top left turret. Without warning his eyes ringed in white, he spasmed, wobbled, did a backward two-step smashing into the van driver's door and slamming it shut. His body pivoted, his feet scrambling for footing as his legs turned on the auto-pilot button to run.

"To hell with this shit!" He yelled. He tore off down the drive as if the devil himself was after him.

The remaining four did not give Harry a second thought, grouping together to unload the van, pushing, rolling, and thrusting the contents across the deck to the top of the ramp and booting it off into the snow.

The five thousand dollar bonus, which had been settled prior to taking the moving job to this particular location, was left by the wayside.

Unopened ... Uncollected.

The hair on the back of each of their necks had been standing at attention since entering the driveway. Half way up, cold shivers began coursing up and down their spines. Since stepping from the cab, they'd all looked over their shoulders time and time again, in-between staring up at the top row of windows. They'd collectively thought they had seen something, something dark, foreboding ... Looking back at them from those top windows.

They had heard the stories.

Everybody in these parts had.

As the last piece of furniture toppled off the side of the ramp, they held one another's eyes. The fear was front and center.

The company's owner winged the documentation of inspection and completion through the air in the general direction of the front porch. The driver started the truck as the other three crammed into the passenger seat on top of one another. The smell of burnt gears and gasoline filled the cab as the van hauled ass down the drive.

The unsecured loading ramps dropped down, swaying, mashing the snow into lumpy mush before ripping free, spinning, following the path of the van like huge grotesque tops. They veered off into the ditch, the one quickly disappearing into the snow; the other teetered, and then moved forward as if it had grown legs, ploughing directly into the massive boughs of a pine.

Marty and Norm Abbott stepped onto the front porch just in time to witness the last of the snow tornados created by the van. They stood side by each, portraying the identical 'Oh My God' body lingo. Their heads swivelled owl like in perfect unison, taking in the disarray of belongings.

"Think anything is broken?" Marty could not believe this. Their entire lives toppled and mangled together like someone's garbage. She zipped up her coat.

"You can count on it," Norm said quietly. He rubbed his hand back and forth across his chin.

"Think they'll be back?"

"Wouldn't count on it!" The words 'Jesus Fucking Christ' were sitting on the tip of his tongue. He sighed heavily instead of blurting them out.

"What are we going to do?"

"Stay up all night." He pulled his hood up and stepped off the porch into the snow.

"Well ... That's the last of it." Norm sat the two wet cardboard boxes that jingled like china bells down in the front hallway. He made his lips disappear into his mouth. He glanced at Marty and then back at the boxes.

"I wouldn't be opening them for a while ... Maybe a long while." He turned them on their sides shoving them tight against the wall, obscuring the wording 'Great Grandmas Crystal ... Dining Room' scrawled in black marker.

Saturday

"Everything's gone from the snow." Dora tucked the small black stool in underneath the telescope that sat directly in front of the side window. The same side window, if one were to draw a straight line from it down across their lawn and through the trees would end up on the Briarwood's front yard and if furthered, the entranceway.

"Did you hear me?"

"Yes ... Something about a doe?" Rodd grabbed the television remote lowering the volume.

She smiled. His hearing was getting worse by the year. "Everything's gone from the snow," she repeated. "They must have worked through the night bringing it all in." She pulled a bobby pin loose, opening it, re-pinning the loose strands of gray hair back into her bun.

"Already? ... That was quick!" Rodd turned off the television and got up from his easy chair.

"Wonder how long these ones will last?" Dora fussed with her bobby pin again.

Rodd shrugged. "Don't know dear ... We could bet a coffee and a piece of pie over at that new restaurant."

"You're on! ... You ready to go say hello?"

"Yes." He drew his thin lips out into a straight line.

"Look more neighbourly, though."

He pasted on a smile. "This good?"

"Not so much teeth, you look possessed."

He sized down his smile. "Better?"

"Better."

They strolled arm in arm along the shoulder of the road, pausing briefly between the two substantial stone pillars. They eyed the engraving on the shiny brass plaque that read nine-ninety-nine Briarwood Gate in large letters with the italics underneath that said 'Built in the year of our Lord eighteen-hundred-thirty-five - ____, the finish build date was blank.

It had always been blank.

It would always be blank.

The box had seen to that.

They looked from the plaque to one other. Neither said a word. They didn't have to. They knew ...

They moved to the side of the mansion's drive as Norm's jeep came up on them slowing and passed them cautiously.

Norm bounded to the house, opening the front door. "We have company," he yelled.

IIe watched the old couple as they struggled through the heaps of snow.

"Sorry about all that," Norm mumbled.

"Hey, 'tis the season," Rodd shouted. He gave a hearty wave.

Marty and the three children joined Norm on the front porch just in time to merge in on the handshaking.

"I'm Rodd Keeper and this is my lovely wife Dora of ..." he paused, he could not say one-hundred-eighty years. He pulled a number out of his hat, "sixty-three years. We are your neighbours, so to speak. We are on this same side and just down the road apiece, on the other side of the forest. We thought we'd come over and give your family a proper welcome to the neighbour-hood."

"Thank you," Norm said. "Thank you so much," he reaffirmed. He abruptly let go of Rodd's hand realizing

he had latched onto it shaking it to death. "We thought that kind of social grace was a thing of the past."

Rodd and Dora pasted on smiles. "We're both things of the past." Rodd chuckled.

"I am Norm. Norman Abbott and this is my wife Martha, everyone calls her Marty though. In addition, directly behind me is our youngest Valerie who is seven, to our right is our middle child Monica who is ten, and to the left here is our oldest Eric who is twelve, and pinned in between my wife's legs is our dog Roger. He is somewhat skittish. Last but not least is our hamster Buffy, who is curled up in Eric's shirt pocket here. "Norm pulled at the material allowing Rodd and Dora a quick peek inside.

They pasted on another smile.

Their curiosity appeased Eric, Monica and Valerie disappeared back into the house.

"All, the move go well?" Rodd said. It seemed like the proper thing to ask, he knew it hadn't. But ... It never did at this address ... In or out.

"All ... The move?" Norm paused clasping his hands together. "The on loading went without a hitch. The off loading, to put it graciously, not so much."

Rodd's eyes traced quickly over the snow with the splinters of wood and remnants of soaked cardboard. "Left sooner than later did they?"

"Yes they did ... A lot sooner than later!" Norm confirmed. "A hell of a lot sooner," Norm muttered.

Dora and Rodd gave one another a quick glance.

"Mom! ... Mom! ... I can't find my night clothes!" Monica's yells from inside the house sounded the other side of exasperated. "Can you come and help me?"

Marty swivelled round. "Just a minute honey," she shouted. She excused herself to Dora and Rodd, quickly disappearing into the house and closing the door behind her.

"It looks like you're in a muddle here," Rodd said quietly. "We should be getting along anyway. There is supposed to be a storm coming. Just wanted to say hello. If you'd be in need of anything come on over or give us a jingle. We're in the phone book." He ran his fingers over the bricks. "These Victorians are sure good and solid. They don't build them like this anymore." He paused, pasting on the same smile nodding to Norm. "Good day to you."

Rodd and Nora toddled off as they had come, through the heaps of snow.

"They seem like such a lovely family," Dora said. She hooked her arm through Rodd's. "These Victorians are sure good and solid." She rocked her shoulders repeating him verbatim, mimicking his voice. "They don't build them like this anymore?" She grinned profusely. "Good thing ... Don't you think?" She added in her own voice.

He smiled for real; she was getting better at mimicking him. "Yes," he said. "One Briarwood Mansion on this earth is more than enough!"

The Following Friday

"Did you have a good day at work?" Marty asked.

"Yes, glad it's done though, it was super busy. I might have to go in tomorrow morning for a few hours." Norm shook the snow from his jacket hanging it on the hook.

"Awe ... Tomorrow's Saturday. I was hoping I could use your muscle power to move around some heavy stuff."

"I'll be home around noon. Will that work?"

"But of course," Marty said. She watched him pick up his tool belt. "Don't get into doing something dinner's soon."

"Okay, I'll get to it after supper." He picked up the jar of nails and set it beside the belt. "Hey instead of me fixing stuff tonight, want to play a board game after supper with the kids?"

She nodded.

He rubbed his hands together, cupped them, then blew in warming them. He eyed Marty; she had her winter coat on. "Why the hell is it so cold in here?"

"I think the furnace quit." She said nonchalantly. She moved a pot onto the burner.

"You think it quit?"

"Yes, I think it quit!" she chirped.

"Did you go look?"

"Nope."

"Why?"

"Still can't find my boots."

"Okay then," he sighed heavily, the last thing he wanted to do was go back out into the cold. "Did you say you think it quit?"

"Yes ... Yes I did. There was a loud rattling through the ducts then a boom, then silence ... Then Walla! ... No more heat."

"Walla?"

"Yes ... Walla!"

"I see." He could not help but smile at his wife, he knew she knew it had quit. Nevertheless, this was just her way of dealing with things, especially things that could cost a lot of money like a furnace repair. Thinking it did is by far better than knowing it did. "And by chance would this also be another one of those colour coded things of yours? Aside from the missing boots of course."

"Yes it is! ... It's definitely blue, and that colour is you."

"Before you decided on this colour code, did you happen to call anyone?"

"Yep, all of the furnace repair places." She chirped. She sat down the ladle and looked directly into his eyes. "No one will come."

"Did they say why?" He pulled out a stool from under the kitchen island and sat.

"Yes and no ... When they found out the address, they had lots of excuses. Most were general, however one did have a death in the family while we were talking on the phone and another just outright hung up. I was going to call you in hopes of a quick 'DIY' instruction session, but then I remembered you'd forgotten your phone this morning."

He pursed his lips muttering things she was not privy too.

Dinnertime with the family all in winter gear passed by quickly ... Too quickly for Norm. He could not seem to warm himself and he was about to get a lot colder.

He pulled on his boots, mumbling away to himself about the old school, outside door to the basement. Why they did that so many years ago was beyond him? Someday, he would do a major renovation, redirecting it inside.

He had not been down in the basement since the first viewing of the house.

He unlocked the door and yanked it open.

He stepped into the doorway.

The basement was blacker than hell and as silent as the dead.

A cold shiver ran up his spine.

He squinted his eyes flicking them back and forth seeing nothing.

His skin goose-bumped.

He could not shake the feeling it was beckoning him in ... Inside its darkness. He was suddenly apprehensive, intimidated in a way indescribable in words. He stood as he was, envisioning the door slamming shut, the lock turning, the blackness engulfing him ... He didn't further his thoughts.

He forced himself to step forward. He stretched his arms upwards, splaying his fingers. He fanned the darkness above his head searching for a telltale sign of the string pull cords for the light bulbs.

He had remembered the bulbs and pull cords in the basement.

This was the only thing he had remembered.

There was nothing but air.

He scrunched up his face kid like. "Shit," he whispered. He put his hood up and knotted the ties under his chin.

He shuffled his feet back and forth. His palms were perspiring. He was suddenly afraid. Afraid to step further into that basement. He shoved his hands deep into his coat pockets rocking his feet in his boots.

He quickly about faced, bounding up the steps three at a time, running full out for the house.

He bent over the front porch railing, shaking, feeling as if he was about to vomit. His heart roared in his ears. His teeth chattered ... A grown man petrified of his own basement.

He cracked open the front door and entered stealth like. "Do we have a flashlight handy?" he mumbled.

"Nope, don't know where it is," Marty said from behind him.

Norm visibly jumped. She was so close ... Too close.

Marty had been watching him out on the porch from the window. He had been out there over fifteen minutes with his head hanging down over the railing. "What's with you?" She asked.

He started unzipping his coat not saying a word.

Marty disappeared then reappeared. "Use this." She handed him her computer tablet. "There's a flashlight app on it."

"Wonderful," he muttered. *'Just fucking wonderful ... Thank-you so much ... What a good wife you are ... Fuck!'*

He re-zipped and trudged back outside, circling the house ... Twice.

His heart was roaring in his ears again.

He compelled his feet to descend the steps. He used the stone walls to steady himself. Why he had to force himself down the stairs and needed to steady himself, were one in the same. A question he did not have an answer to.

He took a breather, and then stepped in through the doorway.

He fiddled with the tablet sliming the screen with perspiration.

He pressed his index finger on the flashlight icon.

The walls and floor about him glowed in a tight circle of blue-white light.

Something small he could not make out scurried out of the light into the darkness.

He flashed the light side to side along the ceiling as if marking out an invisible grid. He ever so slowly inched into the basement keeping in direct line with the open door just in case of ... Of ... Of ... He didn't further.

He couldn't.

He was batting two for two in the unfinished thought department.

He went back to his search mission.

"There you are," he whispered. He breathed a sigh of relief. He unclenched his shoulders. There ... On the far side of the room, quite unobtrusive ... Hung the light bulb.

He held the tablet light close and personal to the fixture.

The cord looked like a mass of dried spaghetti wound round the blub.

Another cold chill ran up his spine.

He glanced over both shoulders and each side flashing the light into the blackness. He could feel it ... Feel it as if it was feeding off his fear.

He gave himself a shake. Then another.

His hands vibrated and shook as he went to work untangling the pull cord. He grimaced, finally freeing it.

"Okay baby! ... Hope you work," he said.

He yanked the cord.

The area flooded with light.

He ran the length of the basement, stopping, unwrapping, and pulling the light cords in succession, filling the entire space with light.

The basement floor was nubby concrete, the walls mortared old stone.

He smiled a real smile for the first time.

His neighbour was so right, when he said the house was good and solid, that they did not build them like this anymore. He estimated the walls to be at least three feet thick. Be a good safe haven for a *Zombie Apocalypse*. He instantly wished his mind had bypassed that thought. "Jesus Christ," he muttered. "Get a fucking grip here."

He averted all upcoming thoughts, running a block by whistling a Christmas tune as he strolled over to the furnace. He placed his hand on the metal. She was sure cold ... Stone cold to be exact. The thing probably had not been on for the better part of the day. His mind rewound to his family in their winter coats. "Correction '" he said." Not probably, it hasn't."

He started to whistle again.

He opened up the lower furnace compartment.

The pilot light was out.

"Easy fix," he said.

The small thing scurried by.

He searched the inner compartment for a pack of matches. All old timers kept a pack or two in the cubbyhole for times like this.

Empty.

Ina Louise Jackson

He journeyed back upstairs into the house.

His family, eyes full of hope, greeted him at the door, complete with coats, hats, and mitts.

He answered them before they asked. "Not yet. Do we have any matches?"

Eric darted off up the stairs, returning and slipping a navy blue lighter into his hand, not saying a word.

"Thanks," Norm said, breaking the silence. The conversation of what his son was in need of a lighter for could wait until another day.

Minutes later, he held the lighter to the pilot.

It lit and went out.

He tried again.

It lit and went out.

He tried once more.

It lit and went out.

He sucked his lips into his mouth, smiling. He had just demonstrated the principle of stupidity. Doing the same thing and expecting different results. "Jesus fucking Christ," he said.

He checked out the furnace's electrics. The wiring resembled a jumbled up ball of different coloured yarns. He pulled them loose, untangling and laying them out. None of the wires were damaged, terribly kinked, but not damaged. He reconnected the electrics.

He tried the pilot again.

It lit and went out.

The small thing scurried by.

He traced the furnace wiring up and through the main base to where it came out at the side and clamped onto the stone wall. He followed it to the far corner of the room where it went through a small hole in a block wall.

He had not noticed this when he'd been turning on the lights.

He inspected the block that held the wiring. It was solid.

He stepped back, studying the two block walls that made the room.

No door.

"Fuck!" He yelled.

The small thing scurried by ... Again.

He went back up into the house.

"Anyone seen the sledge hammer?" he shouted.

Marty's eyes grew like plump grapes in the sun. "Sledge hammer?" she questioned. *'He was supposed to be fixing the furnace not beating it.'* "You need a sledge hammer?"

"Don't ask," he said.

"This thing dad?" Monica yelled, dragging something heavy from the back porch into the kitchen. She was so cold she was ready to do about anything to help the situation.

"That's it." Norm fetched it from her heaving it up on his shoulder.

Minutes later the house filled with the sounds of heavy wallops.

"This damn thing is well made ... I'll give them that." He leaned on the pole of the sledge taking a break.

The small thing scurried by once again.

"What the fucking hell is that?" It sounded too big for a mouse and too small for a rat.

He went back at the hammering, thrusting blow after blow slowly fissuring the blocks. The mortar started to pop and crackle, dime size jagged lumps fell to the floor.

"Come to papa," he yelled clenching his teeth.

He swung the sledge hard ... Full ... Three blocks split and fell. He spaced his feet, battering the wall with knock after knock. More blocks fell. He dropped the sledge stepped back and examined the opening. It was large enough.

He fetched the tablet flashing the light in through the hole. He grinned toothy and full, finding another pull light and the 'piece de resistance,' the fuse panel.

He clambered through.

He had forgotten about whistling, whistling drove the fear back down into the pit of his stomach where it was manageable.

He rushed the pull light, tripping over something, almost going down. "Fuck! Fuck! Fuck!" he yelled. He directed the tablet light along the floor.

There ... Silent ... As if trying to be unobtrusive ... Sat a wooden box.

The hair on the back of his neck stood.

He pulled the light cord.

The bulb exploded.

The room rained glass daggers.

The small thing scurried past his foot.

"What the fucking hell? Now it is in here? Jesus Christ!"

He whipped the tablet light around the room in frenzied erratic stops and starts.

Dead flies and glass shards carpeted the entire floor.

"A fucking sealed room, with a fucking blown light, a fucking wood box, dead fucking flies and a fucking scurrying thing ... Fuck me!"

He shone the tablet along the walls stopping at the fuse panel with trembling fingers. He so wanted to turn and run.

"Fuck! Fuck! Fuck! Okay Norm ... Whistle ... Just whistle ... It worked before ... Come on old man." He pursed his lips and blew ... Nothing came out. He stared to hum beating the system.

He jerked the electrical panel door open.

Fuses, old school round screw in fuses.

The wiring to the fuses marked 'F', 'A', and 'P,' were hanging mid-air, free of cobwebs and dust ... Unlike all the others ... The ends were white and frayed. He knew they had been ripped loose. Moreover, it had been recent. *'Don't think Norm ... Don't do it ... Just wipe the sweat from your palms on your jeans ... And whistle Norm.'* "Norm," he yelled. "Get a fucking hold of yourself! ... Don't think! ... Just fix! ... And yes ... Whistle!"

He felt like his heart was going to pound right out of his chest.

He about faced, stepped forward, tripped over the box ... Again ... Bounded up the basement steps and rushed into the house.

He put the tablet on the kitchen counter, shoved his sweat filled shaking hands into his pockets, and sat.

"You okay?" Marty put her hands on his shoulders. They were hard and stiff like he had been doused in cement that had long cured.

Norm nodded awkwardly.

"You sure you're alright?"

He had been sitting at the counter for the better part of an hour.

"Yes. I need some tools that is all," he mumbled flatly. He got up and went out into the back porch. He rummaged through his toolbox fetching wire cutters, a stripping knife and electrical tape. "Yes. I need some tools that is all ... Yes. I need some tools that is all."

Marty stared at her husband trying to find something to say. He had said the same thing three times in a row, the same damn thing. "Okay then," she muttered. She watched him shuffle down the front hallway, smack into the back of the door, back up open it, and go out.

He scuttled through the hole, tools in hand.

"Now I lay me down to sleep," his voice was high pitched and sing songy.

He tripped over the box.

"I pray the Lord my soul to keep."

He shut off the electrical power.

"If I should die before I wake."

His fingers moved clumsily, swiping back and forth as if puppeteered.

"I pray the Lord my soul to take."

He repaired the wiring in the panel, without the aid of light.

He shut the panel door.

Turned on the power.

Tripped over the box.

Slithered back out the hole.

Walked over to the furnace.

He lit the pilot.

It stayed on.

Minutes later the finance rumbled and blew heat.

He did not notice the small thing directly behind him as he closed and locked the basement door and started up the stairs

Mid-point he stopped, whirled in a one-eighty, went back down into the basement He pulled all the light cords turning them off as he passed by. He then clambered through the hole and stood over top of the box. The small thing came and sat a hair off his left foot.

Hours later, he scooped the box from the floor, tucked it under his arm, and returned to the house, with the small thing in tow.

Norm sat the wooden box on top of a pile of flattened moving boxes on his way into the kitchen, where he joined his family, sipping hot chocolate with whipping cream and coloured sprinkles.

Marty slipped in beside him giving a peck on the cheek. "Thanks sweetheart. Whatever would we do without you?"

He did not reply.

"Honey?"

"Freeze." His voice was flat, stale, and full of gravel. He tipped his mug chugging back the hot chocolate.

"What was wrong or should I ask?" Marty peeked into his cup. It was empty. Hers was full and still too hot to drink, as was everyone else's.

"Some wires were off the panel."

"What was all that booming?" Marty poured him another cup of the hot chocolate.

He guzzled it.

Her eyes flickered from his face to his cup with the steam rising from it.

"All ... That... Booming." He drew out the words.

"Yes."

"House has a room ..."

'Yes I know it has many, many, in fact ... So?' She drummed her fingernails along the counter top waiting for him to finish the sentence.

He didn't. He just stared straight ahead with a blank look on his face.

"House has a room ...," he repeated. He coughed then cleared his throat. "Room fuse panel."

Marty's eyebrows lifted wrinkling her forehead. *'Okay then ... So ...Yes ... And?'* She nodded at the kids to take off. *'Their dad was a little off at the moment ... Off? ... He's goddamn fucked!'*

They did, winging it up the stairs like lightning.

"Norm?" Marty said.

Nothing.

"Norm?" She said again.

Nothing.

"Okay then," she mumbled.

He wasn't there.

'Maybe he hit his head, sniffed up furnace dust, or got a shock from the furnace wiring, or ...?' She could not put a handle on it.

He got up, walked round the island, took the boiling hot pot from the stove, tipped it back and downed the remainder of the hot chocolate.

Steam wisped from between his parted lips.

"House has a room ... Room fuse panel," he murmured.

He coughed out a dead fly.

She gawked at the fly sliding down his chin.

He teetered his stool balancing it on the two back legs. He glared at her neck as if sizing it up for a length of rope.

Marty instinctively put her hand to her throat, covering it. She backed herself into the kitchen cupboards propping herself up with her elbows. Her legs felt like they were made of rubber bands. Rubber bands that were about to let go any second.

Norm had gone into the basement, something disguised as Norm had come back up.

Norm was still fixated on her neck. He started rocking the stool, front to back, front to back. Without warning, the legs skirted out, flipping him backwards onto the floor.

He lay as he landed, motionless, flat on his back; his legs twisted one over top of the other.

Marty studied his chest ... It was rising and falling.

She inched toward him. She stood over top of him inspecting him.

He was as he was.

She clasped his hand. It felt like cold rubbery five-day old 'Jell-O.'

"Norm? ... Norm? ... You okay?" she said barely above a whisper.

His eyes shot open.

A scream stuck in her throat.

Jet black eyes looked into hers. His body suddenly spasmed. His eyes rolled, turning from black to white.

The stuck scream vibrated her throat. Her head bobbed turkey like. Without thinking, she lunged forward, grabbed his head, lifted it and banged it into the floor.

His eyes flickered, opened, closed. "House has a room ... Room fuse panel," he muffled.

"That's it! ... Norm!" She screamed. She jumped on top of him grasping his head lifting it up to her. "Stop this shit! ... Stop this goddamn shit right now!" She dropped his head.

It hammered onto the floor. His eyes opened and he coughed.

No dead fly.

He gazed at her questionably with his own green eyes, rubbing his head. "Fuck my head hurts," he mumbled. "Is there a reason you are sitting on my chest?"

"Yes."

"Do I want to know?"

"No."

He coughed again.

Still no dead fly.

Marty forced a smirk, clambering off him. He was himself again.

He sat himself up. "Bet you didn't know our house has a room ..." He coughed again holding his throat. "God my throat is sore ..." He searched Marty's eyes sensing there was more going on here than he knew.

Her mask was impenetrable.

He started over. "Bet you didn't know our house has a room just for the fuse panel?"

'Oh Norm I know ... Believe me I know!' Marty shook her head back and forth no.

He brought himself to a stand. "It didn't have a door ... But now it does." He right sided the stool.

"I guess that is a good thing then?"

"Yes."

He put his arm around her. "Are you alright?"

'Me? ... Am I all right? ... You are honestly asking me if I am all right? ... Really? ... Cause you're the one that went down into the basement after supper, came back up, hung over the front railing for a half hour, sat staring at the kitchen cupboards for double that time, went back down and came back around midnight like the stuff of horror movies ... Then downed scalding hot chocolate, not once, but three times ... Stared at my neck like you were going to squeeze the life out of me ... Coughed up a dead friggin' fly? ... Had eyes that went all black then all white? ... And kept on saying the same two-asshole sentences? ... And whatever else you did!'

"Yes," she said barely above a whisper. "Are you?"

"Of course." He gave her a hug.

214

"Okay, then." She started to leave the kitchen. *'Holy Christ! ... What the hell is going on in this house?'*

"Hey! Where you going? ... I thought we were going to play a board game with the kids?" Norm rubbed his head again.

She stopped in her tracks, about faced and marched back in the kitchen. "Look at the time!" She pointed to the kitchen clock. "It's after one a.m. I have to get the kids off to bed. The beggars are still up watching television."

"What did you just say?"

She shortened it. "I've got to get the kids to bed. It's after one."

"Are you kidding me?"

"No."

"Shit! ... How can it be after one?"

"It just is."

"Was I in the basement that long?"

"For the most part, yes."

"Really?"

"Yes." He was totally and completely Norm again. She blew out a sigh of relief. "You came back up hours after you got the stuff from the toolbox."

"Hours?"

"Yes," Marty confirmed.

"How many?"

"Five."

They climbed the stairs together.

The small thing sat up on its hind legs watching them from on top of the wooden box.

Sunday

"Wow, look at this thing!" Eric picked up the old wooden box. He shook the dead flies off it onto the floor.

"Mom can I have this?" He yelled.

"Have what?" Marty was in the kitchen fishing through the cupboards.

"This box." He turned it over in his hands.

"Box? ... You want a box?" She smiled; she found what she was searching for.

"Yeah."

"Sure ...What-ever." She started replacing the kitchen light bulbs. Every one of them had blown over night.

Eric rushed out of the dining room and up the stairs.

He shoved the box under his bed.

The small thing scampered after him.

 # Wednesday

Eric and Stu bounded up the stairs two at a time. They had skipped school right after lunch break. They chased one another down the hall into Eric's bedroom slamming the door behind them.

Eric's sisters had dental checkups this particular afternoon, his mom would be with them, and his dad was at work. The stage was set. A completely empty house for himself and his new best friend Stu Williams.

"Come on! ... Give it up!" Stu yelled. He'd been waiting since Eric had phoned him the past Sunday telling him about it. He could not hold on any longer.

Eric and Stu jumped onto the bed. Stu examined the space ships that dangled from the ceiling as Eric pulled the box from under the bed.

"This is what you brought me here to see?" Disappointment rang through his words. "I guess I'll go to the mall."

"No ... Wait!" He brushed off the coating of dead flies, sitting the box on the floor between them.

The small thing scurried from under Eric's bed to beside the nightstand.

They both slid snake like off the bed onto the floor, kneeling in identical poses, directly across from one another. They pulled up their hoodies and clasp one another's hands.

There they remained, silent, still, before the box as if they had been embalmed as hours passed and the small thing darted about the room.

As if caught up in a sudden wind the bedroom door whipped open, back lashing into the wall, denting in the plaster with an exact replica of the doorknob.

Their hands unclasped.

The small thing scurried behind Stu unnoticed.

Stu snapped forward, then backward, forward then back again as if he was made of springs.

He coughed up a dead fly.

He leaned into the box detailing it. The ornate carvings, the tones of the aged wood, the red-waxed coat of arms, the heavily waxed seams, the silver padlock. "Wow!" he said.

Eric was sitting stark upright, his chest heaving in shaky stops and starts. He spit something dark from his mouth into the garbage can.

Stu peered at Eric "Want to open it?"

"Hell ... Yeah!" Eric retorted.

They sprang from the room, galloping down the hall and stairs, through the kitchen into the back porch. They rifled through Eric's dad's toolbox, fetching a hammer, vice grips and knives.

Stu swiped off the thick layer of flies and picked up the box, shaking it. "What d'ya think is inside?" He rolled it over in his hands.

"Don't know ... But ... We're going to find out!" Eric plucked up the hammer and handed it to Stu. "I've seen my dad do this, lots of times." He clamped the vice grips onto the padlock. "Okay ..." Eric's words broke off as he coughed up something the size of a pea. He spit it in the general direction of the garbage can. "Okay," he repeated, "Hit it!"

Stu tapped the lock.

"Hit it hard ... You asshole!"

Stu swung the hammer.

"Keep doing it till it breaks!"

Stu used both hands on the hammer, smashing at the lock until it fell to the floor.

Eric ran his fingers along the waxed edges. "Wonder why someone did this?" He threw a knife to Stu.

They worked together skinning off the wax. When done, they dug their fingers under the lid edge pulling together.

The lid held steadfast.

Stu twirled the box in his hands. "Think the wax is on the inside too?"

Eric shrugged, lifting his gaze to Stu.

They held one another's eyes feeling like pirates about to open a bounty.

"Wait a sec ... I got an idea ... Put your knife right here." Eric pointed to the right front corner of the box. "Shove it in as far as you can." He picked up the hammer beating on the knife.

The lid emitted crackles and pops.

"Turn the knife! ... Turn the knife!" Eric shrieked.

The lid burst open.

The smells of musk, urine, decay, and jasmine permeated the air, wafting in and out like waves coming ashore.

Their stomachs flipped threatening to spew out their contents. They cupped their noses. The smell was the worst thing they had ever encountered in their lives. They gave one another a thumb up as the small thing snatched the long dead carcass from the box unnoticed and ran under the bed with it.

They peered into the box itemizing the contents. Four wheat pennies, a small granite statue, an old yellowed linen handkerchief, a wooden puzzle piece, a goblet, a skeleton key, a dried rosebud and two locks of hair; one blonde and one dark, the dark bound with a cord. A small envelope was pinned to the top of the lid. 'Simple Gifts' penned in blue ink across the front.

Stu unfastened the envelope; turned it over; scratched off the red thumb print wax seal with his knife; pulled out the card and read it aloud to Eric. "To Isabelle: here in lies 'Simple Gifts', best regards Howard."

Stu and Eric both looked at one other scrunching up their faces in disgust.

"This guy gave her all this shit!" Stu stuffed the card back into the envelope. He fingered all the contents, picking up and putting down the wheat pennies several times. He held his hand to his mouth coughing then shoved the same hand into his pocket. "What a crappy ass gift!"

He glanced at Eric's bedside clock.

His eyes abruptly widened.

"Four-thirty p.m.? ... Holy shit!" He jumped to his feet. "I'm going to catch hell for being late coming home from school." He laughed whole heartily.

"Yeah right," Eric said.

The two shared a high five.

"See you tomorrow." Stu flew down the stairs and out of the house, bounding across the snowed in front lawn. He jogged down the shoulder of the road, veering off just in time to avoid Eric's mom and two sisters approaching from the opposite direction in their vehicle.

Eric picked up each of the articles examining them thoroughly. The two wheat pennies, the granite statue, the linen handkerchief, the puzzle piece, the goblet, the key, the rosebud, the two locks of hair. He pulled the note from the envelope, re-read it, shoved it back in upside down and re-pinned it to the top.

He suddenly heard the slamming of car doors.

They were home.

He snapped down the lid, ran out of his room and down the hall carrying the box. He darted up and down the hall suddenly stopping at the linen closet. It seemed like the perfect place to hide it. He reefed opened the closet door, throwing it up and in behind some boxes.

The small thing scurried along the hall, flattened itself out, and went underneath the linen closet door.

Thursday Morning

Eric's class was informed about the premature death of their classmate Steward Howard Williams, Stu to everyone.

He had been rushed to the hospital the night before and had passed away.

Nothing more was said.

But it could have ... An awful lot more could have been said ... Like ... How during his supper he'd suddenly coughed up an entire handful of dead flies ... Or ... How after retiring to his room, something invisible had levitated him from his bed by more than three feet ... Or ... How he'd been hung in mid-air and rotated slowly and purposefully six times ... Or ... How his limbs had all stiffened, morphing his body into the shape of a cross ... Or ... How he had spun in the air so rapidly he'd been nothing but a blur ... Or ... How his body had whipped and smashed on and off the walls and ceiling so many times every bone in his being had broken ... Or ... That both his eyeballs were missing from the sockets and replaced with wheat pennies ... Or ... That his spattered blood on the walls, floor, and ceiling had coagulated and formed into what looked like wording in ancient Hebrew.

The rest of the school day for Stu's classmates was spent waiting on wooden benches outside the counselling offices.

The topic of the day? ... Dealing with death.

Thursday Night

Valerie's bedside clock flashed three-thirty-three a.m.

She sat bolt upright.

Her eyes opened, blackened, rounded, and stared non-blinkingly.

She folded the covers back, swung her feet over the edge of the bed, and stood. She walked stiffly down the hallway, one bare foot in front of the other, toe to heel, shoulders back, chest out swinging both arms in unison. She stopped at her parent's bedroom door, turned the knob and entered. She positioned herself at the bottom of the bed, direct centre and stood statuesque.

At, the first rays of daylight she about faced and returned to her room.

# Tuesday One Week Later

Marty stood on the porch, front door open, arms folded across her chest, hands pulled into her sweater, waiting for the sounds of the school bus engine.

It was exactly four weeks to the day to Christmas.

There was but a few boxes left to unpack and all would be said and done. She was hoping the missing Christmas decorations were among them. If not, the family would be buying a cheap tree and making paper ornaments. The move had been more costly than they had expected, even with the movers unclaimed bonus for relocating them to this address, for reasons unbeknown.

She stepped back into the foyer, the wind had come up, and it had started to snow. She zipped up her sweater turning in a complete circle taking in the ornate decor of the house. At first, she had enjoyed the solitude of being alone in the home investigating its idiosyncratic nature.

Then it had started.

There were bangs, thunks, and scratching coming from within the walls. There was something she never saw but constantly heard scurrying around the second floor hallway. There were shadows of objects they did not own and other shadows in places there should not be any. Pictures came off the wall, possessions crashed to the floor. The entire family were having horrid nightmares. Doors slammed shut then reopened. Water turned on in the sinks and bathtubs. And entire rooms worth of light bulbs would explode all at once. The covers from everyone's beds were on the floors each morning, always draped identical to one another. Roger refused to go up to the third floor and when on the second he would sit and growl up at the far corner of the ceiling foaming at the mouth. Monica's hamster ran backwards in her wheel every afternoon at preciously three-thirty-three p.m. to three-thirty-four p.m. squealing like she was being tortured. The power flickered continually. Then there was the family, Norm, Valerie, and Eric. Norm with his odd behaviour the evening he had repaired the furnace, and not remembering any of it. Valerie sleepwalking, she had been finding her all over the house at night banging on the walls. Eric who kept coughing up little black bits of something he would not show anyone.

Everyone in the household seemed predisposed and not themselves. When she had confided in Norm, all and everything with the exception of himself, he had said it was just adjusting to the new home. It was old and large and all houses had their idiosyncrasies. Their conversation had ended there. However, not once had he looked her in the eye while talking ... Was he hiding something? ... Even lying perhaps? ... She thought so.

The whine of the bus engine and air brakes broke off her thoughts.

Marty could see two heads bobbing up and down through the tops of the bushes. Valerie was invisible. Roger darted from between her legs running at them. She smiled waiting for the screams. He always jumped up on them and knocked them down. She was not disappointed.

Monica and Eric rushed past her into the foyer, throwing off their coats and boots. Valerie stood like a newly cemented figurine on the front lawn, face tilted upward, eyes strained on the top row of windows.

"Valerie? ... What on earth are you doing?" Marty chewed her bottom lip out of exasperation. "Get in the house!"

Valerie remained as she was.

"Now!"

Valerie slowly turned her head fixating on her mother's eyes.

"Now!" Marty repeated. She returned her daughter's gaze. There was something different about her eyes. Something off, dark and unnerving.

Valerie shook her head back and forth no.

Marty went off the porch into the snow in her slippers.

"Come on," she grabbed hold of one of Valerie's mitted hands.

"I'd rather stay out here mom," she said lifelessly.

"What?"

"I'd rather stay out here mom," she repeated verbatim.

"Why?"

"I don't like that house."

Marty firmed her grip on her daughter's mitted hand, inching her forward. She carefully picked out some of Norm's words about the house. "It's too new yet ... You'll settle in ... You'll see."

Valerie planted her feet. She went up on her tiptoes. "We're all going to die ... He opened the box," she whispered.

"What?" She gazed at her daughter, dumbfounded lines digging into her forehead.

Valerie pulled free from her mother's grip leaving her with the mitt. She rushed ahead into the house.

Marty rolled Valerie's words over in her head. *'We're all going to die ... He opened the box.'* It did not make any sense. She shook the snow off her slippers closing the front door behind her. *'We're all going to die ... He opened the box?'*

Wednesday

Monica and Eric soared through the air in the entranceway, dropping, toppling on the floor in a tangled up heap of arms and legs. They had perfected the art of riding the banister.

They both scrambled to their feet running full tilt at Marty, banging into her and knocking her off balance.

"Mom! ... Mom! ... I want to change rooms with Eric!" Monica hooked her arm into her mother's turning them both in circles.

"No ... It's mine!" Eric blurted. He started to chase his sister round his mother.

"Come on ... I want that one!"

Marty caught them both by the arms. "Hold on guys. What is the problem here? There are plenty of rooms upstairs," she said. "More than plenty," she added as an afterthought.

She turned to Monica. "Why on earth have you decided you want Eric's room all of a sudden? You were all given a choice and you chose the one you have, if you remember?"

"I know, but his is in the corner and has lots of windows. And it's the furthest away from the linen closet."

"What is wrong with being near the linen closet, might I ask?"

"It keeps me awake at night."

Marty's eyebrows rose. "It keeps you awake?"

"Yes."

"The linen closet keeps you awake?"

"Yes."

"Should I even ask?" Marty's eyes narrowed.

"Mom ... It makes all kind of noises at night." Monica folded her arms across her chest mimicking a gesture of defiance.

"The closet makes noises?"

Monica nodded her head. "Yes it does. It's like something that's not happy is living in there."

"Pardon?"

"Something that's not happy is living in there." She confirmed her statement by pursing her lips together and nodding.

"Okay and just for my curiosity's sake. How do you know there is something living in the linen closet?"

"'Cause noises come from it like bangs and thumps and stuff. And the door opens and closes all the time."

"And ... Just to further. This thing that bangs and thumps and stuff is not happy ... Because?"

"It growls and hisses and does other things."

"Other things?"

"Yeah other things ... You know other stuff." Monica looked at Eric. "He knows!" She pointed at him, mouthing *'It's all your goddamn fault.'*

If Monica had said anything else about the house, she would have been right there on the same page. But ... *'Something living in the linen closet? ... The linen closet?'*

Marty turned to Eric. "Have you heard any of this? ... Well?"

He looked down at the floor scuffing his feet back and forth, not saying a word.

"Jesus Christ," she muttered. She pointed to the stairs. "March!"

Eric grabbed his coat and boots hurriedly putting them on watching his mother and sister climb the stairs. He rushed through the front door out onto the lawn busying himself making a snowman. Shit was about to hit the fan.

Marty and Monica stood side by side directly in front of the linen closet. The smell emanating was foul, nauseating as if something dead had been left lying out in the warm sun for days.

Monica pulled her sweater up over her nose.

"Holy Hell," Marty fanned the repugnant air back and forth in disgust. She cupped her nose with her hand.

Monica stared directly into her mother's eyes, holding them.

"You forgot to mention the smell." Marty said through her fingers.

"It didn't smell before." Monica muffled.

"I see ... Okay then," Marty muttered. "Shall we ..." She turned the knob. The door popped free of the latch. The stench worsened.

They both took a step back.

Marty took a huge gulp of air, held her breath, and jerked the door open.

Boxes tumbled all over the floor.

She gazed at her daughter then back at boxes. *'Holy hell kid!'*

It looked like a landmine had gone off in the closet, and the stench ... The ungodly, putrid, gut retching stench. She eyeballed the closet. The linens were stained brownish red and hanging off the light, the towels were soiled like someone had used them to wipe mud off their shoes and were all heaped up in a pile in the back corner, the bedding was in compact rolls like camping gear. Most of the boxes contents were scattered, smashed, and appeared as if someone had attempted to grind it into the floor.

"Eric! ... Valerie!" She yelled, "Get the hell up here! ... Now! ... Shit! ... What the hell have the three of you been doing up in here? ... Playing dodge ball, and shitting, and pissing in the closet? ... This is utterly disgusting!"

Monica turned to run.

"Don't you dare young lady ... You stay right goddamn here!" She tented her hands over her mouth. "Eric! ... Valerie! ... I am not kidding around! ... Get damn well up here! ... And I mean now!" She screamed.

Eric could hear his mom yelling from inside the house. She had opened that door.

He dawdled into the house taking as long as he could. He kicked off his boots and threw his winter clothes into the corner. He climbed the stairs one by one.

His mother was on her hands and knees pulling unrecognizable pieces of things from the closet, dry retching as she went.

Monica was standing directly behind her, legs vibrating so hard her knees were clacking.

"Yes mom." He exchanged a quick glance with his sister.

Marty gave him a death stare. "And where is your little sister?"

He reaffirmed his footing attempting to appear nonchalant. He lifted his shoulders up and down. "Don't know."

"You don't know?"

He shook his head so fast he lost his balance and crashed into Monica.

Marty went up on her knees. "Valerie!" She yelled.

Nothing.

"Whatever, I'll deal with the two of you first!"

Eric and Monica's foreheads wrinkled in fear. They had never seen their mother this angry, ever. Their eyes zoomed back and forth like a bolt of white lightening, to one another, their mother, and the closet.

"I want an explanation!"

Monica jerked her head up and to the side, silently signalling for Eric to say something ... Anything.

Eric chewed at the inside of his cheek.

Monica gave him another head jerk.

"We didn't do anything ... Mom," he said quietly.

"Don't you dare lie to me!" Marty slowly rolled her eyes over her son. "Well?"

He shook his head no. "I'm not ... Mom ... It's what Monica said."

"So I am supposed to believe that something is living in here and that whatever is supposedly living in here according to you both," she shot a look between them. "Is not happy and did all this?"

Eric and Monica nodded in perfect unison.

"So where is this thing?"

"Don't know mom." Monica mumbled. "It's not there all the time."

"Jesus Christ." Marty grabbed a wooden box dragging it out of the closet.

Vomit rose in the back of her throat.

She cupped her nose and mouth with one hand, fanning the air with the other. "My good god this thing stinks!" She muffled. "What in the hell is in this?" She brushed off the coating of dead flies from the top.

Monica and Eric went down on their knees.

Marty was already on hers.

The kneeled side by side by side, lifeless, as if frozen in time and space.

The small thing carted off the day old carcass from the box.

Hours passed.

Mucus coated dead flies dribbled out from the corners of their mouths, down their chins and onto the floor.

The small thing watched and then scurried into one of the toppled boxes.

Suddenly, as if a finger had snapped signalling the end, they re-animated picking up exactly where they left off without skipping a beat.

"I don't remember this thing," she mumbled. Her throat was dry. She scraped her teeth backward over a tongue that felt like used up sandpaper. She felt as if she had, had her mouth open for hours and hours.

She ran her hand back and forth across the top of the box swishing off the dead flies.

Eric and Monica shared a quick glance, both silently sneaking backwards.

"Stay! ... Right! ... Damn! ... Here!" She knew they were trying to creep off. She would have too if she were them.

They stopped dead in their tracks.

Marty examined the box. The lid was gouged and scuffed round all the edges ... Newly gouged and scuffed. The metal latch was bent and scraped and sported hammer dents. The wax ceilings were separated.

She sat it back down. "Would either of you two, care to explain this?"

"You said I could have it." Eric garbled to the back of her head.

"What? ... When?"

"It was the day after dad fixed the furnace ... Remember?"

"No. I don't remember, enlighten me."

"You were in the kitchen fixing the lights and I asked if I could have a box."

She did not remember. She did not remember anything, the box, him asking or anything else. The fixing of lights in the house had become a daily mainstay. They were always blowing. "What's in it? ... Something dead?" She fanned the air again.

"I don't know," he looked down at the floor, trying to conceal the lie.

"Eric! ... I am in no mood for horseshit! ... Let's try this again ...What's in it?"

"Not much mom," he said a hair above a whisper.

"Should I even look?"

Eric shrugged.

Marty sucked her lips into her mouth tilting her head back and forth re-examining the box. Curiosity got the better of her and she reached out for it.

It whisked away from her hand as if it had been lying in wait, anticipating ... It rotated and flipped on its side.

Marty pulled her hand back to her chest guarding it with the other.

The box rocked back and forth mockingly, and then whipped across the floor, smashing into the wall, up ending and opening, spewing out all its contents. 'Four wheat pennies, a small granite statue, an old yellowed linen handkerchief , a wooden puzzle piece, a goblet, a skeleton key, a dried rosebud and two locks of hair; one blonde and one dark, the dark bound with a cord.' A small envelope pinned to the lid flapped back and forth like it was caught up in a breeze that wasn't there.

Marty's eyes ringed in white and glued onto the box. Her mouth dropped open, rounded and hung off centre.

She wrung her hands round one another.

She turned, flicking her eyes over her children, petrified was not even close to what was etched in their faces.

She used her hand to close her mouth. She wet her lips with her tongue. She had to say something ... Anything ... For them.

"I knocked with my hand." Her voice was two octaves higher than normal. "I knocked it," she said reaffirming her first statement.

She knew she hadn't.

They knew she hadn't.

Monica and Eric cemented themselves to her sides.

She tucked her legs up underneath her body.

They copied.

They ever so slowly crawled towards the box in stops and starts resembling a dyslexic crab with three heads.

She removed the envelope.

"Sim ... ple ... gif ... fts," she squeaked. She cleared her throat on purpose. "Simple ... Gift ... Gifts," she said again. The squeak was still there but minimal this time. She felt like she was a few fries short of a happy meal.

She removed the card. "To Isabelle; here in lies 'Simple Gifts', best regards Howard." She cleared her throat again.

She unglued Monica and Eric.

Four over size eyeballs gawked at her.

She forced a half-assed smile that resembled more a grimace than anything else. Monica's two words were front and center inside her head, bouncing around like greased up rubber balls. *'He knows ... He knows ... He* knows ...' She withdrew her half-assed smile. '*Just what did he know?*'

She fixated on Eric. '*He knows ... He knows.*'

He opened his mouth his tongue flopped out.

"What do you know about this thing?" Marty murmured.

Eric sucked his tongue back into his mouth. '*There is was ... The question ... That question.*'

He shook his head frantically back and forth.

Marty did not say a word. She watched the beads of sweat drip down from his forehead. She didn't further. She scanned the floor, and then went about picking up the articles slow and carefully as if they were made of glass. She used only the fingertips of her one hand to place them back into the box.

She was still coddling the one she had reached for it with earlier. She closed the lid. She had no idea what it was, why it was, what it stood for, what it meant, where it came from, or why it stunk worse than a two day old road kill underneath the summer sun.

She brought herself to a stand using the wall.

She tucked the box under her arm. All the time feeling as if it was made of cheap after-market rubber.

She pointed to the boxes. "Pick up all this shit," she muttered.

She skated her socked feet along the hallway toward the landing.

The sounds of them scuttling along the wood plank floor echoed through the hallway.

She stopped and turned.

They were still on their hands and knees like baby zombies learning their way in the world.

"After you pick it up, pile it all neatly back in the closet, the way it was before it was totaled."

"But ... But ... It ... It ...Wasn't us ... Us mom." Monica's voice pitched and shook.

Marty forced another slice of a smile.

She hadn't said it was them. She had just said to clean it up. The box was still rotating and flipping around in her head. She so wanted to appear normal to her two children praying even a small sliver of it would rub off.

She held up her hands in the standard mom pose. *'This was an easy safe remedy. Not a good one, but would do. It was like putting a kid size band-aid on an open wound that required twenty stitches.'*

"I don't want to hear anymore ... Just do it! ... When you're done go to your rooms."

"I don't want to go in my room. It's too close to the closet." Monica's eyes brimmed with tears.

Monica was there, with the closet thing again. She needed to put the closet thing to bed. Pretend if need be that there was no linen closet. Never was, never will be.

She watched them crawling towards the mess. "Damn it to hell! Both of you have feet! Get up!"

They used one another to stand.

Monica slowly started swishing stuff into one of the boxes. "You're ...You're not going to put that ... That ... Stinking box back in the closet, are you mom? ... I just ... Just can't be close to the closet with it in there ... I don't think ... Think I can be close to the closet without it in there either ... Something does live in there mom."

Marty sighed heavily on purpose. "Monica, if you want a different room by all means go for it. But you cannot have Eric's! And ... And you can damn well move everything yourself."

Monica pointed at her mother. "Are you putting that ... That back in the closet?"

"For Christ's sake!" Marty turned and started walking.

"Are you mom?" Monica yelled.

Marty untucked the box from under her arm and held it up in the air so Monica could see it.

"But are you mom?" Her tears were running in rivers down her face wetting the neckband of her sweater.

"No!" Marty yelled.

She switched the box to the other arm. It suddenly felt hot, extremely so as if it was about to catch fire. "I don't like this thing," she said. "I don't like this thing at all. I don't know why, but I don't." She forced a laugh. "I'm lying ...Yes I do, know why," she added. She headed for the staircase.

The small thing followed.

Monica swiped her face back and forth on her sweater sleeve drying it. She tapped her brother on the shoulder. "Will you help me move my stuff, after we're done here?"

"Yeah, I guess."

Monica sat the box on the kitchen counter ... The box that moved out of her grasp then flew all by itself across the hallway ... The box that no one is saying a single solitary thing about. The box she surmised all of them, herself included, wished they had never laid eyes on.

They had all watched it go across the hall, smash into the wall and open, spitting out its bizarre contents.

They all, she was sure, wished they hadn't.

She gulped almost choking on the excess saliva that had pooled under her tongue. *'Oh dear Lord ...What the hell is going on in this house?'*

She went over to the sink, pulled up her sweatshirt sleeve, ran the cold water, and stuck her arm under. Her flesh looked charred. She grabbed the margarine from the refrigerator slathering it top to bottom. *'Just fucking great! ... My one arm feels like it is made of rubber, my other one feels burnt to a crisp ... Fucking Hell! ... I'm swearing ... I'm fucking swearing! ... My fucking goddamn thoughts are fucking swearing! ... Fuck me!'*

"Okay ... Now ...Valerie...Where the hell are you?" she said.

She looked over her shoulder at the box.

Cold chills shot up and down her spine. Her nose dripped blood. *'Fuck off box! ... You quit the fucking shit too! ... Jesus Christ! ... I'm losing it here.'* She grabbed a tissue and wiped her nose. *'At least it's not goddamn flies coming out of it.'* She wiped it again.

She left the kitchen, stopped, and peeped around the doorframe at the box.

It was as she had left it.

She darted through the ground floor of the manor yelling for Valerie.

It was almost dark.

She could hear Monica and Eric chattering from the second floor.

She searched the house floor by floor coming up empty.

She made her way back to the kitchen.

The box was gone.

She snapped her eyes shut.

Counted to six and reopened them slow and purposeful.

Still gone.

She ruffled her hair with her hands. *'Fuck! ... Fuck! ... Fuck!... Lord, I need help! ... I so need help! ... Please, please help me ... I'm all fucked up.'* She stood, arms open wide, looking upwards, waiting for a sign ... None came. *'Okay then lord ... Where ever it is ... It is*

... Out of sight ... Out of mind ... And Lord fuck you! ... The bible says ask for help and you will abide ... What was that a fucking misprint?'

She left the kitchen.

"Valerie! ... Valerie? "She shrieked." Come on kid! ... Where the hell are you?"

Nothing.

She pulled on her boots, opened the front door, and stepped out.

A snowman without a head wearing Norm's scarf stood on the front lawn. *'Eric's work.'*

She traipsed around the house ending up at the east side.

She stood motionless, eyeballs clicked on zoom, focusing, and refocusing on the basement steps with the wide open door.

"Valerie?" she said. "Valerie? ... You down there?" *'Please God do not let her be down there ... Please ... Please ... Pretty Please.'* "Valerie?" she said again.

She descended the steps one by one; arms stretched wide, hands trailing the stone.

A third of the way, her one boot tab caught and hooked on the other. She teetered, lost her balance, bashed the back of her right hand on stone wall, and went down. She tobogganed on her back, picking up more than enough momentum to jump the rise at the doorway, allowing her to slide right on through the basement and smash feet first into the back wall.

The basement was dark ... Pitch dark ... Hubs of hell pitch dark.

She rolled onto her stomach, and then crawled in circles trying to find her bearings attempting the impossible. The darkness was total and absolute.

She stood, waving her arms above her head feeling for a pull cord. "Jesus, fucking hell! ... Come on will you!"

Something dabbed into her hair.

She smirked fingering the cord. She pulled it without hesitation. The light snapped and popped, coming to life dousing her with a hollow ghost like glow.

Something faint and delicate caught her ear. It was as if the air was whispering to her.

"Valerie? ... Is that you honey?" *'Please let that be you ... Please don't let it be something that isn't you ... Please ... Please ... I'm having so much trouble with my head today, so much trouble Valerie ... It's just fucked my darling ... From flying boxes to setting something down, that isn't set down any longer... Please ... Please ... Let this little noise be you.'*

Marty moved along the wall pulling the light cords as she went. She halted examining the cement wall with the gaping hole.

Marty leaned into the opening. "Valerie? ... You in here kiddo?" It was just dark enough in there for the shadows and other dark things to skulk off into the corners unnoticed.

She stepped through the opening, her boots crunching down on something that sounded like 'Rice Crispy Cereal.'

She peered through the darkness. "What the hell?" She muttered.

A small obscured figure sat centred in the room.

She ever so slowly reached and touched it with one finger.

Warmth ... It was warm ... *'Thank you God for this one, at least.'*

The small thing snatched up the maggot-filled carcass moving into the shadows with it.

"Valerie?" She put her hand on its shoulder. "Valerie," she said again. *'It had to be Valerie ... Who else could it be? ... Don't you fucking dare answer yourself Marty ... Don't you dare!'*

She gently placed her hand on the shoulder of the figure. *'Hair ... Soft ... Curly ... Long Hair.'* It was her daughter.

She grasped her shoulder.

Valerie face planted.

Dead flies fell from her mouth unnoticed.

Marty scooped her up in her arms, tiptoeing backward for reasons she did not understand.

Valerie's arms and legs flopped to the sides like a rag doll needing stuffing. A lot of stuffing. Her head lulled back. Two wheat pennies fell from her hand to the floor.

A pungent odour bit into Marty's nostrils. An all too familiar odour.

Vomit rose to the back of her throat, halting and threatening to bubble over into her mouth like a too full pot.

She looked down at the floor.

'The box ... That box ... That goddamn fucked up box, that had fucked her up ... Was there ... Right there ... Right fucking there ... Valerie had not been spared keeping company with it ... Fuck!'

Marty held Valerie tight to her chest, twisted round, crossed the room, climbed through the hole, running the length of the basement, up the stairs, and into the house.

The basement light bulbs all exploded in rapid succession about the same time Marty slammed the front house door shut and locked it. The basement now was as before, the way it should be, the way it liked it best, silent and black, oblivious to the rest of the house. Its cement room with the gaping hole in one of its walls with the crunchy carpeting of glass, dead flies, red pentagrams, and hieroglyphics were left undisturbed and solely onto its self to view over and over again at its leisure ... After all ... Not a thing was going anywhere ... Unlike the box which was no longer there.

Marty laid Valerie down on the sofa covering her with blankets. She searched through the kitchen drawers for the smelling salts. She grabbed the counter steadying herself as she kicked out one leg bending at the waist like an obtuse ballerina searching the bottom drawer.

Her hand slid and nudged something hard. *'Please ... Please ... No ... No ... No.'* She slowly lifted her head doing face time with the box.

Time stopped.

She remained as she was, as if a trial item for a time capsule, leg extended, fingers gripping the counter, eyeballs the size of grapes, tongue clenched between her teeth .

Hours passed.

Suddenly she blinked, coming back to life.

She searched through the bottom drawer and the next and next. No smelling salts.

She fetched a cloth, wet it under the cold water, and ran into the living room. Valerie was curled up on the sofa sound asleep with Roger, television blaring away with outdated cartoons, open pizza boxes on the floor.

The mantel clock chimed once denoting the half hour. She eyed it, picked it up, and shook it. Something was wrong with it. It read two-thirty.

She sauntered into the main floor hall. The house was quiet and still.

She went up to the second floor checking in on Monica and Eric, stopping at the linen closet on her way. She ripped open the door. Her eyes ticked over the contents, bedding, linens, and boxes; all neat, tidy ... The precise way she had put it there. A vein of frost crept up her leg and lodged into the base of her spine making her shudder.

She darted down the hall into Eric's room. He was sound asleep, bedside lamp on, video game controller on his chest, homework scattered about the floor.

She backtracked to Monica's room.

It was empty.

"Oh God Monica!" she screamed. "Where are you? ... Monica?" Her words bounced off the walls and ceiling coming back at her like they had been fired from a slingshot. "Monica!" she screamed again.

Monica popped her head out from around a doorframe at the end of the hall. "Yes mom."

"What happened to your room?"

"What do you mean?"

Marty rushed down the hall to where her daughter was.

The room was all done up, painted, curtains up, bed made, pictures and mirrors hanging. "How did you do this?"

"What do you mean?"

"Your room is moved ... And ... And it's perfect."

"Mom you are confusing me."

Marty's eyebrows lifted. *'She was confusing her daughter? ... Really? ... Monica was the one standing at the opposite end of the hall in a space so picture perfect it should have been in a magazine.'* Marty's mouth opened and hung like an unclosed gate.

"Mom, you did say I could move my room remember?"

She stared at her daughter, she did not remember.

"You said I could right after Eric and I put the linen closet back together."

"Linen closet? What was wrong with the linen closet?"

"Mom ... Quit fooling around ...You were so happy with the linen closet ... You sent Eric and I out for pizza and milk and stuff so dad could paint it. Then after we all had the pizza you and dad put my new room together."

"Store? ... Your dad and I? ... Milk and stuff? ... Pizza?" Marty ran her tongue across her lips wetting them, they felt as if they were going to crack and break off. "Your dad's not home from work yet. What are you talking about?"

"Mom it's three a.m."

"What?"

"Its three a.m." *'The mantel clock had chimed two-thirty.'*

"Say again?"

"It's three mom."

"It wasn't me," Marty mumbled. She felt like her mouth was full of cotton batten.

"Who was it then? ... Dad and your double?"

Marty stared at her daughter like she had just beamed down to earth.

"Mom quit joking around ... You're creeping me out." Monica hopped onto her bed.

"Goodnight." She slowly turned and started down the hall. "It wasn't me," she said again. *'What the fuck*

Lord? ... Now I have a fucking double. ... Where the hell am I living? ... In a horror movie?'

The Following Saturday

Marty and Norm stood, out in the snow, gazing up at the turret, the one and only one with a double rectangle window right at the top.

"You sure there's no more boxes?" Norm said, still staring up at the double window.

"Nope, not a one."

"Christ," he muttered.

"All our Christmas decorations, just gone." Marty kicked at the snow. The decorations had been family heirlooms.

"Did you ever get a hold of the moving company?"

"The phone company said the number's not in service any longer."

"Really?"

"Yes, really."

Norm cast an eye over the front lawn with the seven lop sided snowmen wearing all his winter scarves, gloves, and hats. "Not unless they're under the ..."

She cut him off. "Under the snow? I am way ahead of you. The kids and I already dug through it. No boxes."

He looked back up at the turret. "You know ... I don't get it. No inside staircase to the top of that thing." He punctuated his sentence with an upward head jerk in the direction of it. "I'd bet a million there's probably stuff stored up in there ... Maybe even Christmas decorations."

"Why would someone store stuff in a place you can't get into?"

"Maybe you could once."

"I suppose I guess. There are windows to look out of."

He gave her a sideways glance.

"Well sweetheart," she slipped her hand into his. "If there is anything up in there, as you say, it will be up there forever."

"I beg to differ, there's that window."

She glanced up at the window and then back at him, full well knowing what he was suggesting. "Are you out of your goddamn mind?"

He smiled, let go of her hand and put his arm around her. "Could be all kinds of treasures up in there and if we're extra lucky Christmas things as well. You never know. People do keep that kind of shit in attics?" He tucked her hand inside his shoving them both into his pocket.

"It's not an attic."

"Close enough."

"What you going to do? Scale the wall like 'Spiderman?'"

He chuckled. "I was thinking ladder."

"We don't have a long enough ladder."

"Rental city does." He needed to get up in there. It was all he had been thinking about for over two weeks.

"You phoned?" She could not help but smile. As long as she had known him, he had always tried to make her world a better place. She knew he was doing it for her. Christmas was so close. Moreover, just maybe on the off chance he was right, the house would feel like the holidays, instead of thrift store finds.

"Want to come for the ride? I'll buy you a coffee and a donut on the way back."

"A donut too? ... You trying to bribe me?"
"Yes ... Yes I am."

 # Saturday Afternoon

"Think it will reach?" Marty eye balled the metal extension ladder laid full out in the snow.

"There's only one way to find out." Norm flipped the ladder on its side.

"Wait hon, I'll get the kids to help us."

Marty hopped up onto the front porch, yelling the children's names in stops and starts.

Two appeared one didn't.

Monica, Eric, and Marty positioned themselves around the ladder according to Norm's instructions.

"Where's Valerie?" Norm tightened his grip on the ladder, swapping glances between Eric and Monica.

"Don't know," Eric mumbled.

Norm brushed it off; she never seemed to be around much anymore, not even for her favourite foods. "Okay, on three ... Ready?"

He glanced at each of them in turn.

They nodded.

"Okay ... One ... Two ... Three!"

The ladder went up effortlessly, the top resting solidly against the bricks a mere few feet from the turrets upper windowsill.

Norm rubbed his hands together. "Perfect! If I do say so myself. Cross your fingers!"

"Come on guys; stand on the bottom rungs to steady it for your dad." Marty directed Eric and Monica via hand signals.

Norm shoved a hammer into his back pocket climbing the ladder slow and purposeful. He held his arm out upon reaching the top tread giving a thumbs up.

He gave the window frame a whack at the bottom corners then shoved on the glass. He peered inside looking for window locks there wasn't any. He pushed upwards, then lifted and pulled.

It didn't budge.

He ran his fingers along the underside of the wood.

Nails ... A department store worth of nails. *There has to be hundreds and hundreds of the suckers. Why would someone go to this kind of trouble with a window so high up in the air?'*

He ran his fingers back and forth underneath the frame slicing off a piece of skin from his thumb in the process.

Blood dripped onto the windowsill, unnoticed by Norm.

The window frame as if it had been waiting, sucked up the blood greedily.

"Okay ... You won't open so I can get in huh? ... We'll have to remedy that now, won't we?" He pulled the hammer free. "I'm damn well talking to myself," he muttered. He adjusted the hammer in his hand smashing through the window glass with one foul swoop.

He crawled through.

Marty backed off the ladder rung, head tilted, eyes glued to the top window. She shielded her eyes from the sun with her arm knocking Valerie in the head.

"Oh you showed up. I am honoured. You are a little late. Don't you think?" She inspected her daughter's head then gave it a rub.

"Dad shouldn't have gone up there," she whispered. "They won't like it ... He cut his thumb ... They'll like that."

Marty repeated her daughter verbatim. "Dad shouldn't have gone up there? ... They won't like it? ... He cut his thumb? ... They will like that?" She gazed at Valerie.

Valerie shook her head slowly back and forth tapping her foot.

Marty felt like she had taken a mentally deficient pill. "Why not? ... Who won't like it? ... How do you know he cut his thumb? He's way up there." She pointed to the turret.

"They won't. And he did. And they will." Valerie said in a flat monotone.

"Who is they?"

Valerie smiled a smile not of a child and started to hum ... Then sing. "Stayed in bed all morning just to pass the time." She animated her hands like a mime, whipping them back and forth, up and down in fancy moves, then raised both thumbs, pointing them inward at her chest. She bobbed her head side-to-side, continuing. "There's something wrong here, there can be no denying." She hummed again. "It's too late baby, now it's too late." She hushed her voice to a whisper, going up on her tiptoes repeating "it's too late baby, now it's too late." She eyed the turret, then her mother, turned and skipped toward the house barely leaving indentations in the snow.

Marty felt as if she was suddenly floating. There but not there.

Time rewound, repeating Valerie singing and humming over and over like an old time record player needle stuck in a scratch. The vision of her daughter accompa-

nied the rewind as if added window dressing. The singing and vision swirled, mixed, turning black and white. *'Here comes the newest sensation of 'Tiny Talent Time ... Give a big hand for Valerie Abbott only seven years of age belting out a pitch perfect rendition of a 'Carole King' song era nineteen-seventy-one '* Marty folded into the snow like a soggy piece of perforated paper. She opened and closed her mouth frog like. She felt like she was trying to find the square root of 'pie' without a calculator.

"Do you need us anymore mom?" Monica was standing staring down at her.

Marty did not answer, instead just cocked her neck side to side as if she just gotten out of bed with a bad kink.

"Do you mom? ... It's cold out here."

Marty shook her head, rolled onto her stomach and went onto her hands and knees, all her limbs felt like kids toy wobble wheels.

"You coming mom?" Monica yelled back behind her.

She caught her brother by the arm spinning him around. "Has mom been drinking?" she whispered. "She's back there crawling through the snow."

He turned giving a quick glance at his mother, smiled and shrugged.

"You're helpful," Valerie chirped.

Marty crept over to the ladder, used the treads to pull herself up, and sat on the bottom rung. She quietly hummed 'Baby it's too late.'

The air swirled and kicked up in miniature dirt devils as Norm moved about the room. "No one's been in here in years," he muttered.

The room was dusty and heavily cobwebbed. In the far corner nestled into the wall stood Victorian era furniture, other than the dust and spider webs it was as perfect as the day it was made. Nothing else was in the room with the exception of some wooden crates up in the rafters.

Norm pulled out a dresser using it as a makeshift stepladder.

All the crates were identical except in size. Each contained a stamp like that of a sailing vessel with the word 'Briarwood' and the numbers eighteen-hundred-thirty-five. Norm set about opening them carefully one by one with the hammer claw. Most contained old linens, nightclothes, handwritten leather bound books and porcelain dishware.

He beamed as he opened the final crate. He had found the mother load ... All things turn of the century Christmas, hand spun glass ornaments, embroidered garlands, milk paint pinecones.

He set it aside and walked over to the window.

Marty looked like a 'Kewpie Doll' from that height.

"Shit that's a long way down," he murmured. *'No one survives the fall ... No one is supposed to,'* teletyped in front of his face. He stepped back. His palms were perspiring profusely.

He looked back over his one shoulder; Then the other. A thread of fear wrapped around his ankle and tied itself in a knot. He whistled a few bars of an old Carole King song 'Baby it's too late.'

He planted his feet apart, braced his hands firmly on the windowsill, and leaned his head out. "We hit pay dirt!" He yelled. His fear thread had unknotted and was now worming its way up his leg. He broadened his stance.

"You found Christmas stuff?"

"Yep!" He pulled his head back in, whistling the same tune again.

He looked over his shoulders again.

He stared at the crate full of Christmas items. "How in hell do I get you down?" he said. He stood and gazed at it pursing his lips. "Pulley system? ... Ropes? ... Carry it? ... I'll figure it out." *'Fucking hell, I'm talking to a box! What the fuck?'* He started shoving the crate across the floor towards the window. It caught up in something. He went down on his hands and knees running his fingers along the floorboards, his fingertips stubbed into the sides of a scuttle door. He shoved the crate out of the way. It had jammed on the handle. "I'll be fucking damned! ... There is a trap door!" he said. He used his fingernails to trace around the four sides. *'Nailed ... Just like the window ... Hundreds of fucking nails.'*

He fetched his hammer setting to work pulling the nails. He whistled the same old nineteen-seventy 'Carole King' song. At the last and final nail, he threw the hammer off to the side, stood over top of the door, clutched the handle, and pulled. He set the door back behind him, again going down on his hands and knees. A wood and rope ladder was compacted into the cubby ... It was nailed to a wooden framework the size of the opening, directly under the framing was plaster. He ran his hand back and forth across his chin. "Why would someone seal this up? ... Better still, why the hell seal it up with all these fucking nails? ... Jesus Fucking Christ!" *'Why so many nails? ... It is not supposed to be opened that is why.'*

He went over to window yelling he was coming down.

"There's a way in ... I found it ... It's a folding stair-case."

Marty's smiled. *'Yeah! ... Another room in a house with all ready too many rooms ... Thank you dear.'*

"Stay here. I am going to go get some tools and open it up, okay?"

She nodded. "What's the Christmas stuff like?"

"All antique, you're going to love it!"

"How much?"

"A crate?"

"As in one?"

"Yes, but it's a big crate."

A sudden chill attacked her spine, going slowly up and down like a malfunctioning escalator.

She padded down the snow in a circle waiting for Norm to come back out from the house.

Minutes later he was back, shutting the front door holding up a crow bar and medium size sledgehammer as if they were guarded trophies.

Marty looked at him questionably?

"I'm prepared this time. Can you go up to the third floor as soon as I get in the room?"

"Will do."

He started to climb the ladder.

She stood on the bottom rung until he disappeared from sight.

She kicked off her boots running into the kitchen and putting the kettle on, and then galloped up the two flights of stairs to the third floor. She stood in the centre of the hallway glancing back and forth between the ten bedrooms ... Eighteen bedrooms between the second and third floors. Never in her lifetime did she ever envision herself living in a mansion. She tried to imagine what type of people used to occupy the house, where they came from, what they did each day; maybe the third floor was the servant's quarters. The rooms were smaller than on the second ... Or maybe the house was used for ...

Her thoughts broke off at the sound of pounding. She followed the noise along to the end of the hallway, turned right, and strolled to the middle of the small dead ended corridor where the thumps were the loudest. She had always thought the small hallway as odd and misplaced. It wasn't. It had a purpose and the purpose was about to come down from the ceiling.

Plaster started to crack, split and fall. A fist sized hole emerged. A hand jutted through and waved crazily.

She grinned. He always had a way of causing her to smile.

More plaster fell.

"You ready?" Norm yelled.

"Yep, as ready as I'll ever be." A piece of plaster fell into her hair.

"Stand back, here it comes!"

The booms thundered and bounced throughout the third floor. The wooden framing splintered and gave way showering the corridor with wood and plaster. The stairs dropped and swung a foot above the floorboards.

"Holy Hell! ... Who would have known? "Marty latched onto the ropes climbing the stairs. Norm's hand jutted out of the hole fastening onto her upper arm as she neared the top. She wrapped her arms around her dusty husband. "Thank you, I think."

"You think?" He chuckled. "Thank you I think?"

She smirked. "Okay ... Just thank you ... No, I think."

"Good, that's all settled then." He gave her a sly wink. "There you go madam, you have an attic with an

indoor entrance," he swept both arms towards the hole in the floor. "You also have air-conditioning, might I add," he pointed to the broken windowpane. "And ... And we have Christmas decorations to boot." He bowed royal like, then fanned his one arm, pointing with the other to the crate with the stamp that read 'Briarwood' eighteen-hundred-thirty-five.

Marty's eyes lit up. She rushed the crate picking through the decorations. "Holy hell Norm ... They're beautiful," she murmured. She took a glance around the room smiling as the antique furnishings came into view. She gently traced her fingers over it. "I can't believe someone would just walk away from all this!"

Norm knew what she was mulling over. "I'm thinking, you'd like some of this brought down into the house?"

Marty smiled "You read my mind. It is absolutely beautiful. Look at it, just look at it! ... The spinning wheel, the butter churn, the roll top desk, the buffet, the dressers, oh my God yes," she turned facing Norm beaming. "Forget some of it, bring it all down!"

"Bring furniture down a rope ladder?" He started to laugh.

 # Sunday Morning

"I'll hold it, you get the door." Norm wrestled with the Christmas tree trying to keep it from falling over and taking him with it. "You want it in the far corner right?" He muffled from between the pine branches.

"Yes." Marty affirmed.

"Okay, off we go ... Tell me when to stop. Why am I always the one that gets to walk backward with the tree?"

"It's a blue job," Marty retorted. "Just don't trip over the crate on your way through; we don't want to break any of the decorations," she teased.

Norm started to chuckle.

Marty tented her hands over her mouth for maximum velocity. "Come on down guys." She took a quick glance at the tree through the French doors; it was going to be extraordinary this year. "Guys? ... Come on! ... Let's decorate our tree!"

Monica and Eric appeared moments later in socks and PJ's. They rushed the crate like overly excited three year olds, chattering and squabbling as they sat the ornaments out on the floor.

Marty was watching them pull apart the crate. She had not seen them this happy in a very long time. Longtime equated to since they had moved to this house. "Why are you in your pajamas, it's not even lunchtime?"

"We always decorate the tree in our PJ's mom." Monica said.

"It's the Abbott tradition," Eric added.

"True." Norm threw into the mix.

"Okay ... You got me ... You're right ... Say where's your sister?" Marty zipped up her sweater, the room felt chilly.

"Don't know," Eric said.

"What do you mean, you don't know?"

"Haven't seen her since you guys left to get the tree," Eric had his arms buried up to the elbows in the crate.

"We thought she went you," Monica was separating the hand crocheted snowflakes and candy-canes into piles as Eric handed them to her. "Wow mom, look at this!" She held up a snowflake the size of a dessert plate spinning it in her fingers.

Marty stretched her lips into a two-second smile. *'They thought Valerie went with us ... Oh my God! ... Where in the hell is she?'* She gave Norm a quick glance. She turned and ran through the main floor. "Valerie!" she screamed. "Where in the hell are you?"

"I'll look outside." Norm dashed out the front door.

"Valerie?" She bounded up the stairs checking in and out of all the rooms, bedroom closets and underneath all the beds on the second floor.

She came up empty.

She ran up and down the hall one more time yelling for Valerie. She halted in front of the linen closet. The one place she had not checked. She fingered the knob hesitant to open it. She shuffled her feet. "Valerie you in there?" she whispered.

She did not know why, she didn't want to open it other than she just didn't.

She counted to ten.

Turned the knob.

Reefed the door open.

Cold air snapped at her face.

She slammed the door shut.

The third floor was beyond silent. One could have heard a pin drop if they'd had one. She looked back over both her shoulders each and every time she opened a door, and again when she re-closed it.

A miniscule trailer of air whiffed past her face, ever so slight, but enough for her to catch the scent of her daughter. *'Pink-bubble-gum. '*

Marty forced her feet into the small dead ended corridor silently praying to God again to give her strength.

The ladder was down.

She looked up.

The trap door Norm had recently installed was open. She prayed harder.

"Valerie? ... Valerie? ... You up there?" Her words broke and shook in her throat.

The trap door slammed shut.

'Holy Hell! ... Oh, fuck! ... Why oh why, does this keep fucking happening to me? ... Why Lord? ... What the fuck did I ever do to piss you off so much?' She grabbed the ropes putting both feet on the first rung. She slowly, methodically, ascended. She pushed the attic door open.

She crawled along the floor not wanting to look up.

She brought herself to a stand.

And ... There it was.

What she didn't want to see.

"Fuck you Lord," she said.

Her Valerie ... Or what she thought to be her Valerie ... As silent as the snow falling in through the glassless window. ... Squatting, balanced perfectly sedentary on the narrow window ledge ... Facing the front lawn in a picture perfect freeze frame ... Hair, frilly nightcap, and nightshirt flapping in the breeze. It was as if she was staring at a 'Norman Rockwell' painting gone terribly wrong.

Marty worked her jaw back and forth. "Valerie ... Get down ... From ... From there." Her voice was fragile and weak. "Valerie?"

Nothing.

Marty shoved one foot forward then the other. She slowly inched toward the window in silent stops and starts like an old-fashioned pop-up children's book. The light breeze was changing into wind. What if she fell? *'No one survives the fall ... No one is supposed to,'* "Fuck you Lord," she said again.

She rushed her, wrapping her arms around her middle she pulled back hard.

Valerie flew into her like a limp dishrag.

The trap door slammed shut.

Marty gathered her up in her arms.

She brushed the hair from her face.

A strangled cry stuck in her throat.

Valerie's mouth was stitched closed in a blanket stitch pattern, clumps of blood were intertwined with the French knots. Ribbons of blood long dried, marked out where the sewing needle had pierced her flesh. Her eyes were gone and replaced with cheap soulless black glass doll eyes. Her nose had been removed and in its place ran a single black stitch tied in a crude bow at both ends. Her nightshirt was not at all a shirt, but a 'Victorian' era dressing gown. The front was saturated in blood. The matching laced cap was pinned into her scalp with coarse hatpins.

Marty screamed and screamed and screamed screams that fell on deaf ears. The attic was way too far away from the room they used as the living room, three full floors below.

She felt like a newspaper left out in the rain, weighting and shredding.

She hit the floor face first eyes open, staring blankly.

Valerie free from her grasp tumbled across the floor into the wall.

Eric and Monica were busy decorating the tree and singing off key Christmas carols.

Norm had long finished searching the outside, he had noticed the basement door open, and had gone down in.

 # Sunday Afternoon

Marty lifted her head, eyes slowly focusing on the antique furniture along the far wall. She spit out the dust in her mouth then put her head back down gazing up close and personal at the floorboards. *'Why am I laying on my stomach? ... On the floor? ... In the goddamn attic? ... That's a damn good question Marty ... That's a very good damn fucking question.'* She rolled onto her side. Snow was coming through the window. *'Should we answer that damn good fucking question? ... Hell no!'* She went up on her hands and knees, crawled to the trap door, yanked it open and slithered down the rope stairs, running full out down the hallway and two sets of stairs.

The smell of homemade fries and burgers hit her smack dab in the face at the first floor landing. She took a two-second glimpse at the half-decorated Christmas tree on her way through to the kitchen.

She stopped in the archway.

Norm was dishing out hamburgers; Monica and Eric were putting out fries. The table was set, with all the fixings, sliced tomatoes, cheese, onion, dill pickles, mustard, relish, ketchup, mayo, and hot peppers.

Norm smiled and gave Marty a wink as he sat the burgers on the table.

She stayed put bracing herself with her arms between the arches.

Norm traced over her ever so slowly. She had crazy person eyes, and was dusty, cobwebby, and wet. Her hair was sticking out every which way as if she'd just come through a tornado.

"We all figured you were probably busy up there, somewhere ... Doing something." He paused, mouthing 'what the hell happened to you?' Then continued on matter of fact, "So, we decided to surprise you with dinner ... You surprised?" He cleared his throat. "You sure as hell look surprised." He pulled a chair for her to sit. "Maybe try not to look so surprised dear," he whispered brushing off a clump of cobwebs from her back.

"Valerie!" He yelled. "Dinner! ... God, that kid lately." He took a bite of his hamburger. "I'd swear she fell down a set of stairs, lost her head, found it, and put it on backward." He tilted his head back. "Valerie! ... Now! ... I'm not calling you again!"

Valerie suddenly, was there, as if she'd manifested out of thin air. She slipped in beside her mother at the table, buttoned up to the neck Victorian nightgown, frilly nightcap, bare feet, and all.

The entire family's heads turned in total complete unison, to Valerie, to one another and back to Valerie.

Norm coughed, and then cleared his throat. "What do you want on your burger?" His gaze was set onto his youngest daughter. "Valerie!" he shouted.

She returned his stare giving him a toothy smile that sent shivers up and down his spine. "Nothing," she said flatly.

"Plain?" He did not wait for an answer. He suddenly wanted to get dinner the hell over with. "Okay fine ... That's not like you, but whatever ... I want it all gone too young lady!" He talked without looking at her. "You've been picking at your food lately and feeding most of it to Roger under the table ... Don't think I don't notice."

She picked up the hamburger. Turned it upside down. Ripped a huge chunk off with her teeth. Used the back of her hand to stuff it all in. She stared at Norm chewing slow and exaggerated with her mouth open. Bits of the burger and bun fell onto her nightgown and table. "Are you done Norm?" She said through the mouth full of burger.

Norm glanced at the bits and pieces of the burger sticking to her chest and the table. His eyes flickered back to her chewing and smacking like an animal. He banged the table with his fist, jumping everyone's dinner plates. "Quit the goddamn shit! ... And it's dad not Norm! ... And no! ... I am not done! ... When you are finished eating," he reached across the table and closed her mouth. "Get whatever the hell you've got on off and throw it in the damn garbage! ... And don't you dare open mouth eat ever again! ... Now I'm done!"

"But I like my clothes," Valerie quipped. Her tone was sing-songy and obnoxious.

"I don't! ... Neither does your mother by the look on her face." He glanced at Marty she was still spaced out, although not quite as bad and was chewing.

"Where'd you get the damn thing?"

"A crate in the attic." She smiled at him. More food fell. She quickly scooped it up with her hands and jammed it back into her mouth.

"Don't smile when you eat! ... And stay the hell out of there!"

She took another massive bite of her burger, cramming a fistful of fries into her mouth along with it.

"Didn't I just tell you to quit the shit?" He brought the garbage can over. "Spit it out!"

Valerie continued chewing.

"Now!" he yelled.

She pushed the food slowly with the tip of her tongue into the can.

Norm stood there holding the can looking up at the ceiling.

"Is that all of it?" he asked a minute later.

Valerie spit another chunk into the can.

"For Christ's sake kid! ... Eat like a normal human being would you?"

"I'm not a normal human being Norm, not anymore," she whispered too low for anyone at the table to hear. "Yes daddy," she said.

"Mom," Monica looked at her mother.

Marty nodded.

"We waited to finish decorating the tree, so we could all do it together."

"Wonderful honey, we can do it after dinner."

Norm smiled at Marty. "You're back I see."

"Was I gone?"

"We're all going to die ... He opened the box," Valerie muttered.

Again, the entire family's eyes shifted to Valerie's clinging and hanging on her like fly on a glue strip.

"That's enough!" Norm grabbed her by the arm, pulled her from the chair, tugging her towards the stairs. "Go to your goddamn room and stay there!" He gave her a tap on her bottom and pointed to the top of the stairs. "Now," he yelled.

Valerie started doing a mock up tap dance, swirling in circles. "But ... But ... You said to eat all my dinner Norm."

"I'll bring it to you ... And it's dad! ... Call me Norm again and you'll be sorry! ... Now go!"

Valerie put her hands on her hips. "No it's you that'll be sorry!" She turned and ran up the stairs humming 'Baby it's too late,' then started to laugh.

"Jesus Fucking Christ!" He said. "Are you sure that's our daughter or just something that looks like her?" He picked up his burger.

Marty held up her hands in the got me pose. She'd come to use this pose a lot lately. It was the best go to when there were no words ... And there was a definite over abundance of no words. "I'll keep her home from school tomorrow and have a very long talk with her."

"She's seven, good luck with that." He held Marty's eyes. "Can you take her to a doctor as well?" He said a hair above a whisper.

She reached across the table and stroked the back of his hand. "Sometimes you have to have a referral for those kinds of doctors ... But I'll try my best."

 # Tuesday Night

Norm ate his dinner in silence.

Marty slowly sipped at her tea, waiting.

He put his knife and fork onto his plate. "Dinner was good honey ... Okay shoot, let me have it."

"Buffy's missing."

"No, the other."

"She's expelled till January ninth, when school goes back in after the holidays."

He pursed his lips. "So tell me just what a seven year old girl can possibly do in grade two classes to get expelled?"

"The short simple version or the long detailed one?"

"Short, simple."

"She jumped up on the teacher's desk waving a meat clever, threatening to send the whole class to hell."

"What?"

"She waved a meat clever in class threatening to send them to hell," she repeated.

"Fuckin' hell! ... What is wrong with that girl?"

Tears rolled down Marty's face.

"Living hell! ... Just in passing, where'd she get the fucking clever?"

"The school kitchen," she sobbed.

He went around the table, pulled her gently to her feet, and hugged her. "Don't cry hon, we'll get her fixed."

"How?"

"I don't know, but we will."

 # Late Tuesday Night

A shrill scream broke the night silence.

Marty and Norm sat bolt upright.

Their bedroom door slammed shut.

Norm jumped from the bed and bounded toward the door.

Another scream shot through the darkness, drawn, wolf like.

He grasped the knob turning it. "The damn fucking thing won't open!" He yelled back toward Marty. He frantically reefed the doorknob back and forth.

Monica stood catatonic; giving the word petrified her picture, water glass in hand as the thing in the bathroom mirror screamed again, and again, and again.

It ever so slowly pulled its thin black lips back in a horrid grimaced.

The glass fell from Monica's hand.

It pressed its face into the mirror. The off-white pallor of its rotted skin shone like fish scales under the lighting. Long, stringy, dark coloured dread locks framed its head, neck, and shoulders in a grotesque free-floating frame. Blood oozed down its face from the single bullet hole dead centre of its forehead. It puckered up its lips and blew on the mirror, fogging it from the backside. All at once, it backed lifted its arm and shoved through the mirror. It knocked Monica hard in the chest knocking her backward. "We're all going to die, he opened the box," it hissed.

Monica screamed, screams that danced along the ceiling and back down into her throat. She tore off into her bedroom banging the door shut. She pulled her bedding off the bed crawling in underneath it.

As if in applaud, all the doors on the third floor opened and slammed closed, methodically one by one, down the one side of the hall and up the other.

Roger stood staunch and erect, tail bristling, growling up at the ceiling near the stained glass window of Marty and Norm's bedroom.

Norm was still working the doorknob. "Fucking hell Marty," he yelled. "I can't get the fucker open!"

Marty wrapped her hands around his, tugging and pulling with him.

Something thumped outside their bedroom door. Then again ... And again ... Repeating in a steady rhythm like something hard, being bounced.

The thumping ceased.

Norm put his ear to the door listening. He shoved his hands into his pajama pockets stopping them from shaking.

The thumping all too quickly resumed, sounding as if it was travelling up and down the hallway.

It stopped, re-commencing on the third floor, going the length of it then silenced.

Norm kicked at the doorknob, pulled, yanked, and kicked it again. The door moaned and flew open, sending him backwards into the wall.

"Stay here," he yelled over his shoulder.

He dashed out into the hallway. Stopping ... Listening through the silence for the one small piece of the puzzle that did not fit.

The thumping re-started.

He ran down the hallway to the landing. Again halting, listening.

The tone of the thunks was different as if the walls were being used instead of the floor. He tilted his head back and forth doglike concentrating. "It's a goddamn fucking ball," he muttered. "I know it is."

'Someone in this fucked up house is bouncing a fucking ball.'

He grabbed onto the banister pivoting the top half of his body out into the staircase. "Valerie!" He yelled. Her name had been on the tip of his tongue first and foremost, running a close second had been Eric's.

The thumping stopped.

Something heavy fell. The lights flickered and went out.

He turned round and ran the length of the second floor hall. The light bulbs buzzed as if hundreds of bees had invaded them, sputtered, and came back on.

He opened the door to Eric's room.

Sound asleep.

He peered into Monica's room.

Asleep.

He opened Valerie's.

Sleeping.

The thumping re-commenced.

'Marty? ... It had to be, there was no one else left.'

He ran back to the landing.

A lone leather baseball was bouncing down the stairs, one by one slow and controlled as if being piloted.

It rolled across the landing leaving a long ribbon of red in its wake. It came to rest at his feet ... He gawked at the ball ... The red looked like blood ... Every hair on his entire body stood erect poking through his pajamas like needles.

He moved the ball with his foot.

His foot smeared with red.

'That is blood!'

Horror etched into his eyes.

He turned and ran.

The ball followed as if tethered to his foot.

He halted, turned, jumped over the ball, and bounded up the stairs to the third floor.

All the doors whipped open, back crashed into the wall, sprang forward, slammed shut, opened, shut, over and over picking up momentum. The house boomed in tune. It was as if it had come alive and was breathing.

Norm pivoted round.

Valerie and Monica were standing side by side on the landing looking at him with toothy smiles that bordered on grotesque. "We're all going to die. He opened the box," they said as one.

They went back down the stairs.

Norm crept along behind them.

Monica picked up ball.

The two of them bounced it back and forth to one another on their way down the second floor hall. They both entered their rooms closing the doors behind them.

The ball was nowhere in sight.

Norm shuffled down the hall slow and clumsily, his gate measurably off and more zombie-like than human.

He steadied his one hand with the other slowly opening the bedroom doors. His sanity hung on them all still sleeping in their beds ... The other stuff ... He would convince himself was part of a nightmare. He stepped through the doorways each in turn ... All empty ... No children ... No wife ... No furniture ... No nothing ... Nothing but the eerie echoing rendition of his breaths.

"Marty! ... Eric! ... Monica! ... Valerie!" he screamed. "Where the fuck are you?"

The ball bounced behind him.

He whirled around.

Valerie was standing a mere ten feet from him bouncing the baseball.

She gazed up at him smirking.

"Where ... Where ... Is ... Is ... Everyone?" He stuttered and choked out his words in stops and starts.

His gaze swept over his daughter with the bloodied baseball in her hands. He took a step back. She felt too close.

"They're up there daddy," she pointed to the ceiling giggling.

Norm took off up the stairs, searched the third floor, went up into the attic and came back down.

"They're not up there."

Valerie laughed so hard her eyes teared. "No silly, not upstairs, up there." She pointed to the ceiling again.

He titled his head. His eyes went wide, white. His body started to twitch.

He'd found them.

Found all of them, up on the ceiling, clinging, with their hands and feet like giant flies.

Valerie snickered sauntering off down the hall towards her room bouncing the ball.

Norm was still as he was, head tilted, eyes wide, body twitching.

The air in the hall seemed to be dropping in temperature. His skin goose bumped.

They started moving spiderlike along the ceiling. They stopped directly above him. Their heads swivelled in a three-sixty in total unison, and then turned his way. Their glassy black eyes sought out his, staring. Their tongues lulled out of the left corner of their mouths. Saliva dripped onto his head. "We're all going to die, he opened the box," they whispered in harmony.

Their heads rotated in another three-sixty, slowing down and halting facing back to the ceiling. They hung there motionless, dry washed their heads with their hands, then flattened, shot across the ceiling to the wall joint, formed a single line head to toe, slid down the wall to the floor, humped up their backs cat like, romping off on their fingers and toes into their rooms.

He just stood, eyeballs glassed over, mouth wide, tongue dried, limbs fixed as he ever so slowly sunk to the floor curling upon his side in a fetal position..

 # Wednesday Morning

"Hey you," Marty said, keeping her tone natural. She had found Norm curled in up a ball in the middle of the hallway in the early morning and when she had fetched a blanket for him, he was gone. "Hey," she said again.

He was sitting at the kitchen island staring straight ahead, coffee mug in hand, as if he was cast in stone.

She glanced in the pot ... Empty.

"I'm a bit late coming down this morning." She was lying; she had been all over the house looking for him. "I was cleaning the upstairs bathroom. Did you know the mirror was shattered and all over the floor?" This was not a lie; it was smashed beyond belief up there.

Norm stayed transfixed holding his mug.

"Hon?"

Nothing.

She glanced at the kitchen clock. "Aren't you late for work?"

"Not going," he muttered off key.

She put her hand on his forehand. "Not well?"

She pulled out a stool, sitting facing him.

His face was shiny and wet.

"What's wrong hon?" *'Aside from the fact you slept in the hall on the floor then just vanished.'*

"Roger's gone."

"What?"

"Roger's dead ... I found him hanging this morning upside down and gutted on the hook on the front door, where the Christmas wreath was ... All his internal organs are missing, except his intestines which are looped around him like garland ... The decorations from the wreath are tacked into him with old fashioned hat pins."

"Say that again?"

"I can't."

"Oh my God ... No." Marty started to cry. She got up walking in circles around the island.

He caught her by the arm. "Don't you go out there; I haven't washed the blood from the door yet. And, he's rolled up in the sofa blanket on the porch."

She ran to the sink, dry heaving.

Norm stayed as he was.

"The kids I should ..."

Norm cut her off. "Don't say anything to them, I'll drive them to school." He cupped his head in his hands. "Except Valerie," he added. "I'll take them outside through the back porch."

He got up from his chair and walked straight into the wall. He stopped, turned, and stared at Marty. "We're all going to die, he opened the box." He backed by way of a two-step, sauntered through the kitchen, out into the back porch, opened the door, went down two stairs, and fell face first into the snow.

Marty clung onto the windowsill, watching Norm sinking and forming into the snow as if he was part of it. *'Lord you up there? ... I so need help Lord ... Lord?... Please hear me ... Help me ... Help me please... I think I'm losing my mind Lord... I think everyone in this god-damn fucking house is losing theirs too ... Lord God please.'* She clasped her hands together looking up at the kitchen ceiling. It was crawling with flies. She left her prayer where it was, that wasn't God up there.

She tripped over her feet all the way to the bottom of the main floor stairs.

"Hurray up you're going to miss the bus," she yelled.

Monica and Eric sledded down the banister both landing on their feet. They gave one another a high five and scampered into the kitchen.

"Hey mom, where's breakfast?" Eric's disappointment rang through his words.

"Have cereal, I have to take care of something outside." Marty went out the front door, closing it behind her.

Tears soaked her face as she rubbed at Roger's blood with her housecoat. It was useless, it had frozen.

She hung her robe on the wreath hook and pulled out the sides, covering up the blood on the door.

She picked up Roger, holding him tight to her chest. She wrapped her arms around him and sobbed her heart out. She had him before the kids were all born. He was her first baby even if he did have four legs and a tail. She stroked the blanket. "I'm sorry sweetheart. I'll have to set you in the bushes, just for a bit." She picked a tall bush under the front window and laid him down.

She went back in the house.

She let Monica and Eric out the front door, then stood and watched them pitching snowballs at one another. All seemed so normal.

She stepped back slamming directly into Valerie.

"You're good ... You should get an 'Oscar' for that performance!" Valerie held her mother's eyes not in the way of a seven-year-old child. She darted into the house and up the stairs.

Marty could hear the slamming of doors, one after the other, coming from the second floor. She slowly closed her eyes picking up her kitchen prayer not looking up at the ceiling this time. *'Lord?... Can you hear me?... Lord, please, please help us! ... Something is so terribly fucking wrong!'*

She pulled on her boots, went through the house, through the back porch and out into the snow prepared to drag Norm into the house.

He was gone ... Yet again ... Just gone.

She ran back into the house, right on through the kitchen, and out into the front hall. She stopped dead, and turned round.

Norm was standing at the kitchen counter making a fresh pot of coffee.

'Fucking hell Norm, you friends with Houdini?'

He sniffled and pulled a handkerchief from his shirt pocket ... An old, yellowed, linen handkerchief. He casually wiped his nose shoving it back into his pocket.

She had seen it before. She cleared her throat before speaking. "Where'd you get that?" *'She knew where he'd gotten it from. That box.'*

"Get what?"

"That handkerchief?"

"What handkerchief?"

"For Christ's sake! ... The one you just wiped your nose with!"

He searched all his pockets, pulling them inside out, smiling idiotically.

Marty pointed to his shirt pocket. "You missed that one!"

He ever so slowly pulled out the handkerchief. "This?" His voice held a childlike overtone.

"Yes ... That!"

"I don't know it," he muttered looking at the floor. "It was just in my pocket." He shuffled his feet side to side.

'It was just in your pocket ... Just in your goddamn pocket! ... Fucking hell!' She snatched it out of his hands, throwing it into the garbage.

"Hey! ... Why the hell did you do that?"

"It's filthy and not right!" She yelled.

"I like it." He fished it from the garbage shoving it back into the same pocket. "I think I'll go lie down for a while, I'm cold."

'I wonder why Norm ... I wonder why ... Napping face down in the snow might make one cold ... You think ... You go lie down ... You just do that!' She scrutinised him as he climbed the stairs, his legs wobbling, his arms dangling loose and free.

There was a loud thunk at the second floor landing.

Marty went part way up the stairs.

Norm had face planted again.

She went back into the kitchen, made a tea and sat at the counter, elbows splayed, chin resting in her palms. She gazed out the window watching the snow ... Something was very, very wrong with everyone in this house.

She looked up at the ceiling.

The flies were gone.

The light bulbs started to hum.

The dishes suddenly flew from the top cupboards, hitting the wall, dropping down onto the floor spinning like tops.

She got up and walked through the house and out the front door, got in the back seat of the car and just sat there. She made her lips disappear into her mouth. "That asshole of a thing is haunted," she whispered.

# Thursday Evening

"Valerie!" Marty yelled. "Bath time!" She strolled up and down the second floor checking in all the rooms and under the beds. "Valerie ... Where are you?"

"I thought she loved a bath," Norm whispered.

Marty jumped. She had not realized he had been following her up and down the hall. "Jesus Christ! ... Don't sneak up on me like that!" She rapped him in the shoulder.

"Jumpy are we?"

"No," she shot back too quickly. *'Am I jumpy? ... I'd be putting a much different name on what I am Norm.'*

"So? ... What's up with her lately?"

"I don't know. She literary hates anything to do with water since we moved to this house."

"What does she do, steam when she touches it?"

"Norm!" Marty gave him a look.

"Sorry. I'll go find the little devil." He really was not sorry, not by a long shot. She could have gotten the lead in the 'Exorcist' hands down, just by being herself. No acting required.

Friday Early Evening

"You want what again, from the basement?" Norm threw on his coat and boots.

"Two of those blocks from the wall you took out." Marty picked the Christmas tree up off the floor. "Our tree keeps falling over. I thought I could wedge the base in between the two to prop it up."

"Okay, I'll grab them. I'll be right back."

"You promise?" She rested the Christmas tree against the wall.

He gave her a thumb up and disappeared out the door.

He pulled every other light cord as he made his way over to the pile of blocks, suddenly wishing he hadn't piled them in that room with the hole in the wall.

He looked over both shoulders then glanced in through the hole. He put one leg in looking back over his shoulder again.

He stood just inside the opening allowing his eyes to adjust to the darkness. Something other than blocks was in there.

He did a double take.

There was a chair in the room.

He'd never put a chair in there. He leaned towards it not lifting his feet from the floor. There was something in the chair.

His chin started to tremble. He became afraid.

The blocks were piled up on the far wall. The other side of the chair he didn't put there with the something in it that he didn't put there.

He tried to whistle. He couldn't.

He had promised Marty he would be right back with the two blocks. He dragged his legs by pulling his pant legs forward with his hands. He inched along awkward and slow.

'Don't look at the chair, don't look at the chair.'

He picked up the two blocks, turned to leave.

The light bulb buzzed and lit.

The blocks fell from his grasp.

A life-size ragdoll was slumped in the chair. Filthy and weathered. Its head lulled on its chest. Its woolen hair hung down in thick dread locks obscuring its face. Its yellowed linen nightgown draped about the floor.

He inhaled deeply, exhaling slow and long shaking his head at himself. He picked back up the blocks.

'Fucking hell!' He poked the doll in the foot.

The head lifted.

The woolen hair fell back from its face ... The round faded eyes jumped to life ... The mouth widened ... The lips drew back exposing jutted teeth ... It started to hiss and grow.

Norm's body jerked like a fish stabbed by a spear.

A gagging groan escaped his throat.

The doll hooked its hands around the chair arms. It started to stand.

He could feel himself screaming. He raised his arms as if to throw the blocks, losing his balance. He crashed into the wall and went down. He rolled up onto his knees crawling out of the room as if the devil himself was on his heels.

He ran full out through the basement smacking into Valerie in the doorway.

"Looking for me Daddy?" she cooed.

"Na ... No ... Na." He croaked. "I wa ... Was ... Ju ... Just ..."

She cut him off. "Very well daddy."

She went up on her tiptoes ... Hauled up her nightgown .... Kicked off her panties. Grabbed hold of her crotch with both hands ... Squatted ... Opened her legs, peeing, whipping her body side to side, channeling it into the spray soaking him in urine.

His eyes widened and glazed. His lips disappeared into his mouth. He cemented in place.

Valerie laughed hysterically.

She sauntered through the basement, climbed through the hole, and retrieved the chair and doll. She used the chair to reach the pull cords, turning the lights off.

She sat the chair against a pile of boxes. Placed the doll in it fussing with its nightgown making sure it was draped absolutely perfect.

"Night Daddy," she whispered.

She closed and locked the basement door.

 # Saturday

"Come on answer," Marty said. She hung up and hit the redial button.

"One, tee, three ..."

Marty cut in hearing the women's voice. "Hello? ... Hello?"

The woman spoke over top of her. "One, tee, three ... The number you have called is not in service."

Marty rolled her eyes. "A recording ... A goddamn fucking recording." She said.

She grabbed her coat and hat, threw on her boots, and ran out the front door.

She hustled along the streets to the reality office.

She needed answers. If anyone had any ... They would.

She stood stationary in front of the huge plate glass window, gawking into the empty run down office. A for rent sign hung cock-eyed on the door. The office looked as if it had not been used in decades.

She collapsed against the glass sobbing.

Someone tapped her shoulder.

The reflection of the old woman blurred in the glass.

"Get out of that house," she whispered. "Get out now!"

Marty turned.

The woman was gone.

Christmas Eve morning

"Where's your dad?" Marty did not lift her eyes from her last minute shopping list.

Monica and Eric were performing an animated rock, paper, scissors as a means to determine who got the biggest muffin.

"Excuse me." She put down the pen looking from Monica to Eric.

"Don't know mom." Eric mumbled.

She gazed at Monica. "And, what about you? You seen him?"

The air in the kitchen seemed to thicken; one could have cut it with a knife. Monica started fidgeting with the Christmas table ornament.

"Well?" She herself had not seen much of him if any, since she had asked him to get the blocks for the tree the past Friday. She had thought she'd seen him from the back walking through the halls, but he had never stopped nor turned her direction. When she'd called out to him. He had not shown up for any meals or come to bed. She had searched the house several times looking for him, almost afraid to find him, relieved when she hadn't.

"I think I've seen him kind of, but not really." Monica got up from the stool and flew up the stairs. She did not want any more questions. What she'd thought she saw in the upstairs hallway escaped words.

Marty went out, finishing up the last minute er-
rands.

Christmas Eve afternoon

"I'm back! ... Hey guys," she yelled. "Come help bring in the stuff."

The house sat silent.

She mumbled away complaining about the lack of help, as she went back and forth to the vehicle lugging the bags into the entranceway. She closed the front door throwing off her boots and hanging up her coat.

"Guys!" she yelled. "Come on down." she furthered.

Silence, dead eerie pin drop silence.

She walked into the hallway her back facing the French doors that lead to the living room. "Come on guys." She started turning towards the living room, she just loved the tree this year. "Let's get this all put aw..." The words abruptly broke off in her throat.

Her tongue curled back and rolled.

Her fingers trembled.

Fear in its purest of form crawled up inside her.

Her eyes, the only thing of functioning movement flickered ... To the tree ... To her daughter ... Back to the tree with the ornaments spinning counter-clockwise ... Back to her daughter Valerie sitting cross-legged in front of the tree ... To the floor where the angel topper lay, its wings torn off, its halo shredded, its throat slit, its gown bloodied.

Marty's face filled with horror. Her breath came in hollow gasps.

Valerie as if she had been waiting for this precise moment put her hands, palms down, at her sides. Unfolded her legs and turned towards her mother.

"Hello momma," she slurred.

Marty screamed and screamed and screamed.

Valerie's eyes were gone. Big, black plastic buttons were sewn into the eye sockets. One of her ears was severed, and crudely stitched to her neck as if something had missed the doll making for dummies course. Her lips were thin and bluish-grey. Her skin opaque and paler than any vampire's. A large caliber bullet hole, dead centre of her forehead, trickled blood down her face. She stretched her lips back exposing black canines.

She looked like the epitome of evil.

She gently lifted the wooden box from her lap holding it out to her mother as if an offering. "We're all going to die, he opened the box," she croaked.

She heaved the box at Marty, hitting her square in the chest.

She tilted her head back and laughed and laughed.

Marty screamed silent scream after scream after scream, her voice stolen by terror.

She took off at a dead run into the kitchen, all at once skidding through a massive blood pool on her heels.

She smacked hard into the island, almost going down. She grabbed the edge steadying herself.

Her pulse pounded ... Her tongue went thick ... She went pale as death ... She vomited all over herself.

She stared at the counter, there but not, lost in this nightmare.

Monica was bathed in blood, eyes wide and fixed, lying on her back, ax protruding from her chest, head dangling off one side of the counter, legs off the other.

She stood blank, dizzy, empty, trying to comprehend the uncomprehendable, then she started to scream.

She ran in wild panic through the main floor. She slammed into the French doors, slipping and sliding in her socked feet into the living room.

Valerie was gone.

She flew up the staircase tripping and falling, sprawling out into the hall. She lifted her head ...

Eric ... Still, lifeless, lying in a pool of dark red blood, face up, legs splayed, bare feet, one eye staring up at the ceiling, the other dangling down the side of his cheek from the optic nerve. Both arms hacked off at the shoulders. The entire set of kitchen knives were handle deep in his neck.

She couldn't remember how to breathe. She couldn't remember her name. She stared straight ahead her face horribly pale.

She heard a heavy thunk, then another, then another.

She sat up swivelling the top half of her body in the direction of the sounds. Someone was clunking towards her slow and awkward using a cane. Her consciousness rocketed her into clarity. Norm ... It was Norm clunking towards her.

Then she saw him ... Really saw him, and started to scream.

His eyes had been replaced with big black buttons that were crudely kept in the sockets with hatpins. His hair was a solid mass that moved and swayed back and forth all on its own as if alive. His skin resembled old yellowed linen. The flesh just below his chin was sewn

together in a crude blanket stitch that ran all the way round as if his head and neck had separated and been hand stitched back together. His toothless mouth was open and drooled profusely. His one leg was turned at an odd angle and dragged as he walked. He held a noose in one hand, a sledgehammer in the other, a carving knife handle protruded from his front jeans pocket. His clothes were tattered and blood soaked.

Marty's screams echoed throughout the house as she scrambled to her feet, ran up the stairs to the third floor, down the hallway, climbed the ladder into the attic, and slammed the trap door shut.

She could hear the sledge hammer thumping and banging off the stairs.

He was coming.

She crawled in behind the furniture pile, shut her eyes, clasping her hands together, whispering the 'Lord's Prayer.'

Something brushed the back of her hand.

Her eyes shot open.

Valerie ... Right there, up close and personal, staring at her with the same black button eyes. She hooked her arm into her mother's, rested her head on her arm, and started to sing. "And it's too late ... Baby now ... It's too late ... Though we really did try to make it ... Something inside has died ... And I can't hide ... And I can't fake it ... Oh, no, no." She pulled away from her. "Bye momma," she whispered and disappeared.

Marty's brain snapped and let go of the lifeline.

Her body was on its own.

The trap door thundered open.

She flattened in to the wall.

The furniture slid away.

He grabbed her by the throat and hauled her out into the middle of the room.

Marty was gone, though she breathed in and out and her heart still beat,

He bent over picking up the rope and sledge.

Her eyes glazed and rolled white.

He pulled the knife, shoved it handle deep into her abdomen, and pulled it sideways.

Her intestines spilled out onto the floor.

He put the noose around her neck, dragged her over to the window, tied the loose end to the pillar, smashed her head in with the sledge, heaved her up, and tossed her out.

She felt no pain. She felt absolutely nothing. She had been long gone since she'd been sung too.

Blackness came engulfing and taking its prize.

Norm climbed up on the windowsill, and jumped.

# Christmas Eve early evening

"Time yet?" Dora was standing behind Rodd with her hand on his shoulder.

"Let me check again, just to make sure."

He scooted the stool up closer to the telescope. He moved it slow and steady tracing back and forth across Norm's body. Norm was lying face down, just to the front and right of the hedge.

His flesh was as white as the snow itself. There had been no movement in the last hour.

There was still none.

Rodd grinned toothy and full. He could just imagine the sights in that house. He turned to Dora and nodded.

Dora breathed in and out through her mouth until she was breathless.

She dialed nine-one-one.

Early evening

Two squad cars pulled up to the 'Briarwood Mansion.'

The officers all looked back over their shoulders as they got out of the cars. The cold shivers had set in midway up the drive.

Sergeant Riley strolled over to the body of the man splattered on the cement walkway just to the right and front of the hedge. The officers followed. He shook his head.

He stepped back and looked up at the body of the woman soaked in blood hanging from the turret. "Jesus Christ," he muttered.

He went into the house. Two officers followed. One stayed at the front door.

Fifteen minutes later, they were in a huddle with Riley writing in his notepad.

He flipped the notepad shut shoving it and the pen into his front coat pocket. He gazed from one officer to the next in turn. "We're all good then?"

They nodded.

"Okay get out of here, it's Christmas Eve." Riley leaned against his squad car watching the taillights until they disappeared.

He looked back over his shoulder.

A half hour later, the coroner and crime scene cleaners arrived.

He opened the notebook notating the time of arrival directly underneath the traffic fatality report, where it said head on collision highway thirty-seven, mother and three children killed instantly along with the lone man in the other car.

He walked over to the coroner handing him the chains and padlock for the front gates. "When you're done."

Both men nodded to one another.

No words were spoken.

None were needed.

Everyone knew the drill.

They all met at the same place, on the same day, every two years.

 # Christmas morning

'Briarwood' sat lifeless, as if estranged from the town and its inhabitants.

Rodd and Dora had been over at first light to retrieve the box and the little creature.

As the minute hand of the town clock caught up to the hour and the bell tolled twelve noon 'Briarwood' started to stir.

The lights flickered, and then blew.

The windows slammed down.

The contents crumbled and turned to dust.

The stone foundation moved loosening the mortar joins, then rocked back and forth.

The house rattled ... Exploded ... Debris grouped, gathered ... Shot skyward, in a mushroom cloud formation not unlike that of a nuclear blast.

The cloud gently drifting over top of the town and dissipated.

'Briarwood' was no more.

One Year Later

Clara Stewart hung up the telephone smiling the same smile that adorned her picture encased in the gold oval on the real estate sign in the front window.

She got up from her desk and walked to the next room.

"They bought the 'Briarwood Mansion', deals being taken over to the law office as we speak."

"No kidding?" Adam said. He paddled his chair back from his desk with his feet.

"Nope, possession date is four weeks."

"Box waxed?"

Clara nodded.

"Padlocked?"

She nodded again.

"It's ready to go back where it belongs?"

Clara smiled toothy and full. "Of course my darling." She gave Adam a sultry wink. "Rodd and Dora are taking it over tonight."

"The demon Stfig-Elpmis back in its box?"

"Yes." He shuddered. He had seen it once. He never, ever wanted that particular pleasure again.

"The little creature ready to go back over?"

"No, it's going to stay with the Keepers until the new family moves in. They'll take it over when they go say hello, like last time."

"Doesn't it bother them?"

"No, it's just the demon's familiar."

"What did they write on the 'Simple Gift' card this time round?" Adam got up from his chair.

"To Miss Thelma Louise Pettihurst; from the Honorable Phillip Theodore Page. And of course the usual ... Here in lies 'Simple Gifts'."

"The box keepers gave it 'savoir-faire' this time!"

Clara's smile broadened showing off her decayed teeth. "Yes they did! ... However, after one-hundred-eighty years of keeping the box and the little creature safe each time the house explodes and rebuilds for its next interval. They're duly entitled. Don't you agree?"

"Yes I agree, my lady." He held out his arm for her to hook onto. "You know my dear madam, if you had not been so inclined to dabble in the dark arts way back in nineteen-hundred-thirty-five, we would not be in this mess taking care of a demon, its familiar, and his house for all of eternity."

"Her," Clara corrected. "Simple Gifts is a her."

"Excuse me ... The good lady Elpmis-Stfig!"

"Oh just stop it!"

Cackling laughter echoed throughout the office.

They both stopped and turned looking over the empty run down office.

It was always the same.

As soon as the papers were signed for 'Briarwood', everything dissipated back to rubble, dust, and cobwebs. Even their clothing metamorphosed back into their eighteen–hundred-thirties death attires.

Adam lifted Clara's hand gently kissing the back. "C'est la vie, my love ...Till the next sale," he whispered.

She smiled.

They joined hands, vanishing into the brick wall.

Epilogue

Energy cannot be created or destroyed ...
It can only change form.

Author's Note

Moments in time are divided into three parts ...
Before this, this, and after this.
Thank you for sharing this.

Sincerely
I.L. Jackson